I0565710

FOOL'S
GOLD

FOOL'S GOLD

Stanley Hart Page

COACHWHIP PUBLICATIONS
Greenville, Ohio

To my mother and father, with all affection
and gratitude, I dedicate this little tale.

S. H. P.

Fool's Gold, by Stanley Hart Page
© 2025 Coachwhip Publications edition
Introduction © 2025 Curtis Evans
Cover: Coins (CC-BY 2.0) Portable Antiquities Scheme
    https://creativecommons.org/licenses/by/2.0/deed.en

First published 1933
Stanley Hart Page, 1902-1979
CoachwhipBooks.com

ISBN 1-61646-623-5
ISBN-13 978-1-61646-623-7

ANOTHER ONE FOR THE PHILO BRIGADE

STANLEY HART PAGE AND THE CHRISTOPHER HAND MYSTERIES

CURTIS EVANS

In 1929 the prestigious firm of Alfred A. Knopf published Dashiell Hammett's tough and violent crime novels *Red Harvest* and *The Dain Curse* (*The Maltese Falcon* would follow the next year), forever altering the face of crime fiction with what reviewers dubbed the "hard-boiled" style. Yet at the very same time that Hammett commenced his great crime sweep, traditionalist American mystery writer S. S. Van Dine (Willard Huntington Wright), whose best-selling Philo Vance detective novels were published by Knopf's rival Scribner's, stood resplendent at the height of his popularity, having also in 1929 produced *The Bishop Murder Case,* the book which proved the most popular and enduring of his mysteries. Although the future of American crime writing might lie with the tough guys, what Hammett's Sam Spade or the Continental Op might have termed the "pantywaist" genteel amateur detectives were hardly down for the count. Indeed, that very same year Frederic Dannay and Manfred Lee, the two New York cousins who wrote as Ellery Queen, introduced, in *The Roman Hat Mystery,* a monocled amateur detective named, appropriately enough, Ellery Queen, a gentleman who in his studied affectations shared considerable affinity with Philo Vance, particularly in his early years in print. Five years later, Rex Stout's obese, orchid-loving eccentric genius,

Nero Wolfe, would make his first of many fictional appearances in the detective novel *Fer de Lance*. In between those epochal events in American mystery genre history, myriad Philo Vance wannabes made brief their own brief struts on the crime fiction stage. One member of this troop of toff tecs was Christopher Hand, who between 1932 and 1935 appeared in a quintet of novels by forgotten American mystery writer Stanley Hart Page.

Stanley Hart Page, who, ironically enough likely was distantly related to native Marylander Samuel Dashiell Hammett through mutual Dashiell ancestors of French Huguenot lineage, was born in prosperous circumstances in Chatham, New Jersey, on March 10, 1902, to Laurence Stanley Page and his wife Emma F. Jowett. Stanley's colorful entrepreneurial paternal grandfather was self-made millionaire coal tar king George Shephard Page (1838-1892), originally of Reading, Maine, and Chelsea, Massachusetts. Upon his death at the age of fifty-four George Page, the renowned "millionaire chemist" who was then an inmate of the New Jersey State Insane Asylum ("his mind was broken down by the worry introduced by a severe attack of the grippe" according to the newspapers), bequeathed to his four sons and one daughter the substantial fortune (about thirty-five million dollars in modern worth) which he had accumulated through his various business ventures, the best known of which today is the Vapo-Cresolene Company. This profitable enterprise with great success marketed Vapo-Cresolene, a therapeutic vaporizer used in the United States during the late nineteenth and early twentieth centuries in the hope of providing lasting relief to sufferers from such ailments as asthma, bronchitis, croup, whooping cough and diphtheria, despite the fact that the American Medical Association reported with dry derision in 1908 that "Vapo-Cresolene is a member of that

Stanley Hart Page

class of proprietaries in which an ordinary product is endowed, by the manufacturer, with extraordinary virtues."

Perhaps to salve his moral conscience George before his breakdown became a great advocate of both alcohol temperance, founding the New Jersey Temperance Association, and of universal free public-school education. He also founded Chatham's Stanley Congregational Church. After his death, Page's own rather more fortunate offspring inherited from the family patriarch his highly profitable, if arguably somewhat dubious, patent medicine business, over which they maintained firm control, with Stanley's uncle Albion Lambert Page serving as president, his uncle Henry de Bacon Page serving as vice president, and his own father, the aforementioned Laurence Stanley Page, serving as secretary. All three men additionally served as directors of the company, the remaining two of whom were Stanley's youngest uncle, Raymond Page, and his aunt, Florence Page.[1]

With a family fortune behind him, Stanley Hart Page might simply have lived a dilettante life, like the fictional Philo Vance, Albert Campion and Lord Peter Wimsey, taking a sinecure job from the firm; yet he went to work, rather, as the manager of the Montclair bureau of the *Newark Evening News* (then New Jersey's newspaper of record), after attending the Pawling and Peddie prep schools and Brown University and taking a token vagabond year out west employed as a cowboy and farm-hand. Yet in 1930, as he approached the age of thirty, he was still single and living under his parents' spacious roof in Chatham, New Jersey, the 64th wealthiest inhabitation in the United States in 2018, according to *Bloomberg News*. However, the next year he got himself an apartment in nearby Short Hills, where he found time—having been "[s]ince his boyhood . . . absorbed with mysteries and fictional detectives"—to write a pair of detective novels, *Sinister Cargo* and *The*

Resurrection Murder Case, which he successfully placed with none other than Alfred A. Knopf's Borzoi Books imprint.

Knopf evidently was on the hunt for another Philo Vance, judging from the back flap blurb description of Page's book, which boldly, if perhaps a bit precipitately, proclaimed that the author's sophisticated dilettante sculptor and amateur criminologist, Christopher Hand, already belonged in the pantheon of Great Detectives:

> We nominate Mr. Christopher Hand for a place in that distinguished company of detectives whose work has thrilled so many readers of crime fiction in both England and America. His ability as a forger, his utter disregard of such ordinary necessities as food and sleep, the fact that he is a dilettante of the arts and sciences, and his uncompromising persistence, make him worthy in every way to stand behind those masters—Sherlock Holmes, Philo Vance, Lord Peter Wimsey, Father Brown, Hanaud, Poirot, Dr. Thorndyke, Charlie Chan, Reggie Fortune and [Knopf's own] Sam Spade.

Certainly Knopf was no wallflower when it came to boosting its detective fiction to the American mystery-reading public. Beginning in 1919, the publishing firm had launched a hugely successful effort to boost the middling mainstream English novelist J. S. Fletcher as the greatest British mystery writer since Arthur Conan Doyle. In this aggressive commercial campaign Knopf made great use of the fact that President Woodrow Wilson had read Fletcher's detective novel *The Middle Temple Murder* (1919) and expressed his enjoyment of the tale.

"PRESIDENT WILSON HAS BEEN READING THE MIDDLE TEMPLE MURDER A Fine Detective Story by J. S. Fletcher," boasted Knopf's advertising in the November 22, 1919, issue of *The Publishers' Weekly*. Knopf made a similar effort with Stanley Page's Christopher Hand mysteries, though nothing was said on their part about the admitted detective fiction predilections of President Herbert Hoover, who was highly unpopular as the nation staggered through its third year of crushing economic depression.

Knopf, which published Page's first three Christopher Hand mysteries (*Sinister Cargo,* 1932, *The Resurrection Murder Case,* 1932, and *Fool's Gold,* 1933), excelled itself in the production design of the books, with each volume in the series having a striking dust jacket and an appealing uniform board design of serpentine lines. *Cargo* had dark green lines on a lighter green background, *Resurrection* blue lines on an orange-brown background and *Gold,* the fanciest of all, red lines on a faux gold leaf background. The jacket to *The Resurrection Murder Case* in particular is memorably ghoulish, but all three jackets are fine indeed.

Sinister Cargo, about endangered New York financier Robert Garrison and his retired stage musical actress spouse, begins with a miraculous country house murder and goes to some very queer corners indeed, was praised by Isaac Anderson in the *New York Times Book Review,* who in his notice avowed: "This story offers a continuous succession of thrills . . . . Christopher Hand has methods of his own. Sometimes they are more than a bit high-handed, and sometimes they are without the law, but they get results. This is Mr. Page's first detective story, but we gather that he intends to give us more stories of the exploits of Christopher Hand. We'll be waiting." In the *Saturday Review* William C. Weber was equally enthusiastic, writing, in a notice which made the book sound more like a Doyle

Sherlock Holmes or Hammett Continental Op novel: ". . . the story does stand up. . . . There are two picturesque villains named Spitz and Spawn, a variety of successful and unsuccessful attempts to kill a wealthy New Yorker and his friends, and a pitched battle finale on a little island off the Maine coast. . . ."

Sinister Cargo's weird and colorful climax on a "haunted" Maine island at times seems like an anticipation of John Carpenter's classic ghostly fright film *The Fog* (1980). For this final section of the tale the author drew on the "many summers he had spent with his family on the coast of Maine." The narrative is punctuated by a series of

wild criminal episodes which sometimes savor of pulp fiction, with Christopher Hand's slavishly loyal chronicler,
Ralph Clark, getting more pieces of the action, as it were,
than Philo Vance's poor pale shadow Van ever did. As in
Doyle's *The Hound of the Baskervilles*, Hand is absent from
a substantial chunk of the narrative but returns to the
scene to elucidate all of the remaining mysteries. Despite
their social standing Christopher Hand and Clark prove
something more of men of action than the cerebral Philo

Cover courtesy Curtis Evans

Vance and Van, at least until the late Van Dine's late Vance detective tale *The Kidnap Murder Case* (1936). The body count in the novel ends up rather high indeed.

Upon the appearance of Page's follow-up, *The Resurrection Murder Case,* the reviewer in the *Boston Transcript* huzzahed: "The many friends of Christopher Hand will rejoice to meet him again . . .The devious paths followed until the crime is brought home are sufficiently interesting to hold the attention and to make it difficult to lay down the book. . . . One reads many pages half expecting the crack of a bludgeon on one's own head." For his part A. P. Bryan in the *Lexington Herald-Leader* wrote: "Mr. Page takes the most complicated plot that has come to the attention of this reviewer in many months and weaves it into a logical and interesting, yet baffling story of mystery and adventure. . . . [Christoper Hand] eventually solves the entire mystery by one of the most ingenious devices yet introduced to detective fiction." In the *Philadelphia Inquirer,* E. W. P. raved of the novel: "Hand the investigator is brilliant, and the dénouement is breath-taking."

Page dedicated *The Resurrection Murder Case* to retired New York police captain Grant Williams, a pioneering specialist in reconstructing faces from the skulls of murder victims (Dominick La Rosa and Lillian White were two of his most noted cases) whom the press in the Twenties dubbed a "modern Sherlock Holmes."[2] The so-called "sculptor-sleuth" headed New York City's Bureau of Missing Persons, between its organization in 1914 and his retirement in 1928. Read the novel to see wherefore the dedication. It is set in and around Mill Ridge, New Jersey, "a fashionable community of larges estates" located on a ridge above the Great Swamp, which sounds a lot like places where the author himself had lived, like Chatham and Millburn.

Page's third mystery, *Fool's Gold,* which he penned in 1932 and published with Knopf in the Spring of 1933, reads rather like a Sherlock Holmes pastiche, allowing for the fact that it is set in Depression-era America rather than Victorian/Edwardian England. In the novel it appears that some criminal fiend has murdered a pair of grizzled gold prospectors, who had traveled to New York to find investors in their Alaska mining concern, and purloined from them the bills and gold they had kept stashed in their money belts. Unhappily involved in the problem are the congregants of the Hendley Congregational Church, who contributed to the ill-fated venture the sum of $50,000 (over a million dollars today), constituting their life savings.

The presence of the Hendley Congregational Church recalls the real-life Stanley Congregational Church, which Stanley Hart Page's grandfather as mentioned had founded and which Stanley would attend all of his life. Along the way to the solution of the various crimes Hand confronts a locked room murder problem as well. The notice in the *Los Angeles Times* declared of the inventive novel: "[T]he reader will be caught and will hold on until the [culprits] are discovered. . . . [T]here is a trick in this tale that will almost fool an experienced student of mystery yarns." Almost! The reviewer for Kentucky's *Lexington Herald-Leader,* on the other hand, avowed that "there's no chance of [readers] beating the author to the solution," adding: "You'll be flabbergasted by the number of clues that appear and the amount of action that is jammed into a 24-hour period." On May 7, 1933, the *San Francisco Chronicle* listed the novel as the Bay Region's #6 fiction bestseller of the week.

Page's mysteries won praise as well in the United Kingdom, where the author did not even have a really prestigious publisher behind him. When the second Hand opus, *The Resurrection Murder Case,* was published by Stanley

Paul in England in 1933 (the author's name was abbreviated there, for some reason, to S. Hart Page) an anonymous reviewer for the *Manchester Evening News* roundly praised the mystery as "[a]n American thriller of the most intense kind." In the *Leicester Mercury,* the writer of the column "From My Library Table" reflected that "with the thousands of 'thrillers' that are turned out every year it is amazing that we can still be mystified over any plot. But

Cover courtesy Curtis Evans

S. Hart Page keeps us in suspense throughout and then gives us the necessary jolt at the end. . . . *[The Resurrection Murder Case]* stamps him as one those few writers who can be relied upon to give us breathless adventure and a mental puzzle."

No less a figure than British mystery writer Richard Keverne lauded *Fool's Gold,* when it was published in England the next year, humorously writing: "Quite early in the story I thought I had guessed the solution to the mystery of *"Fool's Gold"*. . . . but later on the idiot police detective tumbled to the same solution, and of course it was wrong. So it was left to the Sherlock Holmesian Christopher Hand to put us both right, and Mr. S. Hart Page makes him do it in a most agreeable manner." The *Leicester Mercury* pronounced the novel a "really gripping yarn" and the Daily Mirror found it "very readable."

As has been seen above Stanley Hart Page drew upon his own privileged background for his mysteries. His Grandfather George was a noted trout angler in the state of Maine, in 1867 founding, in the remote village of Oquossoc, an angling club on the shores of Mooselucmeguntic Lake. According to *The American Fly Fisher,* George Shephard Page's "reputation and fame as a fish culturist were international in scope." Christopher Hand's detecting companion and chronicler Clark is a devotee of trout fishing, declaring in *The Resurrection Murder Case:* "I had heard of the excellent fishing in the vicinity of Mill Ridge. . . . It was with a light heart that I fell asleep that night. I visualized myself wading in a trout stream." Recalling Philo Vance's enthusiasms in *The Kennel Murder Case* (1933), George Shephard Page was also a breeder of Scottish Deerhounds. With such a background it is perhaps not surprising that one of their scions ended up writing a detective fiction series headlined by a Philo-esque gentleman detective.

Stanley Hart Page grew up in privileged circumstances in Chatham, New Jersey, along with two elder brothers, George Shephard Page and Lawrence Stanely Page, Jr., an elder sister, Elizabeth, and one younger brother, Henry de Bacon Page. Despite their fortune, there was tragedy in the family's life. One Sunday morning in January 1919 Stanley's sister Betty died at the age of twenty-one from the Spanish flu then raging around the world. At her death Betty Page, whose obituary avowed had been "universally beloved" from childhood, was doing Red Cross work and taking a "special course in domestic science" at Centenary Collegiate Institute in preparation for her impending marriage. Less than a year earlier, Stanley's brother George Shephard Page, a professional aviator, had been killed in the Great War.

Described on his 1942 draft card as 5'11", 155 pounds, brown-haired (though balding) and blue-eyed, Stanley Hart Page in late 1931, not long before publishing his first detective novel, wed Beatrice Bayard, daughter of an affluent old-money New Jersey magazine publisher and descendant of Anne Stuyvesant Bayard, sister of Peter Stuyvesant, the ill-fated seventeenth-century Director General of the Dutch colony of New Netherland. Beatrice Bayard, a lovely, doe-eyed twenty-four-year-old actress who had graduated from the American Academy of Dramatic Arts, had acted in traveling company and played small parts in two Broadway plays, the hit 1929 Edward G. Robinson comedy *Kibitzer* (2nd neighbor) and the 1928 revival of John Colton's 1926 melodrama *The Shanghai Gesture* (apprentice mouse). She had spent the summer before her marriage traveling around Europe with an auntly chaperone. She and Page were married in a small private ceremony at the Episcopal Church of the Transfiguration in Manhattan, popularly known as "The Little Church around the Corner," which liberally catered to theater folk and other bohemian types.[3]

Page credited his imaginative wife with having helped inspire him to start writing mysteries and he dedicated his first novel to her. The couple dwelt at the roughly $500,000 (in modern value) Millburn, New Jersey, home of Beatrice's parents, along with her siblings Stuyvesant and Martha. The Bayards employed a single maid, a young black woman from South Carolina memorably named Ida May Neville.

In 1933 Stanley and Beatrice produced one daughter, Martha Pintard Page, and Stanley produced two more

Beatrice Bayard Page

Christoper Hand mysteries, the aforementioned *Fool's Gold*
and *Murder Flies the Atlantic,* the latter of which innova-
tively is set on a zeppelin flying between London and New
York. It was published by a rather less distinguished concern, Alfred H. King. Despite Knopf's vigorous pushing
in the press and his supposed winning of "many friends,"
Christopher Hand sadly had not in fact become the Next
Big Thing in the way of dilettante detectives. Two years

later there followed from Page's hand, as it were, Christopher Hand's finale *The Tragic Curtain,* which was published by The Dial Press. The author appears then to have laid down his pen, at least as it concerned crime writing.

Page continued to receive press praise for his last two detective novels, however, with, for example, the *Boston Globe* labeling *Atlantic* "a tense and thrilling story that is admirable written" and the *Houston Post* avowing of *Curtain:* "It is well-told, complicated and interesting." With *Curtain* Page provided a fitting end for the series. "There is a certain ingenuity in this work, one which makes it difficult to put it down," reflected the reviewer of the novel in the *Baltimore Evening Sun.* "Mr. Page . . . has thought up a solution to his crimes which pretty completely baffles the reader until the denouement is reached. Moreover, he plays fair and doesn't break the established rules of the game."

Although his detective thus vanished seemingly without a trace ninety years ago, Stanley Hart Page himself lived on for over four decades. For years he and Beatrice were actively involved in the Chatham Community Players, who in 1941 performed Stanley's play *A Welcome Stranger,* which the Chatham Press called a "lively, uproariously funny farce." Hardly in need of money, Page retired relatively young from the news business in 1952 and passed away after a lengthy illness at the age of seventy-seven on August 4, 1979. For nine decades now Page's sleuth Christopher Hand has waited to experience his own miraculous resurrection. While admittedly, despite all the puffing from his first publisher, no Philo Vance, Christopher Hand for a very short time was a name much bruited-about in mystery-loving circles. See for yourself what you think of this clever fella.

ENDNOTES:

[1] On Vapo-Cresolene and George Shephard Page and his children, see the online accounts provided by John Langlois, "On Beyond Holcombe: Vapo-Cresolene," *1898 Revenues: United States Revenue Stamps That Financed the Spanish American War*, 12 November 2012, and by Dan Edminster, "Lamps Designed for Medicinal Purposes: Vapo-Cresolene and Schering's Formalin Lamps," *The Lampworks: An On-Line Resource for Lighting Researchers and Collectors of Oil and Kerosene Lamps, Burners and Other Trimmings*, at http://www.thelampworks.com/lw_vapo_cresolene.htm. On the AMA's 1908 report on Vapo-Cresolene, see *Nostrums and Quackery* (Chicago: American Medical Association, 1912), 626. On the overall dubiousness of Vapo-Cresolene, see James Harvey Young, *The Toadstool Millionaires: A Social History of Patent Medicine in American before Federal Regulation* (Princeton, NJ: Princeton University Press, 1961), 215. George Shephard Page, bluntly notes William D. Eddy *in Stone Pond: A Personal History* (1982; rev. ed., White Plains, NY: Plain White Press, 1988), was "colorful, eccentric and ultimately mad. . . . In the quaint phrases of his obituary, he was 'deprived of his reason and removed to the State Insane Asylum at Morris Plains, NJ'" (p. 51. n. 4).

[2] A 1936 letter writer to *Time* detailed the Lillian White case:

> In April 1922, acting Captain Grant Williams of the New York City police department was imported to Rockland County, handed a skull and other bones found on Cheesecock Mountain and asked to solve the mystery of its presence there. Sterilizing the skull, he placed it on an artificial neck made out of a curtain pole shaved down to fit the opening of the spinal column. Inside the skull on either side of the pole, he wedged two radio tubes to hold the head steady. The other end of the pole he fitted in a stand made of a soap box.

Greasing his fingers, Williams then coated the skull with modeling clay. He spread it thinly, following the contour of the bone evenly. Gradually he applied other layers, feeling his own jowls & forehead for guidance. The length of the nose he determined by measuring the distance between the bridge and the roots of the upper teeth: its contour by following the curve of the nasal bone. To get the fullness of the cheeks he held a pencil from the cheekbone down to the jawbone and allowed a little for normal rounding. He used the same instrument to determine the set of the eyes, holding it slantwise from the eye socket to the cheekbone. . . . The brows he determined by beginning at the inside corner of the eye socket and following around the upper edge of the bone; the fullness of the lips by the protrusions and recessions of the upper and lower teeth. And so on. . . .

Until, 56 hours later, when he had dipped the flesh-colored clay in wax, inserted glass eyes and dressed the victim's original hair, which providentially had been recovered near the skull, he had before him the snub-nosed, sullen face of a temperamental Irish girl.

The rebuilt corpse was subsequently identified as Lillian White, an inmate of Letchworth [a New York residential institution]. The identification was upheld by Justice Arthur S. Tompkins of the New York Supreme Court; and her murderer, Joseph Blunt, was subsequently caught in Maine.

[3] The Church of the Transfiguration was built and consecrated in 1849. During the New York City draft riots of 1863, Rector George Hendric Houghto, gave shelter to African-Americans who were targets of a draft-protesting white mob. Houghton was said to have turned the rioters away, sternly admonishing: "You white devils, you! Do you know nothing of the spirit of

Christ?" The church's nickname came about thusly: In 1870 the rector of the Church of the Atonement refused to conduct funeral services for a deceased actor, airily telling his friend, famed thespian Jefferson Farjeon (grandfather of English mystery writer Jefferson Farjeon), "I believe there is a little church around the corner where they do that sort of thing." Farjeon allegedly responded: "If that be so, God bless the little church around the corner!"

I

CORPUS DELICTI

For a man who regards entertainment as one of life's un-
necessary frills, Christopher Hand was gratifyingly appre-
ciative. But it was a good play that I had literally dragged
him off to that evening.

He sat beside me, scarcely breathing, his eyes on the
stage. Except for his cramped attitude, occasioned by
jamming his long, lean body into the theatre seat, he
appeared, I noticed with pleasure, to be enjoying the performance immensely. Hardly a word had I got out of him
during the intermission between the first and second acts.
But toward the end of the second act he suddenly snapped
his fingers. The action of the play, from that moment, no
longer seemed to enthrall him. He fidgeted in his seat,
took things from his pockets, examined them and put
them back; and altogether he became the general nuisance
to those round us that he always is when he condescends
to accompany me to the theatre. As the curtain rang down
on the second act, he turned his sharp face to me.

"What went on in those two acts, Clark?" he asked,
innocently.

"Eh?" I said. "What went on? Didn't you see for yourself?"

"Of course not."

"Of course not? Why, you were looking right at it!"

25

"Oh, was I?" he asked serenely. "I hadn't realized it. While you were wasting your time watching that play, Clark, my mind was dwelling upon a subject of the utmost importance. I came to quite a conclusion about it, too. My theory concerns the deterioration of the criminal mind. And, my boy—would you believe it?—I evolved it by applying versions of the theories of Darwin, Weismann and the Chevalier de Lamarck to actual facts! Let's go out for a cigarette, and I'll explain it."

"I refuse to ask these people to allow us to climb over them," I retorted, indicating the row of people between us and the aisle. "You have got them all on edge, anyway, with your fussing about."

"All right," shrugged Hand. "I wouldn't have time to expound it; so perhaps it's just as well. But then, we might go back to the rooms. You're anxious to see the rest of the play?"

"Oh, I don't care," I replied, irritably. "We might as well go; you've spoilt it for me."

"I don't want to hurry you along, Clark," said Hand, reaching under the seat for his hat.

"It's quite all right," I said, bitterly. "But let's get out before the curtain rises. Hold on, we're too late. The curtain is going—oh, well."

Hand was plowing his way through the maze of legs that filled the space between the seat-rows. We left a mutter of ill-will behind us as we started up the aisle. I decided then and there that I would never entice Christopher Hand to the theatre again.

I was not in a receptive mood for Hand's theory, but I had to listen to it, nevertheless, all the way home in the taxi. As we started up the stairs to our rooms, a sudden thought struck me.

"See here," I said, catching him by the arm. "This is your month for paying our rent. I hope you remembered to do it, for it should have been done last week."

"Oh, yes," said Hand, vacantly. "That's too bad."

"You mean you haven't paid it?"

"Inexcusable of me."

"Well, it really is. Mrs. Flemming needs the money, and you know as well as I do that she'd never ask us for it. But here, I have my checkbook with me; I'll pay the rent now, and you can do it next month."

"Splendid, Clark, splendid! Come right up after you've given Mrs. Flemming the check. I'll just go on up now."

I passed a few moments with Mrs. Flemming at her door; then I went on up to the rooms. Hand sat sprawled in his Morris chair, gazing glumly at his feet. After watching him for a moment, a smile got possession of my lips.

"Don't take it so much to heart," I chuckled. "I know how details of that sort bother you if you think you must attend to them."

"Why do people get so excited?" he sighed.

"But my dear fellow, I'm not!" I protested.

He seemed not to hear me. I turned to the closet to put my hat away. As I was returning to go over to my chair, there came a peremptory rap at our door. I glanced sharply at Hand, who remained immovable. It was impossible that the caller could be one of his creditors coming round at such an hour. I crossed to the door and threw it open.

In the hallway stood Inspector Gerrity, looking, as usual, as if he were carved out of the hardest kind of rock. Puffing on the cigar between his lips, he blew a cloud of smoke into the room, following in after it. I closed the door after him. Hand stirred in his chair.

"Obviously, Inspector," he said, "a man's dead body can't get up and walk away."

The cigar fell from Gerrity's lips to the floor. His eyes popped wide open.

"Blast it!" he exclaimed. "I believe you hover over the city like a disembodied spirit, watching every move the entire population makes."

"The trouble with you, Inspector," said Hand, cocking an eye at the police official, "is that you are too blunt. I've said it before. You have no flare for the subtleties. The mere fact that I, without preamble, make a statement concerning a murder that has just been committed takes you completely off your feet. You begin to think that I have read your mind, or that I have accomplished something supernatural."

"Well, what in blazes do you call it, then?" demanded Gerrity.

Hand quietly ignored the question.

"You should let everything that you see, everything that you hear," said he, "filter through your mind to the innermost recesses of your truly excellent intellect. Don't let it bounce right out again through your mouth, Inspector. Had you thought for a moment, you would have realized that I have a client, a man who has a lively interest in the case, a man who has called me on the phone and given me some meagre details. Why do people get excited? He hung up before he had so much as told me where the crime was committed. But he is on his way over here."

"Oh," growled Gerrity, sinking into my easy chair.

I made shift to get the inspector's cigar off the rug, where it had lain unnoticed. It did not altogether look out of place there, for Hand had been doing some clay modeling in the living-room during the afternoon. I had had no chance to clean up the mess, and he, of course, would not bother about it. But after all, the cigar was burning a hole in the rug. Gerrity accepted it from me and jammed it back between his powerful jaws.

"Your client the nephew?" he asked.

"The nephew," affirmed Hand. "Mr. Woodford Amesbury."

"Coming here, eh?" growled Gerrity. "He told me when I spoke with him on the phone he'd come right over to his uncle's place."

"It would be interesting to know where that is," said Hand.

"Right round the corner here," replied Gerrity. "They're over there now looking for finger-prints and so on. Thought I'd drop in and tell you about it."

I knew that he thought more than that. Gerrity, if he had told the truth, also thought that Hand might give him a few very helpful suggestions. But I was completely in the dark about the whole thing. I immediately set about correcting my ignorant position.

"As far as I'm concerned," I complained, "you fellows are talking like a couple of magpies. What's all this about dead bodies getting up and walking round?"

"The inspector might enlighten us both," suggested Hand.

"All right," agreed Gerrity. "It's like this. The deceased, if there is a deceased, is Jeremy Amesbury."

"Never heard of him," I said.

"Neither have I," shrugged Gerrity. "Not until a few minutes ago, that is. We might well have, though. He was something of a character. He was a prospector for gold. Found it, too, recently in Alaska. He was here raising money for mining operations, he and his partner. Both men were unusual, as far as New Yorkers go. They wore their hair long, and both had beards. Between fifty-five and sixty years old, both of 'em. I found that much out about 'em from their landlady."

"Were you able to find out anything else?" asked Hand, stirring slightly in his chair.

"Yes," replied Gerrity, dubiously, "but I don't know what to make of it. Amesbury was in the habit of having coffee served to him in his room about ten-thirty every night. He and his partner, who lived in the same house, would sit there and drink it. Well, tonight when the land-lady took the coffee in she found only one of 'em there. That was Amesbury, and he was dead."

"Must have been quite a shock to her," I observed.

"How did she know he was dead?" demanded Hand, his gray eyes peering sharply at the inspector.

"She was pretty sure he was," replied Gerrity, "and I guess he must have been. There was a long bowie-knife sticking into his heart. She says Amesbury was lying on the floor with his beard sticking straight up in the air. I've got the bowie-knife, and it's covered with blood."

"But you haven't the corpse?" asked Hand.

"That's the trouble!" cried Gerrity, banging his huge fist on the arm of the chair. "The landlady ran out and got a patrolman. When they got back to the room the body was gone!"

Hand thought for a moment. Gerrity looked expectantly at him, and so did I. At length his eyelids flew up and he shot a glance at Gerrity.

"What about the partner?" he asked.

"Don't know," growled the inspector. "He's the man I want, though."

"You can't locate him?"

"We've been looking all over for him. He's gone."

"You think he murdered Amesbury?"

"I'm sure of it. They had a lot of money; I don't know how much yet, but it was a lot. They've been here all summer. The minister of the Hendly Congregational Church over on Sixth Avenue was a friend of Amesbury. They had trouble raising money through the regular channels, and the upshot of it was that they got a lot of people belonging to that church to put their private savings into this venture of theirs. They were due to leave for Alaska tomorrow, and they had the money with them."

"You don't mean that they had it in cash?" asked Hand, in astonishment.

"As nearly as I can make out they did," replied Gerrity. "They were a funny pair, as I said before. They didn't operate the way city people do. But my information is too sketchy. If you're in this case, let's work together, as usual. But let's get started. Want to visit Amesbury's room?"

"Yes," said Hand, "but first I have an appointment to meet my client here. It seems to me that we might get some valuable information from him."

"I don't think you will," averred Gerrity. "He just got in from Washington. He called his uncle on the phone while I was there."

"Nevertheless," said Hand, "I think we are about to see him, if I'm right in assuming that it is his step I hear on the stair."

I had not heard a step on the stair, but Hand's ears are far sharper than mine.

"I might ask you, Inspector," said Hand, quickly, "what is the name of Amesbury's partner?"

"Nick Haggerty," replied Gerrity. "From what I've learned, the description I gave you of Amesbury would do just as well for his partner. But I've only touched the surface of this case."

A moment later there came a rap on the door. I crossed the room and opened it.

The man, in the neighborhood of thirty, who stood there was large and raw-boned. A mop of black hair sur-mounted an angular face, and from under quite bushy black eyebrows a pair of incongruously gray eyes peered sharply at me. He wore an ill-fitting blue suit, and in his right hand he held a pair of pigskin gloves and a new light gray fedora. Shifting his eyes from me, he glanced into the room.

Hand rose slowly from his chair and smiled upon our visitor.

"Mr. Amesbury?" he asked.

"I am Mr. Amesbury," affirmed the man. "Am I speaking to Mr. Hand?"

"You are," said my friend. "That gentleman holding the door for you is my friend, Mr. Ralph Clark. Also let me introduce to you Inspector Gerrity of the police department. Won't you come in?"

Amesbury, bowing respectively to Gerrity and me, solemnly entered the room. With a diffident air he stopped before the inspector.

"I believe I talked with you on the telephone," he said.

"Yes," said Gerrity succinctly, remembering, no doubt, that Amesbury had broken his word to him.

Hand offered his client a chair, which the man dropped into with a sigh. Although Amesbury was tall, he had to look up into Hand's eyes when he passed him.

"Have you discovered anything new?" he asked, becoming a little animated. "You aren't sure it's murder? You can't be positive!"

"No," grunted Gerrity. "I don't know any more now than I did when I talked to you before."

"Why—why this seems unbelievable," cried Amesbury. "I came to New York to see my uncle before he left for Alaska and—why, he must have been murdered almost at the very minute that I arrived here to see him!"

Hand, who had remained standing with arms folded, turned to Amesbury.

"When did you arrive in New York?" he asked.

"Well," replied the man, wrinkling his brow, "I arrived at the hotel about ten-thirty. I got a room, got my luggage in, and then called my uncle. Inspector Gerrity answered and gave me this frightful news."

"And got your word that you'd come right over there," frowned Gerrity.

Amesbury, for a moment, seemed mildly disconcerted. "I'm sorry about that, Inspector," he said. "But on my way down in the elevator I got to thinking that I should do something to find my uncle. I mean," he hastily added, catching the gleam that had come into Gerrity's eyes, "that I couldn't feel at all easy unless I did something myself. Do you see what I mean? Well, I asked them at the desk whether they could recommend a good criminologist, and they advised my getting hold of Christopher Hand. I thought I'd drop in here, pick him up, and then go on to confer with you. I hope I haven't done anything to offend you."

"No, indeed," cut in Hand, as Gerrity was about to make a retort. "How did you arrive in New York, Mr. Amesbury?"

"By automobile."

"From Washington?"

"Farther than that," smiled Amesbury. "I came from Texas. But I didn't expect to get here so soon. I had intended to spend a day or so in Washington, sight-seeing, but when I reached my hotel there I found a letter waiting for me from my uncle. He said he had had splendid success in raising his money, and was leaving for Alaska the eighteenth, which is tomorrow, of course. I wired that I'd try to get here before he left. I set out for New York right away; didn't realize I could make it in such a hurry. And now I find this. As I said before, I can't believe it!"

Gerrity fished into his coat pocket and produced a yellow slip of paper. He passed it over to Amesbury.

"That your wire?" he grunted.

"Why, yes," replied Amesbury. "Where'd you get it?"

"At your uncle's room," said Gerrity.

"See here," suddenly objected Amesbury, "I've told you all about myself; how about telling me something about this fearful affair? I came here for information, Mr. Hand."

"I have none," said Hand. "Inspector Gerrity has a little." Amesbury looked questioningly at the inspector, who gruffly outlined what he had learned about the case. Then Amesbury turned to Hand.

"What is to be done?" he cried. "My uncle may not be dead at all. He may have been carried off somewhere. Perhaps he needs help. Can't we do anything? Come, Mr. Hand, what do you suggest?"

"I fancy that Inspector Gerrity has taken measures to locate your uncle," replied Hand. "For the moment they will have to suffice. We shall get much further by starting from a given point, if we can find one, than we should by rushing headlong into the dark. You yourself may be of inestimable value in that connection. I want to ask you a few questions. I'll make them as brief as possible, and I'll hasten through them. Then we will go out and see what we can accomplish."

"Well, then—" prompted Amesbury.

"You see my purpose, Inspector?" said Hand. "If a murder has been done, and if robbery was the motive, why, anyone, bar none, could be the perpetrator. I grant you that at the moment it certainly looks like robbery, and it also looks as if Haggerty is our man. On the other hand, there may be some reason, something deep and underlying, that has culminated in a tragedy. We have here a close relative of the victim; perhaps he can tell us something about his uncle from which we can construct a case."

"I'll tell you anything I know," promised Amesbury. "But, for heaven's sake, let us get started!"

"Very well," said Hand. "Mr. Amesbury, how close were you to your uncle?"

Amesbury paid close attention to Hand's questions. His answers to them tumbled forth almost before his interrogator had stopped speaking, as if the man wished to speed up the business.

"My uncle and I were not very close," he said. "That is cause for regret—now. He was a wanderer, and so am I. A pity that our trails were not more convergent."

"When did you see him last?"

"About two years ago. When he left the first time for Alaska."

"Where did this meeting take place?"

"In Los Angeles."

"But you have communicated since?"

"Intermittently. For long stretches my uncle was cut off from civilization. He provided me with a forwarding address, and I gave him mine."

"At your last meeting, or since through his letters, did your uncle give you any intimation that he had earned the enmity of anyone?"

Amesbury, for the first time, paused and frowned thoughtfully.

"Yes," he slowly replied. "My uncle found it easy to get at odds with his fellows. I'm afraid it is a family trait. But those who knew him well paid no attention to his occasional irritability. In fact, it amused the few intimates that he had. His partner, Nick Haggerty, was much the same way. Probably got that way from his long association with my uncle, who was very strong-willed and could impress his personality upon others. At any rate, they squabbled incessantly."

"Very interesting," nodded Hand, with approval. "Gives us a most helpful insight to your uncle's character. But, if you happen to know, did this trait gain your uncle any real enemies?"

"I doubt it. But, as a matter of fact, I don't know. I can tell you, though, that there was a man who was playing a dangerous game with my uncle and Haggerty."

"Ha! And this man was—"

"A renegade Portuguese. His name was—hum-m—I'm afraid I have lost it."

"Think!"

"I—no, I can't recollect it. Perhaps it will come to me. Peculiar name."

"Then what was this dangerous game he was playing?"

"Why—and you may not know this—my uncle and Haggerty had staked a claim in Alaska. They had reason to believe there were rich gold deposits on it. The Portuguese, whatever his name was, attempted to jump their claim. He failed, although there was some desperate business before he was eliminated. My uncle, as was his habit in writing, furnished me with only the barest details. The episode, however, holds no interest for us, because it ended with the death of the Portuguese."

"Dear, dear. But then, what you do know of it would be interesting."

"Oh, very well. The claim is situated in a particularly wild country. The matter evolved into a race for the assayer's office. This the Portuguese attempted to win by the expedient of ambushing my uncle and Haggerty with the intention of killing them. But he was pitted against two such formidable opponents that the tables were turned. The Portuguese himself was shot."

"And killed?"

"There was no absolute proof that he was, but there seems no likelihood that he survived. He escaped on horseback, but he was so sorely wounded that he left a trail of blood behind him. Later in the day my uncle and Haggerty came upon his riderless horse, the saddle soaked with gore. As it was a fearsome country with no habitation within miles, the man must surely have perished."

"Yes, indeed. It would be as well, however, to learn his name. Your uncle wrote you of this unpleasant affair, so you said. Have you the letter with which to refresh your memory?"

"I haven't; I destroyed it. Ordinarily, I don't hang on to correspondence. Fact is, the letter from my uncle which I received in Washington is the only one of his that I have.

Here it is; he has given me his address and telephone number, you will notice. That is why I preserved it."

Hand took the letter and, extracting it from the envelope, rapidly scanned it. He gave it to Gerrity, who also read it. Taking the letter back again and putting it into his pocket, Hand turned to Amesbury.

"If you don't mind," he said, "I shall keep this. It has one or two items of interest that might prove useful."

"By all means," agreed Amesbury, with a shrug. "You will notice the paucity of information concerning the writer. My uncle loved to entertain a group of listeners with accounts of his adventures, and at such times, I feel sure, he put no curb upon his imagination. But unless he had figured in something that would make a good story, he scorned to mention it."

"He wasted no ink on personal tidbits, eh?"

"None whatever."

"Just let me get this straight," interposed Gerrity, leaning forward in his chair. "You came all the way from Texas to see your uncle for a few hours before he left for Alaska. That right?"

Amesbury regarded Gerrity a little resentfully. I could see that the pair were not going to get along together.

"Why, no," drawled Amesbury, and let it go at that.

"Perhaps," said Hand, "since the inspector wants to know, you could be a trifle more explicit, Mr. Amesbury."

"All right," agreed the man. "It has been my intention for some time to come east. I had hoped to get here sooner, but somehow or other I couldn't seem to get started. I planned, naturally, to make my visit to New York coincide with my uncle's being here. He seemed to be having trouble raising his money, and I thought he would be here a good deal longer than it turned out was necessary. After I received that note in Washington, I hurried right on."

"Then," said Hand, "upon arriving in New York, you went right to the Skelton, engaged quarters, and called your uncle from your room—seven hundred and two, isn't it?"

"I—I beg your pardon," cried Amesbury, flushing slightly. "I was not aware that I had given you the name of my hotel, but, by thunder, I'm sure I didn't give you my room number!"

"You were rather excited when you called me up," pointed out Hand, moving over to the closet. "I presume that was to blame for your neglecting to leave your room key at the hotel desk. The tab of it, at any rate, is protruding above your waistcoat pocket. Insecure place for it. Only the tops of the numerals are displayed. Seven hundred and two, isn't it?"

Amesbury snatched the key from his pocket. He held it up and sharply scrutinized the tab. Then he thrust it deep into his trousers pocket.

"Seven hundred and three," he snapped.

"Ah," said Hand, emerging from the closet with his hat on his head. "I suppose your uncle was a native of New England, as you are yourself."

Amesbury commenced to look a little wild.

"How do you know I come from New England?" he demanded.

"Travelling has not taken that New England twang from your voice," smiled Hand. "Vermont, I should say."

"New Hampshire," corrected Amesbury. "My uncle and I are both natives of Meadowbrook, New Hampshire. Before you go finding it out from the way I breathe, or something, I'll tell you that my uncle is my only living relative."

"The only thing your breathing tells me," laughed Hand, "is that you have a splendid pair of lungs. But come, Inspector, let us go over to Jeremy Amesbury's room. We have reconstructed the man; now let us attempt to reconstruct what has befallen him."

2

DEDUCTIONS

A short walk took us to our destination. On the way over,
Gerrity, who seemed very much interested in Hand's client,
elicited more information concerning Amesbury. Grudg-
ingly the client told the inspector he had inherited from
his father a business in his native town together with a
comfortable income from investments. Since he had been
graduated from college eight years before, he had sold the
business and knocked about as his fancy directed him.

We stood before a brick building of ordinary appearance. Against the iron lattice of the small porch leaned a
policeman. As the inspector led us up the steps, he quickly
assumed a more business-like attitude.

Hand, on the way over, had walked like one in a dream.
His head was bowed on his chest. As we rounded a corner, he would have marched right on without us had I not
grasped him by the sleeve. But as we entered the building
where had been enacted the mysterious scene, perhaps the
last in the drama of Jeremy Amesbury's life, a swift change
came over him. His whole body became electrified, his
head snapped erect, his hands flew out of his pockets, and
there came that gleam to his gray eyes that means they are
alert to the most minute detail that they chance to fall
upon.

"We will go first to Amesbury's room, Inspector," he snapped.

"But I thought you might like to question the landlady first."

"On the contrary, I should like to question her afterwards."

Gerrity shrugged and led the way up a dark flight of stairs. The house had that musty smell that belongs to all old brick buildings of that sort. A bulb of low candlepower shed a feeble light at the stair-head, sending a long, slanting shadow of Gerrity's broad shoulders along the wall beside us. We gained the gloomy, narrow hall on the second floor and followed Gerrity round a turn to a door in the right wall. Before it stood a second policeman, his brass buttons shining dimly. Gerrity turned the knob and thrust the door open.

A table-lamp, with its shade cocked up at an angle, stood on a small table in the far corner of the room. It sent its rays across the floor toward an iron bed in an opposite corner. A chair before the table lay on its back. Against the wall beside the table, on the side nearest us, lay a duffle-bag, its contents strewn about the floor in disarray. On the floor at our feet lay several pieces of broken china and two silver tea-spoons. The threadbare rug was stained dark with some liquid. The only other objects in the room, with its blank white walls, was an old easy chair, the seat almost sagging to the floor, and a battered chest of drawers across from the table.

"Nothing has been touched?" asked Hand, quickly.

"Nothing," grunted Gerrity.

"I see that the finger-print men have been at work."

"They should have."

Hand crossed quickly over to the table. There his body froze into an alert attitude, but his eyes darted rapidly over the table-top. On it, beside a leather tobacco-pouch bearing the appearance of long use, lay a charred pipe, the bit all but worn through. There was also a pile of burnt matches and a scattering of tobacco ash. The most significant articles to be found there, however, were an open bottle of ink, a pen with a stub point, and a sheet of white paper. Upon it someone had commenced to write. I leaned over my friend's shoulder and read:

Dear Woody—
If you don't get here before we leave, I want to

"I recognize my uncle's tobacco-pouch and pipe," announced Amesbury, crowding up to us. "He's carried them for years."

"Perhaps you recognize your uncle's handwriting here," said Hand, pointing to the sheet of paper lying on the table. "This note was intended for you, I should say. He was interrupted before he got far. Yes, it's his handwriting; no doubt of it," he said, comparing it with Amesbury's letter, which he had snatched from his pocket.

"He must have been attacked while he was writing to me," said Amesbury, in a strained voice. "Oh, this is dreadful! We must find him!"

Hand swung about, regarded the overturned chair for an instant, looked searchingly at the bed, which was all made up, and then walked quickly over to the easy chair. There he remained for several minutes, peering sharply down at it. The rest of us remained by the table watching him.

Just as I was beginning to think Hand would never cease bending over the chair, he turned with one of his quick, furtive strides and reached the stain on the rug near the door. Dropping to one knee, he glanced critically at the broken china and the two spoons. Even I could tell that the debris had once been two cups and saucers, probably filled with coffee. A little brown liquid remained in one concave fragment. Hand raised it to his nose and sniffed it.

"You were right, Clark," he observed, "the landlady did get a shock. You notice, Inspector, there is no evidence here of sugar and cream having tumbled with the rest of this. But then, the typical outdoor man does not take such frills with his coffee. This fits in properly. Some pieces of the china are missing. See, there is only one cup-handle here. Your finger-print men no doubt could account for that."

Next he rose to his feet and crossed quickly to the only window in the room. It was open, as the night was warm. Thrusting his head and shoulders out, he remained thus for fully a minute. Finally he withdrew his head and turned to us, fixing his eyes on Gerrity.

"No blood-stains," he said.

"The knife was covered with blood," said Gerrity, almost defensively.

"Where was the body when the landlady saw it?"

"About the middle of the room."

"You questioned her quite acutely on that point, I presume. Indicate exactly where the body was when she saw it, Inspector, if you will."

Gerrity took a piece of chalk from his vest pocket. With it he traced the rough outline of a man's body on the floor. Hand looked it over carefully from one side; then he crossed over to the other. After carefully measuring with his eye the distance of all objects in the room from the sketched figure on the floor, he turned once again to Gerrity.

"Where did you find the knife, Inspector?" he asked.

"Under the front stairs."

"There is a closet under the front stairs?"

"That's it. It was in that closet that I found the knife."

"You moved not only swiftly, but adroitly, Inspector. You reasoned quickly."

Gerrity strutted across the room and sat on the arm of the easy chair.

"Not very difficult," said he, with much importance. "The moment I got here, I saw the whole thing. Of course, Hand, I've got to admit to you that I have withheld one of the most important facts."

"I'll wager that there was a car at the front!" cried Hand, crossing his arms and glancing sidewise at Gerrity.

"Who told you that?" demanded the inspector.

"It would be necessary to your deductions," replied Hand. "You see, Inspector, after all, you are leading me. Let me give you your views. Upon arriving here and looking over the situation, you reasoned that the murderer, just after committing the crime, heard the landlady arriving with the coffee. He hid in that closet over there until she had gone bustling off after help. Then he emerged, shouldered the corpse, and made for the front stairs. After the landlady and the policeman had raced up the stairs, he came out of his sanctuary, rushed out of the house, deposited the body in the waiting car, and drove away. The knife either slipped from the wound while the body was in the closet, or the murderer removed it in order that no one should see it by any chance when he carried the body outside."

"You have to admit," cried Gerrity, "that I was the first to deduce it. And there was a car outside. The patrolman who answered the landlady's alarm saw it when he went in; and when he went out, it was gone!"

"Naturally," agreed Hand. "Now, it remains to deduce how this crime was committed. Have you formed any theories on that, Inspector?"

"Before you do that," interrupted Amesbury, who was becoming more and more agitated by the deductions that had already been made, "why don't you try to form some theories to the effect that no murder has been committed at all?"

"That is really a corollary," explained Hand, "to the hypothesis that there has been a murder. If we can't form a theory supporting a crime, it must mean that there was no crime. But I'm terribly afraid that there was one."

"How about yourself?" Gerrity asked Hand. "Have you formed any theory on how this murder was committed?"

"I'm too fresh on the case," replied Hand. "My ideas are not set. But surely you, who have been on the case from the outset, have formed a very definite opinion. What is it, Inspector?"

"Well," began Gerrity, once more filling with self-importance, "I think I can explain that for you, too. It's obvious enough that this man was attacked. Nobody thrust that knife into his heart when he wasn't looking for it. He had no visitor, because he was writing over there at that table when he heard someone behind him. He jumped up, overturning the chair and knocking the lamp-shade over the way it is. Then he grappled with his assailant, but the knife put an end to the struggle. The rest of it, which is the very deductions that I made on the spot, you have already told us."

"Excellent!" cried Hand. "Inspector, you excel yourself. But there is one thing that you have overlooked."

"Something I have overlooked?" asked Gerrity, incredulously.

"That rifled duffle-bag over there," pointed out Hand.

"Oh, yes," admitted Gerrity, rather crestfallen. "I forgot about that. The money was in the duffle-bag, and Haggerty, of course, pulled the contents out to get at it. He carried the money away with him along with the corpse."

"What money?" asked Amesbury.

"The inspector believes," explained Hand, "that your uncle and Nick Haggerty had here in this room the money they had raised. He thinks it was in cash."

"What on earth would they have it in cash for?" demanded Amesbury. "And if my uncle was murdered, what explanation can there be for his body's being carried off?"

"That's something we've got to find out," replied Gerrity.

"Do I understand," asked Amesbury, glancing sharply at Gerrity, "that you suspect Nick Haggerty of having murdered my uncle?"

"He's disappeared," said Gerrity, with a shrug.

"Surely you don't believe that, Mr. Hand?" cried Amesbury.

Hand had moved over to the duffle-bag. He appeared not to have heard his client. He stood looking down upon the assortment, mostly rough clothing, that was strewn about.

"I've looked that all over very carefully," said Gerrity. "Nothing there except what you'd expect a man heading for the wilds would take with him."

"Do you know who owned that bowie-knife?" asked Hand, abruptly.

"I think it probably belonged to Amesbury," replied Gerrity.

"Just to make sure, I suppose you are having the substance with which it was stained examined."

"It's blood, all right."

"I feel sure that it is. It would be as well to determine that it is human blood. An analysis should be made, Inspector."

"Well, all right. They're examining it for finger-prints now. I'd better call them right away and tell them to take it to the laboratory."

Gerrity strode out of the room, and Hand turned his attention to the closet, situated across the room from the table. I looked out the window. It opened, I found, into a dark, narrow alley running between the building we were in and another, similar to it, next door. The distance between the buildings, I judged, was approximately twelve feet.

When I turned back to the room, Hand was emerging from the closet. In his hand he held a somewhat battered sombrero.

"Is this your uncle's hat?" he asked Amesbury.

"I suppose it is," replied the client, walking over to examine the head-piece. "He always wore one."

"There is nothing else in the closet," said Hand, returning the hat to its hook. "Ah, there is the inspector back again. Do you know where Haggerty's room is located?"

"They're not connected," replied Gerrity, "but it's right next to this one. Are you through in here?"

"Yes," said Hand, making for the door. "Let's see what we can find in Haggerty's room. I hope we have as much success as we had here."

With the exception of a more orderly appearance, Haggerty's room was much like his partner's. The room was in darkness, but, upon lighting it, we saw a duffle-bag, similar to Amesbury's, resting against the wall. It was fully packed. Hand immediately untied it and pulled it open.

"You haven't examined the contents of this, Inspector?" he said.

"No, I haven't."

"This knot told me as much."

"But we really have no right to go through his stuff—yet."

"Bah!" growled Hand, up-ending the bag and tumbling the contents out on the floor. Haggerty's possessions were almost duplicates of Amesbury's. But, with an exclamation, Hand reached down and picked something out of the pile. He lifted it up, and I saw that it was a bowie-knife, sheathed in a leather holster.

"That's almost the same kind of knife that I found!" cried Gerrity.

"I dare say," said Hand, taking the knife from its sheath, being careful to touch only the tips of the guard. "They are all more or less alike. The fact is, however, that it is not the same knife. If Haggerty killed his partner, he used Amesbury's knife to kill him with. Mr. Amesbury, did your uncle carry a pistol?"

"He did," replied Amesbury. "And carry is the right word for it. He always had it on him except when he slept, and then it was under his pillow, if he had one. If he had no pillow, then he slept with his head on his saddle, and his gun under that."

"If Haggerty has a pistol," said Hand, "he must be just as attached to it. It must be with him now, for it is certainly not here. There you are, Inspector; perhaps you can match the finger-prints on the handle of this knife with those on the one you have. It should be significant if you do. And now let us interview the landlady."

Gerrity took the knife. He carefully wrapped it up in his handkerchief and placed it in his inside coat pocket. Then we trooped from the room.

Down the stairs the inspector led us and then toward the back of the house. Here the hallway was almost in complete darkness. He halted before a door, under which there was a faint streamer of light. He rapped energetically. I heard a woman's soft exclamation and the sound of someone crossing the room. A moment later the door was timidly opened.

Immediately I felt sorry for the little woman who was revealed to us. She looked no stronger than a bird. Nervously clasping and unclasping her thin fingers, she looked fearfully out at us.

"Have to trouble you again, Mrs. Ackner," said Gerrity, briskly. "Come right in, Hand. This is Amesbury's land-lady."

I never felt quite so ashamed of myself as I did when we crowded into that poor little woman's apartment. But once inside, I found something else to take my attention. Seated in an invalid's chair on the far side of the room was a man, all hunched over. His fingers fumbled at a shawl spread over his drooping shoulders. His lantern jaw was firmly set, and his dark eyes gleamed at us resentfully. Long, unkempt iron-gray hair fell over the collar of his coat. I am afraid we all glanced at him quite rudely.

"That's Mrs. Ackner's husband," said Gerrity, swinging about to face the woman. "Mr. Hand here wants to ask you a few questions about the murder, Mrs. Ackner."

"Oh—oh, my gracious!" she exclaimed, her hands fluttering to her breast.

"Seems to me you could let a poor woman alone," whined the old fellow in the invalid's chair. "She told you all she knows a'ready. Go plaguing at her!"

"I know my business, and I'll carry it out," growled Gerrity, turning back to glare at the invalid.

"We pay good money in taxes to support the police," said Ackner, "and what do we get for it? Why didn't you prevent this thing 'stead of coming round afterward bullyin' women? One of the tenants has a'ready give notice since this thing happened. It was hard enough for my wife before, but now—"

"See here," cried Gerrity, "if you think the police can—"

"Just a minute, Inspector," said Hand, sharply. Then he turned smilingly to the cripple. "I can understand your complaint, and I certainly sympathize with it," he said. "It is indeed unfortunate that we must trouble you further, but I'm sure that you want the mystery that clings to your house cleared away. We merely wish to help."

Mr. Ackner seemed inclined to sulk. He hitched his shoulders and whined something under his breath.

"He's not well," said his wife, glancing appealingly at Gerrity.

"What's the matter with him?" sniffed Gerrity.

"He has rheumatism something awful," said Mrs. Ackner. "He hasn't been out of that chair for two years, except to get into his bed. That's all life means to him any more. Please don't—don't get him excited."

"I assure you we won't," complied Hand, heartily. "May I suggest diathermic treatments? Really quite wonderful for rheumatism. But now, Mrs. Ackner, if it is not asking too much, will you tell me of your connection with this deplorable affair tonight?"

"Why—why, I told the inspector here everything I know," she replied, glancing nervously about as she lowered herself into a chair. "I'm sure I can't tell you anything more."

"What time was it that you went to Mr. Amesbury's room?"

"I always took him his coffee at half past ten."

"Then it was at half past ten that you came upon him tonight?"

"Yes."

"Now then, we aren't going to refer to that again. But can you tell me what Mr. Amesbury had been doing earlier in the evening?"

"He went out to dinner. Him and Mr. Haggerty, both of them."

"And where did they go to dinner?"

"To some friends, but I don't know who."

"What time did they return?"

"I don't know. You see, I take care of little Marian Skelly on the third floor evenings. Her mother and father both work in a movie house over on Broadway."

"Oh, I see. How late do they stay there?"

"About eleven. Mrs. Skelly gets home then; her husband's a little later."

"But I thought you took Mr. Amesbury's coffee to him at ten thirty?"

"Yes, sir, I do. I skip down here and make the coffee and leave it with him and then go back to Marian."

"Why, of course. Now, Mrs. Ackner, did Mr. Amesbury say anything to you about having a large sum of money in his room?"

Mrs. Ackner appeared a little frightened. She moistened her lips and glanced with a worried expression over at her husband, as if seeking moral support. Ackner paid no attention to her; he was too busy scowling at Inspector Gerrity.

"Well—well, he did say something about it," she said, at length. "I saw him in the hall just as him and Mr. Haggerty were going out. But he told me a few days ago that he'd raised a lot of money and was going away. He said—"

"How many days ago was that?"

"Oh, why, it was the first of the week. That was when he told me he wouldn't want the room after this week."

"I see. But what did he tell you tonight about the money?"

"He was very happy about it. He was an awful nice man, though a little peculiar, both him and Mr. Haggerty. I met them just as they were going out. Mr. Amesbury laughed and said something about money, but I thought he was joking. I mean, it didn't sound sensible."

"What did he say? His exact words, if you can remember them."

"I can remember them. They were so odd, you see. He said: 'Hello, there, Mrs. Ackner. Maybe you don't believe it, but Nick and I have got more money round our middles than you ever dreamed of.' And then he laughed fit to kill himself, and Mr. Haggerty laughed too."

Hand nodded and veiled his eyes. A moment later he glanced down again at Mrs. Ackner.

"Mr. Amesbury didn't say where he was going to dinner?" he asked.

"No," replied Mrs. Ackner, energetically shaking her head. "But he did tell me he was going to have dinner with friends. He said they were the people who gave him the money."

"Just one more thing, Mrs. Ackner. How long did it take you to locate that policeman?"

"Oh, not very long. I ran down to the corner as fast as I could. I—I don't just remember much about it. I mean, to tell how long it took, and all."

"I see. You haven't seen Mr. Haggerty since he went out to dinner?"

"That was the last I saw of him. I do hope he's all right."

"I guess he is," growled Gerrity.

Hand reached quickly into his pocket and produced a flat, shiny, thin piece of metal, about three inches long by two inches wide. In the center of one end was a small round hole. I recognized it as a highly polished, nickel-plated mirror from a man's toilet kit. Holding it at either side by his finger-tips, he allowed Mrs. Ackner to look at it. She glanced up at him, completely puzzled. Hand smiled down at her.

"Ever seen this before?" he asked.

"My gracious, no!" she replied, appearing very much startled.

"I didn't think you had," he said, dropping the mirror on the palm of his hand and looking at it. "It's rather insignificant, anyway. That will be all, Mrs. Ackner. Thank you very much for your patience, and you have been very helpful."

As we turned to leave the room, Mr. Ackner's whining voice came after us.

"I hope you're through with us now!" he said. "I should be in bed hours ago, and here I am up yet! Don't go coming back again. If you've got anything else to ask, you better do it now."

Hand turned briskly and, with a chuckle, walked over beside the invalid's chair. Ackner glowered up at him from under his eyebrows.

"Mr. Ackner," said Hand, "I'm a neighbor of yours, and I want to apologize for putting you out like this. I also want to tell you that you can go to bed now without fear of further molestation."

"I'll go to bed," whined Ackner, "but I don't think it'll do me a bit of good. I can't sleep a wink after all this. I'll be sick tomorrow, wait and see. Who are you, anyhow, if you're a neighbor of ours?"

"My name is Christopher Hand."

"You Christopher Hand!" exclaimed Mr. Ackner. "My, my! Why didn't you say so to begin with? I'm mighty proud to know you, Mr. Hand."

Hand laughed as he grasped the shaky hand that Ackner held out to him. With a cry of alarm, as their hands met, Ackner jerked his back again. Hand, with a start of surprise, glanced down at his right hand. In it he was absentmindedly holding the nickel-plated mirror. He glanced back at Ackner and laughed good-naturedly.

"By Jove!" he cried. "I'll wager you thought you had grasped a snake when you felt that in my hand. Here," he said, thrusting the offending mirror back into his pocket, "I'll get rid of that. Now then, Mr. Ackner, here's my hand, and good luck to you."

Ackner eagerly took the proffered hand. He even went so far as to essay a hard, cracked laugh. Mrs. Ackner smiled timidly. Altogether, it was in a much more congenial atmosphere that we made our departure than had existed when we entered the Ackners' apartment.

Back in the hall Gerrity turned to Hand.

"I want to give that man upstairs some additional instructions," he said. "Be right down again."

As his heavy step receded up the stairs, Amesbury walked over to the door and looked gloomily out through the glass panel into the street. I spoke in a low voice to Hand.

"Gerrity," I said, "has been right on the job."

"Most assuredly."

"He has excelled himself in his deductions, don't you think?"

"Without question. But then, of course, almost all of them are wrong."

"Wrong!"

"Precisely. And now, my dear fellow, I hear the inspector returning. We must not waste time, you know."

Gerrity came briskly up to us. After glancing over toward the door at Amesbury's back, he turned to Hand.

"Well," he asked, "what's to be done now?"

"The trail ends here, Inspector," said Hand. "We must back-track."

"How's that?"

"We don't know who acted as hosts to our two partners tonight, but it should be easy to find out. Yes, I think our next move should be to call upon the pastor of the Hendly Congregational Church. He, at least, should be a fixture. Perhaps he can put us on the trail we must follow."

We silently left the building where the mysterious tragedy had been enacted. As we passed the alley, I looked up at Jeremy Amesbury's window. The light was still burning. Where was the hand that had turned it on?

3

VICTIMS

The parsonage of the Hendly Congregational Church, like the church itself, did not appear prosperous. I had passed the church dozens of times, since it was right in the neighborhood, but not until now had I taken any interest in it.

We congregated in a small vestibule at the front of the parsonage. Through the glass of the door, we could see that a light was burning somewhere at the end of a hallway. Gerrity pressed his thumb to an electric bell-button and kept it there. Presently a large woman appeared in the rear of the hall and bustled toward the door. She opened it quite energetically. Although the light was not good, I could see that she was regarding us with disfavor.

"Dominie in?" inquired Gerrity, brusquely.

"Mr. Bothwell has retired," coldly replied the woman.

"All right," grunted Gerrity, walking deliberately into the house.

Hand immediately followed the inspector inside, leaving Amesbury and me behind in the vestibule. After an uncertain glance at each other, we also brushed by the woman. She suddenly came to the conclusion that we had taken liberties with her.

"You can't come in here like that!" she reproved, sternly.

"No?" said Gerrity. "We are in, aren't we? Go tell Mr. Bothwell that Inspector Gerrity from police headquarters wants to see him."

"Police?" exclaimed the woman, with a start. "My soul and body, are you policemen?"

"Go tell Mr. Bothwell I want to see him," growled Gerrity.

The woman, without further ado, went puffing up the stairs. We stood silently in the gloom of the hallway and waited. Soon after a light-bulb over our heads, operated, no doubt, by a switch on the floor above, sent a gleam of light through the hallway. A creak of the stair caused us all to turn about and glance upward. There, coming slowly down to us, was a tall, stoop-shouldered, thin man in a dressing gown. On either side of a long nose, set close together, a pair of small blue eyes looked sadly down upon us, accentuating the doleful appearance of the long mouth. None of us spoke until he had joined us in the hallway. Then Gerrity stepped up to him.

"Mr. Bothwell?" he asked.

"I am Mr. Bothwell," said the clergyman, in a voice quite hollow. "What seems to be the trouble?"

"We have come to see you," said Hand, "on a mission of importance. I believe you were a friend of Mr. Jeremy Amesbury."

"You speak as if I no longer am a friend of Mr. Amesbury."

"I spoke of your friendship in the past tense because we have every reason to believe that Jeremy Amesbury is dead."

"You don't say so." Although Mr. Bothwell's words were those of a man startled by a revelation, the tone of voice in which he uttered them was as quiet as any he had thus far used. Without another word, he walked through our group and passed through a door, disappearing in the darkness beyond it. A moment later, however, a glass-shaded table-lamp lighted the room into which he had gone. Sinking into a chair at the far end of the table, Mr. Bothwell rested his head on his finger-tips. We walked in and gathered round the table. Hand opened the conversation.

"This is a shock to you," he said.

Mr. Bothwell appeared not to hear.

"So Jeremy Amesbury is no more," he muttered.

"No more what?" demanded Gerrity, with some spirit.

"How's that?" asked Mr. Bothwell, with a start.

"How long had you known Mr. Amesbury?" impatiently asked Hand.

"How long had I known Mr. Amesbury?" repeated Mr. Bothwell. "Why, I've known him all my life. He was somewhat older than I, but we grew up together in the same town in New Hampshire."

"Then," said Hand, "you should know one of us here, for a native of Meadowbrook is standing right before you. I notice from the marks of them remaining over the bridge of your nose that you are accustomed to wearing eyeglasses. Also, the manner in which the pupils of your eyes have enlarged since you joined us tells me that you are quite near-sighted. Let me show you the one of whom I speak."

Taking Amesbury by the arm, Hand led him over beside the clergyman's chair. Mr. Bothwell half raised himself and squinted at Amesbury's face. Of a sudden he gave a start, the first sign of emotion I had seen him evince. Then he sank back into the chair, continuing to stare up at Amesbury.

"You are—" he said, his voice trailing off to nothingness.

"I am Woodford Amesbury," said the client. "I'm afraid I don't—but yet, you do seem vaguely familiar to me."

Mr. Bothwell once again assumed his doleful air.

"Farthington Amesbury's son," he mused. "Yes, I remember you as a lad. I went off to the seminary when you were about nine, I should say. Your uncle told me about you."

"We came here," said Hand, briskly, "to learn the movements this evening of Jeremy Amesbury. I believe he dined with friends. Do you know who they were?"

"Of course I do," replied Mr. Bothwell. "He dined with the Blakes. I was there myself."

"Splendid! Mr. Haggerty also was there, was he not?"

"Mr. Haggerty, as well as some other friends."

"When did they leave?"

Mr. Bothwell passed his hand over his brow.

"Your questions," said he, "lead me to suspect that there was foul play in the death of my old friend."

"There is every indication that there was," said Hand. "Let me repeat my question. When did Mr. Amesbury and Mr. Haggerty leave the Blakes'?"

"Must you be so specific as all that?"

"It might help tremendously."

"Very well. Mr. Amesbury, although he was one of the two guests of honor, as it were, left rather early. He was departing tomorrow for Alaska. He always retires quite early, and before he went to bed he wanted to write a message to his nephew, who was due to arrive tomorrow. Mr. Amesbury felt that he might miss him, and, in that event, he wanted to leave a note."

"I see. Could you fix the approximate time at which he left?"

"I should say it was about a quarter of ten."

"And when did Mr. Haggerty leave?"

"He left with the rest of us. I can fix that time definitely. It was at a quarter past ten."

"How far from the house where Mr. Amesbury and Mr. Haggerty were staying did this party take place?"

"It is only a step. In fact, the two houses almost back up to each other. They are on opposite sides of a small court."

"Then it is not far from here, either. Did Mr. Haggerty walk round this way with you?"

"No, he did not. It is shorter for him to go round the other block. I suppose that is the way he went."

"Hum-m. But you are not sure?"

"No, I really could not say in just what manner Mr. Haggerty reached home."

Hand paused and concentrated deeply. It seemed that his spirit had gone off to investigate this latest information, leaving his body, like a graven image, to stand there waiting its return. In the meanwhile Mr. Bothwell insisted upon particulars concerning his friend, and Gerrity gave them. As suddenly as he had left off, Hand again took up the questioning.

"I take it," he said, "that you had lost touch with Mr. Amesbury for a number of years."

"I had," affirmed Mr. Bothwell. "It was only by the merest chance that we were ever brought together again. Mr. Amesbury, after he came to New York, chanced to run across a small account of me in a newspaper. The name struck him, and he looked me up. It is gratifying, after what you have just told me, to realize that it was I who brought him back into the fold, and that he is now safe in the church."

"Why didn't you say so before?" howled Gerrity. "The church is right next door, isn't it?"

"I—I—what do you mean?" stammered Mr. Bothwell, blinking his eyes at Gerrity.

"I think," said Hand, turning impatiently to the inspector, "that Mr. Bothwell means it was he who persuaded Mr. Amesbury to confess his faith and return to religion."

"Why, of course," said Mr. Bothwell, blinking some more at Gerrity.

"Well, I didn't know," complained the inspector.

"As his spiritual advisor," asked Hand, turning once again to Mr. Bothwell, "did Mr. Amesbury ever mention that his life was in danger?"

Mr. Bothwell thought the question over. Finally he squinted at Hand, the shadow of doubt on his face.

"Mr. Amesbury," he said, "was a most peculiar man. He was fond of dwelling upon certain adventures that he had experienced. I do not say that he deliberately misled people, but it might be said that occasionally he confused facts with fantasy. Between the time that I last saw him as a young man in New Hampshire, and the time that we were brought together again here in New York, he had not led what might be called—ahem—what might be called a saintly life. He had, praise be given, repented of his sins, but I fear he had been selected by the Power above to be the agency of destruction that cut short the wicked careers of one or two of his fellow men."

"Ah," said Hand, "you are intimating that there might have been looming in Mr. Amesbury's background the shadow of vengeance."

"I did not go so far," pointed out Mr. Bothwell. "But you may have spoken the truth, nevertheless."

"Have you anything more specific in that connection?"

"Nothing. As I said before, it is just possible that Mr. Amesbury had more imagination than he had experiences."

"He never told you that he had been threatened?"

"Never."

"Did he ever tell you that while in Alaska he felt a call to exterminate a certain Portuguese?"

"That was one of his tales. It was one, too, that Mr. Haggerty bore him out in. Most regrettable."

"Why most regrettable?" asked Gerrity. "Amesbury saved his own life; I don't call that regrettable."

"Ah, but violence!" deplored Mr. Bothwell, raising his hands in holy horror.

"Then," said Hand, "do I understand that there is no one whom you know of that might have slain Mr. Amesbury for vengeance?"

"There is no one whom I know of," replied Mr. Bothwell. "Mr. Amesbury never mentioned names, and, as I said before, it is quite possible that some, or perhaps all of the terrible deeds he liked to credit himself with never took place outside his imagination."

"What makes you think so?" asked Hand.

Mr. Bothwell spread his hands.

"Some of them seemed incredible," he said. "And then, too, I have heard the same story told with so many variations that I was led to doubt it altogether. He did tell them convincingly, though."

"I see," said Hand. "You have been most helpful, Mr. Bothwell, and I am sorry that we were the bearers of such sad news. We came here to find out where this dinner party was given tonight. If you will supply us with that information we will be on our way."

Mr. Bothwell gave us an address near by, and we prepared to depart. The minister accompanied us to his door.

"This is most unfortunate in a great many ways," he said. "I had entrusted my own small fortune with Mr. Amesbury, but that doesn't matter; I have no use for money. But a number of people in my congregation had money with Mr. Amesbury, some of them all they had. This will be a catastrophe to them."

The place we were looking for was a rather small and not very elegant apartment house on the next street. We went to the second floor, arrived at the door we wanted, and Hand rapped. The door was soon opened by a middle-aged man who carried himself with quite a little importance.

"Yes?" he said, with a lift of his eyebrows.

"Are you Mr. Blake?" asked Hand.

"That's me. What can I do for you?"

"May we see you on a matter of importance?"

"You are seeing me, aren't you?"

"Yes. May we come in?"

"Well—all right, step in."

We crowded into a small, square hallway. Mr. Blake, who did not seem disposed to invite us any farther into his domicile, looked us over in rather haughty inquiry. Hand doffed his hat and turned to the man.

"Is Mr. Haggerty here, by any chance?" he asked.

"You friends of Nick Haggerty?" countered Mr. Blake. "If you are you won't find him here; he's gone home."

"Ah. I hardly thought we should find him here. But we came here, Mr. Blake, to tell you that Mr. Jeremy Amesbury has been done away with."

Like all men of artificial bearing, Mr. Blake was incapable of absorbing startling news at once. He glanced about at us, as if he were trying to make sure that we were real. Then he looked up at Hand, but the best he could do was to gulp.

"We fear that Mr. Amesbury has been murdered," said Hand.

"I—I don't understand," complained Mr. Blake, feebly. "What's that!"

I glanced quickly about to behold a thick-set man standing in the doorway to a living-room. At the same time, from within the living-room, I heard a woman's cry of horror. The man at the door came over and glared anxiously at Hand.

"What's that?" he repeated. "You say Jerry Amesbury's been murdered."

"Yes," replied Hand shortly. "Perhaps if we were to go where there is more room we could avoid all this confusion."

Not waiting for an invitation, he strode into the living-room. Mr. Blake and his friend, as we followed in after Hand, set up a clamor for more information.

Entering the living-room, I found there two women, clinging to each other on the far side of the room. One of them was middle-aged, and the other, who resembled her enough to be her daughter, was a young woman of no more than twenty-three or four. She was willowy and strikingly beautiful, with black bobbed hair, soft full lips, and a pair of large brown eyes that, at the moment, were filled with dismay.

Mr. Blake, who had regained his self-importance, elbowed his friend out of the way and confronted Christopher Hand.

"I want to know what you mean by all this!" he cried. "Look at my wife and daughter, frightened to death!"

"This," said Hand, indicating Gerrity, "is Inspector Gerrity from police headquarters. He will tell you the whole thing."

As Gerrity brusquely unfolded the strange tale, the Blakes and their friend became more and more agitated. More than once I saw the girl smother a cry of compassion. Mr. Blake no longer could contain himself. He seized Gerrity by the shoulder.

"But the money!" he cried. "What about the money?"

"Yes, what about the money?" insisted the other man, almost hoarsely.

"Who are you?" demanded Gerrity, swinging about on him.

"My name is Anderson," he replied, "and I had a heap o' money in this thing!"

"Well," growled Gerrity, "the money's gone along with Amesbury's body."

A heavy, bewildered silence fell upon those people. And then, with a pitiful cry, the woman threw herself into a chair.

"Joe, Joe, I told you it wouldn't be safe!" she wailed. "All our money! Gone! Oh, what will we do?"

"Be still!" cried her husband. "Good Lord! Let me think. Let me think."

The woman wept softly. Her daughter dropped to her knees beside her and, throwing her arms about her mother's sob-wracked shoulders, whispered consolingly in her ear.

"Where is Haggerty?" demanded Anderson, wildly. "He had half the money."

"That is something that I wish to clear up," said Hand, briskly. "Mr. Amesbury made a remark this evening to his landlady, one which she did not understand. I think that I do. He said something about having a large sum of money about his middle. Haggerty also. I presume that they were carrying the money in money-belts."

"They were," affirmed Blake.

"It was divided equally?"

"That's right."

"How much did it amount to altogether?"

"Fifty thousand dollars! All of it in cash!"

"But where is Haggerty?" Anderson almost screamed.

"Haggerty," said Hand, slowly, "is not to be found."

Anderson fell into a chair and mopped his brow. Blake took to pacing up and down the room, trying his level best, I could see, to collect his thoughts. I felt so sorry for them that I looked appealingly to Hand.

"I have been engaged," said he, "by Mr. Woodford Amesbury, Jeremy Amesbury's nephew, to fathom this mystery. This is Mr. Woodford Amesbury," he added, indicating his client.

Amesbury was standing near where the girl knelt beside her mother, looking compassionately down upon her. Everybody focused his eyes on him. Even the girl looked up. She gazed steadily into his face for a moment; then she gave a start, and a curious expression came to her face. I glanced about at Blake and Anderson. Both were regarding Amesbury quizzically. Mrs. Blake, continuing to sob, paid no attention to him. Hand glanced rapidly about at the ring of faces.

"You seem to have met my client before this," he said.

Anderson slowly shook his head.

"I never have," he said. "But he's a walking picture of his uncle. A good deal younger, and he hasn't got a beard, but from his eyes and nose and forehead I'd know him in a minute."

"I do resemble my uncle a good bit," said Amesbury.

"And who are you?" demanded Anderson, turning to Hand.

"My name," he replied, "is Christopher Hand."

Anderson impulsively grasped Hand by the shoulder.

"You are going to get our money back for us, aren't you?" he cried. "You've got to get it back for us! You will, won't you?"

"My duty," said Hand, "is to find Jeremy Amesbury, to determine what has befallen him, and, if it is foul play, to bring the guilty person to justice. But you may rest assured, if it is in my power to do so, I will get your money back for you."

"You must!" said Anderson. "We're not rich, none of us. We can't afford to lose that money! By thunder, I'm glad you're here!"

"Then co-operate with me," pleaded Hand. "Let us sit down and get a few matters settled as expeditiously as possible. In the first place, what was the exact nature of the business between you and Jeremy Amesbury?"

"I'll tell you," offered Blake, quickly. "There's nobody better able to do it than myself. Mr. Amesbury and Haggerty discovered gold in Alaska. They didn't have any money, and they came to New York to raise it so they could go on with mining operations. They tried to borrow everywhere, but they felt they were being gypped—ah—cheated by all the places that would agree to loan them money,

do you see? We got in with them over at the church—I'm
pretty important over there myself. We decided to form
a private corporation and raise the money ourselves. We
formed the Ajax Mining and Engineering Corporation. I
am vice president."

"You were satisfied that the gold mine was a good prop-
osition?"

"Of course it was—is! And that reminds me, we're not
so bad off, after all. We still own sixty percent of the gold
mine. Mr. Amesbury and Haggerty each owned twenty percent of the stock in the corporation we formed. I suppose
Mr. Amesbury's nephew," he added, with a half resentful
glance at Hand's client, "will inherit his uncle's share. But
Haggerty's, by Harry, should go to the stockholders!"

"If I ever inherit from my uncle any stock in this company," promised Amesbury, "I will certainly give it to the
stockholders."

The girl kneeling beside her mother glanced gratefully
up at Amesbury. He smiled down at her, and the two exchanged a long glance. Finally the girl blushed and turned
back to look after her mother, a duty that she appeared to
take even more interest in than she had before.

"Now, tell me," said Hand, "what was the reason for
those two men to be carrying round such a large amount
of cash?"

"Well," said Blake, with a dismal shrug, "we didn't altogether like the idea, but you couldn't do anything with
them. They knew the conditions in Alaska where they had
their claim better than we did, and they said they'd have to
have it. They expected to have a pretty large pay-roll right
off, and they had to build roads and things to get the ore
out. They were also going to buy a lot of equipment from
another mining company up there. We were going to get
along as best we could for a while on that fifty thousand.
Then, after we'd made some money, we were going to buy

more equipment here and ship it to them as they needed it. Mr. Amesbury was president of the corporation, and I was vice president to look after things here."

"Very well," said Hand, "that settles that point. Now then, we understand that both Mr. Amesbury and Mr. Haggerty were over here to dinner tonight."

"Yes," sobbed Mrs. Blake. "W-we were all so happy."

"Do you know anything of their movements after they left here?" asked Hand.

"No," replied Blake. "Amesbury left early. We had a crowd, all the stockholders. We were celebrating, because Amesbury, Haggerty and Anderson, here, were leaving for Alaska tomorrow."

"Ha! Mr. Anderson was going with them?"

"Sure I was," said Anderson.

"This is most interesting," said Hand. "Tell me about it, Mr. Anderson."

"Why—well, I don't just know what you want me to tell. I lost my job a couple of weeks ago, and—well, I think it was Mr. Amesbury who asked me to go with them. Wasn't it, Joe?"

Mr. Blake thought carefully for a moment.

"I don't know," he said, at length. "I don't know whether he suggested it or me. He was mighty tickled to have you go along, though."

"Sure," said Anderson. "After I decided to go we all thought it was a good idea. I could sort of represent the other fellows here, you see. Besides that, Mr. Amesbury showed me how I could help out in a business way up there."

"It was a splendid idea," said Hand. "Too bad your plans will have to be changed, for a while, at least. Alaska is a marvelous country. But, to get back to the subject. Mr. Amesbury left here earlier than the others. What time, would you say?"

Again Mr. Blake pondered heavily.

"It was a little before ten," he said. "I remember I kidded him about running off so early. He wanted to write a note to his nephew."

"And that was the last that you saw of him?"

"The very last!"

"And Mr. Haggerty?"

"He left along with the rest. Along about ten fifteen, I should say. That's the last I saw of him, too! Anderson and I have been here talking ever since. You see, as vice president, I thought I'd better go over some matters with our representative in Alaska before he left."

"To be sure," said Hand, absently. "Now, I might as well tell you that I have formed a theory to the effect that someone intimate with Mr. Amesbury, probably Haggerty or some other member of this corporation of yours, was the man who committed this crime. If Haggerty continues to remain missing, we can more or less consider him our man. But he may just have dropped in on somebody. In that event, if he is innocent, whom do you consider the most likely to deserve our suspicion?"

"You mean who amongst our stockholders could have killed Jeremy Amesbury?"

"No; anybody could have. But who is most likely to be the one?"

"Hum-m, gosh, I don't know," mused Mr. Blake.

Hand looked expectantly at Anderson, who was knitting his brows and staring vacantly at the floor. For the first time the girl broke her silence.

"I can't believe that Mr. Haggerty would kill his friend," she cried. "And there is no one among the people who formed this company who could possibly have done it! A common thief and murderer, Mr. Hand, must have done this. Why, we are all friends; we are all members of the same church!"

"So I understand," said Hand, bowing kindly to the girl. "Well, you have no ideas. Nevertheless, you have given us some very helpful information. At least one obstacle has thinned away before us. And now, Inspector, I think we should be getting on. Before we go, however, I should like a list of your stockholders, together with their addresses, Mr. Blake. It might prove very useful; who knows?"

Blake sat at a small desk and copied the list, which he gave to Hand. Armed with this, Hand led us back to the street. Behind us we left a household from which the happiness of great expectations had been ruthlessly snatched. My heart went out to them, and, evidently, Amesbury's did also.

"This is ghastly, Mr. Hand!" he cried. "Those poor people. That poor little woman and her brave, wonderful daughter touched me very deeply, very deeply indeed. We must redouble our efforts!"

"Yes," agreed Hand, but in quite a bored fashion. "Now, Inspector, we have here a list of thirteen people. Unlucky number, what? Three of them we have interviewed, and two, Haggerty and Amesbury, we can't interview. That leaves eight. I suppose there is nothing for it; we must look them all up. One of them, I notice, lives at the same address as Haggerty and Amesbury did. That is mildly significant. We might start on him, particularly as it will give us a chance to determine whether Haggerty has returned."

The distance was not great; so we walked back to the house where Jeremy Amesbury had lived. Again Hand walked as if in his sleep. Once he all but stopped, nodded very briskly, and continued on.

The house seemed even darker and gloomier than it had on our first visit. As we rounded the corner of the second-floor hallway on our way to Haggerty's room, a short, compact young man pounced upon us. In succession he glanced closely at all our faces; then, with a mutter, he turned about and commenced resolutely back in the direction whence he had come.

"Who are you looking for?" called Hand.

The fellow turned about and regarded us silently for a moment.

"I'm looking for Nick Haggerty!" he savagely replied.

"I wonder now," said Hand, "are you Mr. Alfred Schmidt?"

Almost pugnaciously, the man walked up to us and regarded Hand intently. There was a flash in his glance that made me nervous.

"I'm Alfred Schmidt," he said, grimly. "Who are you? I never saw you before."

"I dare say you never did. But you seem to be looking for the same man that we are, and that would indicate your identity. Alfred Schmidt, Inspector, is the stockholder who lives in this building."

"Oh," growled Gerrity, who had been keeping his hand suspiciously near his hip.

"But who are you?" cried Schmidt, thrusting his face closer to Hand's.

"I am not important," replied Hand. "One of my companions is Inspector Gerrity, however. He is from the police, and he is attempting to clear up this mystery. I see that you are aware of it."

"I am," growled Schmidt. "My neighbors told me about it. The police have got to do something! All my money is gone! I've got to have it back, do you hear? I have a wife and family, and I can't lose that money!"

"Well, then help us find it," snapped Hand. "I take it that Nick Haggerty has not returned here."

"No, he hasn't. He has half the money, too."

"He has all of it," corrected Gerrity. "What in blazes did you let 'em carry it round like that for? A fine way to handle fifty thousand dollars. And then we try to keep crime down!"

"I didn't want to let them carry it round like that," howled Schmidt. "Mr. Blake said it would be all right, and everybody took his word for it. Amesbury and Haggerty did look as if they could take care of it. Both of them wore guns, and they knew how to use them. The policeman outside Amesbury's door said Haggerty did it. How was I going to know he'd kill Amesbury?"

"See here," said Hand, sternly. "You may be able to give us some valuable information. We are trying to get your money back, do you understand? Tell me, did Haggerty walk home from the Blakes' with you?"

Schmidt took a deep breath and fought to control his emotions.

"Part of the way."

"Where did he go then?" snapped Hand.

"Well, I know where he went," muttered Schmidt. "He isn't there now, though."

"Where did he go?" barked Gerrity.

"I don't know," declared Schmidt, hastily. "I don't know where he went. I was mistaken."

Hand took the young man by the arm and peered sharply at him.

"Your actions are peculiar, Mr. Schmidt," he said. "In one breath you tell us that we must find your money, and in the next you cause us to believe that you are trying to throw us off the track. Before you find yourself down at police headquarters explaining this incongruity, you had better do it here."

Schmidt looked sullenly at the floor, chewing his lip.

"Where did Haggerty go after he left the Blakes'?" insisted Hand.

"He went over to the laboratory," grumbled Schmidt.

"Where is this laboratory?"

"Right in back of here. It's just across the court."

"Whose laboratory is it?"

"What difference does that make?"

"It may make a tremendous difference. Come, whose is it?"

Schmidt took a turn a few yards up the hallway and back. He stopped before Hand, his chest slowly heaving with emotion.

"I'll tell you the whole thing!" he blurted. "The reason I didn't right off is because Larry White is mixed up in it. He's—"

"Ah, one of the stockholders," breathed Hand. "Go on, Schmidt."

"He's a friend of mine," cried Schmidt. "He hasn't anything to do with this murder! I knew you'd go thinking things if I told you."

"My dear young man, I am thinking no things about your friend White. I merely observed that he is a stockholder in the Ajax Mining and Engineering Corporation. Rest assured that we will attach no undue significance to his name being linked with anything that you may tell us. Please proceed."

"Well, all right. We were coming home from the Blakes'. There were five or six of us in the crowd that walked round this way. Haggerty was with us, but I was talking to Mr. Hinkle, and I wasn't paying much attention to the others. Then Mrs. Hinkle says she dropped her favor. They gave us favors over to the Blakes', little gold-bags filled with candy. I looked back and saw it lying on the sidewalk behind us, ten or fifteen feet. I ran back to get it, and then I heard Haggerty and Larry talking."

"Where were they?"

"They must of been standing at the end of the alley. There's an alley there, about half way down the block. Has a solid wooden gate in a ways from the sidewalk. It's kept locked, but Larry has a key. He can get in to his laboratory that way."

"You didn't see them?"

"No, they were round the corner from me."

"But you heard them talking. What did they say?"

"Well, Haggerty was saying: 'What do you want to see me about, son? Is it the same thing? I can't do anything, you know.' I'm pretty sure that's just what he said."

"Did your friend White make any reply?"

"Yes. He said: 'I'll tell you when we get to the laboratory.'"

"Hum-m. Did you hear anything else?"

"No. It was none of my business. I picked up the favor and went on."

"What time was this?"

"Oh, I don't know, exactly. It was a little after ten. I came on home, and later on I heard about this murder. I remembered, then, about Haggerty going off to the laboratory with Larry. I beat it out there, but they'd gone. The place is all in darkness now. It's up to you fellows. You've got to get that money back!"

"We will do our utmost."

"I don't know what'll happen if you fail us; a lot of us put all we had into that corporation!"

"Well, don't lose hope," advised Hand. "Thank you for your help. Inspector, we have yet to make a number of calls. Let us get about them at once. And now, Mr. Schmidt, we shall say good night."

4

NICK HAGGERTY

Once again we left the building. Hand stepped to the curb and glanced up and down the street.

"Never a taxi in this neighborhood when you need one," he grumbled.

"It's pretty late," said the inspector, glancing at his watch. "I'll phone to headquarters and get my car."

"Take too long," said Hand. "We'll walk over to Broadway and get one. Come on."

Off he went, his long legs going like a couple of stilts. The inspector paced rapidly along beside him, and Amesbury and I followed after them.

"I can't tell you how dismal I feel," said the client. "It's bad enough to have the fate of the one relative I have in the world hanging in this mystery, but then along with it comes this miserable business of the money. What a pity! I feel almost morally responsible for the return of that money. And yet, to find it seems impossible!"

"It does seem so," I admitted. "But I have such unlimited faith in my friend that I would almost be willing to wager he will fathom this mystery. Something about him, I tell you, as he walks on ahead of us there seems to say that he is on a warm scent. Don't give up hope, Mr. Amesbury, until Hand tells you to. He doesn't always succeed, but he has done some remarkable things."

"But you can see for yourself," whispered Amesbury, "that he has got nowhere. He has said nothing optimistic all night, and what facts we have uncovered have been of no help whatever."

"You don't know him," I smiled. "Perhaps he hasn't heard any more than we have tonight, but I'll wager he's seen twice as much. I have an idea, although he has divulged nothing to me, that he has formed some sort of theory already. You won't hear of it until he is sure he is right. No doubt I shall be kept quite as much in the dark as anyone else. But—all I can advise you to do is to wait."

"I'll have to do that anyhow," shrugged Amesbury. "I can't seem to forget that pitiful episode at the Blakes'. I wonder what that girl's name is. That made a terrific impression on me."

With a smile I wondered whether it was the girl or the episode that had made such a terrific impression upon him. I remembered quite clearly the look in his eyes as he had gazed down upon her.

We had reached Broadway. A cab Hand had summoned was drawing over to the curb for us.

"Where are we going?" Gerrity suddenly demanded. "What do we want with a cab, anyway? All these people live right in the same neighborhood, don't they?"

"All but Larry White," replied Hand, getting into the cab. "We have not far to go, but we can reach his address quicker this way."

He gave his instructions to the driver, and off we started. The cab soon stopped before a building not unlike the one that had seen the tragic end of Jeremy Amesbury. Telling the driver to wait, Hand bounded out and was at the front door before we had joined him. The door, which was not locked, let us into a small, dark hallway. A flight of somber stairs was just visible before us.

"I haven't been in one place tonight with a decent lighting arrangement," complained Inspector Gerrity.

Hand got out his electric torch. With its beam he explored the walls. With an exclamation, he held the light on a row of push-buttons near the door. Beside each button was a name and a number.

"L. White, number two fourteen," he read. "Inspector, we have but one flight of stairs to go."

Using his light, he led us up the stairs. Then he went along, inspecting the numbers on the doors. Finally he stopped before two fourteen. We stood breathless and listened. Not a sound broke the stillness of the house. Hand quickly reached out and rapped on the door.

Again we stood motionless and listened. There was no response to Hand's rap. Again he rapped, this time much louder. Still no response rewarded our diligent ears. Next he tried the door-knob. The door was locked. Hand suddenly produced his master keys.

"You may be too touchy to follow me, Inspector," said he, "but I am about to break into this fellow's quarters. We should have a warrant, but—"

Silently he inserted the key into the lock. A moment later he had the door open. A blank wall of darkness greeted us. Hand shot the beam of his light through the door.

The room, as much as I could see of it, had the appearance of a poorly-furnished, small living-room. The inspector, finding that he could forget the law he was bound to uphold, followed Hand inside, warrant or no warrant. Amesbury and I followed him. Hand snapped on a light. He crossed quickly to a door on the other side of the room. Throwing it open, he disappeared through it for a moment, and then reappeared. He glanced quickly about the room.

"That's his bedroom," he said, jerking his head toward the door he had just investigated, "and Mr. White is not in it. Here's another missing person for you, Inspector."

"What's it all about?" growled Gerrity, peevishly. "What's been going on, anyhow?"

Hand abruptly strode over and snapped out the light.

"We are here illegally," he reminded us. "I think we had better depart."

He locked the door, and we started off down the corridor we had passed through to reach it. Suddenly Hand stopped, so suddenly that Gerrity, with a soft grunt of surprise, collided with his back. Dimly I could make out Hand's raising an arm for silence. Then I heard a step upon the stair ahead of us.

The shadowy figure of a man turned the corner of the corridor. For a moment he rested his hand against the wall. Then, with bowed head and a heavy sigh, he proceeded to pace straight for us. Not until he was a yard from Hand did he spy him. He uttered a sharp cry and recoiled as though he had been struck.

"I beg your pardon," said Hand, quietly; "by any chance, are you Mr. Larry White?"

As the man waited to reply I could hear him breathing deeply.

"Yes," he finally said. "Yes, I'm Larry White. Who are you, and what do you want?"

"I am sorry to have startled you," said Hand. "We have been looking for you. May we see you in your room?"

"Not until I know who you are," retorted White, quite spiritedly.

"Oh, very well," complied Hand. "My name is Christopher Hand, and I have here with me, among others, Inspector Gerrity from police headquarters."

"Christopher Hand and Inspector Gerrity," cried White, with a forced laugh. "I've heard of you fellows before. Come along, I've no objection to inviting you in."

He pushed his way by us and went up to his door. He quickly had it open and preceded us into the room, switching on the light. Then he crossed over and stood eyeing us.

Larry White was a tall, dark, good-looking chap. The smile that was showing his white, even teeth seemed a trifle set, and there was nervousness in his brown eyes if I ever saw it. I felt, however, that in the circumstances I could not blame him for that.

"Are you satisfied with who we are?" smiled Hand. "If you like we'll go to greater pains to identify ourselves."

"You don't have to do that," conceded White. "You were pointed out to me once, and I'll never forget your face."

"Bad as all that?" said Hand, his eyes twinkling. "But, to become serious, Mr. White, have you any idea as to why we are here?"

"Sorry, I have none."

"I see. I fear we bring distressing news."

"What is it? Let's hear it!"

"Jeremy Amesbury," said Hand, peering intently at White, "we believe, has been murdered; Nick Haggerty is certainly not to be found; and the money that they carried with them tonight is most certainly gone."

We all watched White very narrowly, each anxious to have no detail of his reaction escape us. The young man veiled his eyes and dropped his head. Abruptly he swung about and threw himself into a chair beside a small table. There he sat, his eyes gleaming at the floor. Suddenly, to the surprise of us all, he threw back his head and burst into as wild laughter as ever I had listened to. Just as suddenly and incongruously as it had burst upon us, his laughter ceased. He sighed and turned his face from us.

"What's so funny?" demanded Gerrity.

For answer White merely shrugged his shoulders.

"The culmination of bad fortune, Mr. White?" asked Hand.

White turned and glanced sharply at Hand.

"What—what made you say that?" he asked, almost breathlessly.

"Why," replied Hand, as if in surprise, "when a man's laboratory with all its equipment is about to be taken from him for non-payment of rent, and when he receives word that an invention he has been banking on has already been patented, together with the information that his account has been overdrawn at the bank; then, I say, when he is told that the money he has placed in an investment is stolen it must be the culmination of bad fortune."

"How did you know all that?" asked White, huskily.

"Is it not so?" countered Hand.

"That's my business!" snapped White, his face flushing darkly.

"Yes," agreed Hand, "I'll admit that it is."

"But maybe it's ours, too," growled Gerrity. "Where have you been, Mr. Larry White, since you left the Blakes' party tonight?"

White commenced to show signs that he had decided to refuse to be interviewed. He turned from Gerrity and stared at the wall before him.

"We might amend that a bit," suggested Hand. "Where have you been, Mr. White, since you visited your laboratory tonight with Nick Haggerty?"

White flashed about and turned upon Hand, quite savagely.

"What makes you think I visited the laboratory with Nick Haggerty?" he shouted.

Hand strolled deliberately over to a chair and sat himself quietly down in it. Then, looking over at White, he shook his head sadly.

"My dear young fellow," he said, "you are taking a most stupid attitude. You don't mind my telling you that, do you? No? Sooner or later you have got to account for your actions tonight. Why don't you make a clean breast of it now? You are only gathering suspicion about yourself by foolishly attempting to conceal something that must be told before so very long. I have told you one or two things that I know about you; it would be better to tell something yourself than to have me tell it all."

"Well!" exclaimed White indignantly. "I have nothing to conceal. If I'm suddenly so important that what I do interests you, I'll tell you every blessed thing I've done tonight!"

"Now you have suddenly become intelligent," smiled Hand. "I am all ears."

"Well," began White, glancing thoughtfully at the ceiling, "I did go to my laboratory with Nick Haggerty after we left the Blakes'. We stayed there only a minute or two. I—I had a favor to ask of him. He couldn't do anything for me; so we left. After that I strolled round. Then I came back here. That's all there is to it."

Gerrity snorted disdainfully.

"It's now after one o'clock," he said, displaying his watch. "You left the Blakes' about quarter past ten. We'll say you left your laboratory about ten thirty. Mean to say you've been kiting round the town for two hours and a half?"

"Yes!" said White explosively.

"Did you leave your laboratory at ten thirty?" asked Hand, mildly.

"Before that," replied White. "Fact is, we didn't go in. I was arguing, or trying to argue with him, but Nick wouldn't listen to me. I wanted to get him inside so that I could talk to him better, but Nick turned round and walked away from me. I had unlocked the door, and by the time I'd locked it again Nick was almost out to the sidewalk. I ran after him and pleaded with him some more. He wouldn't talk, though, and I had to give it up."

"Tell me, my boy," said Hand, in a voice incredibly soft, "what were you pleading with Nick for?"

The softness of Hand's voice, together with the kindly
light in his eyes, took White, who had been desperately on
the defensive, quite off his feet. He stared at Hand for a
moment; then he swallowed hard, as if a lump had come
into his throat.

"Do you have to know that too, Mr. Hand?" he all but
groaned.

"I'd like to," replied Hand.

White clasped his hands between his knees. His eyes
seemed to be looking straight through the wall, miles away
into the distance.

"I was pleading for money," he said. "You are right,
Mr. Hand, all my dreams are blowing away—my house of
dreams, my beautiful house of dreams is tumbling down.
I have an idea, a wonderful idea for an electric furnace. It
will take me time to perfect it, though, and I need my laboratory and all my equipment. I haven't much, not nearly
enough. There's a fortune in it, a fortune. Why, I—I could
marry Judy. Poor Judy, she's waited for me so long, and
now—"

His voice trailed off, and he continued to stare as if
into the distance. Hand waited long before he softly put
the next question.

"You are engaged?"

"Yes, to the finest girl in the world."

"Might I ask who she is?"

"Mr. Blake's daughter, Judith."

Hand rose to his feet. He crossed one arm over the
other and rested his chin on the knuckles of his hand.
When he spoke he was gazing at the floor.

"So," he said slowly, "after Haggerty refused to lend
you money, you were so downcast that you paced the
streets, wondering what was to become of you and your
sweetheart."

"I'm still wondering," said White, dismally.

"Will you tell me this, then? If you were so badly in need of money, why did you put some into the Ajax mining company?"

"To make more! When I did it I thought my invention of an electric anti-aircraft gun was the first of its kind. Now I get word that it has already been patented. I've tried to sell my shares to the others, but everybody has already invested all the money he could spare. I had only a thousand dollars in it. It wasn't much, but Mr. Blake fixed it up so that I could get into the company. I thought maybe Nick Haggerty or—that Nick Haggerty would lend me the money, and then I'd pay it back before long, do you see?"

"Yeah, I see," said Gerrity, significantly.

Suddenly Hand turned briskly to the young man.

"Mr. White," he said, "I don't like to do it, but I must request you to accompany us to your laboratory. I think it vital, Inspector, that we visit the laboratory at once. Besides showing us exactly where it is, Mr. White's presence is necessary in case anything comes up that might demand his assistance."

"Suits me," growled Gerrity. "Come on, young fellow."

"All the way down there?" protested White. "I'm fagged out. Besides that, I don't see what you want me to go along for."

"No?" grunted Gerrity. "Maybe you'll find out before morning. Come along now, I want to keep an eye on your welfare."

I was beginning to think that Gerrity was giving little thought to Larry White's welfare, in spite of what he said. Between his peculiar actions and the information Hand had got out of him, a rather complete net seemed to be weaving about the unfortunate young man, a net that appeared to be holding him close to the mysterious core of the case. I was sorry that this was so, for, in spite of my

everlasting efforts to remain impartial while accompany-
ing Hand in his work, I had begun to like the poor chap.

With a sigh White rose from his chair. Gerrity, taking
him by the arm, led him dejectedly from the room. As we
also were leaving, I pulled Hand back, allowing Amesbury
to precede us. Walking slowly down the corridor after the
others, I whispered to him.

"Will you tell me," I asked, "how under the sun you were
so well informed concerning Larry White's difficulties?"

"You mean those concerning his laboratory, bank
account, and so on?"

"Certainly."

Hand sighed and shook his head.

"You won't learn, Clark," said he. "And neither will the
inspector. The Lord gave both of you a pair of eyes, but
you simply will not use them."

"I swear I thought nothing escaped me."

"Something did, I assure you. It was this very series of
calamities that has befallen our young friend there. They
were in the form of communications, every one of them,
and they were spread out on the table in his room. Why
didn't you read them?"

"Why, I didn't see them. I didn't see you looking at
them, either."

"Well, I did, nevertheless. I looked at them when we
broke into the room."

"Surely you hadn't time to read three letters. I was
watching you very closely."

"No, I didn't take the time to read them. But I glanced
rather sharply at each in turn, furnishing my mind with a
photographic impression of each one. I am able to do that,
and so would you be able to do it if you had trained yourself as have I. I tell you, my boy, that at this very minute
I can conjure up those notes, one at a time, and read them
from beginning to end, every word, with my mind's eye

just as accurately as I could by holding the actual notes before me and reading them with my physical eyes."

"My word!"

Never do I cease to marvel. This was a new accomplishment to me, and one requiring stupendous schooling. Yet in the light of those of his that I had perceived before, perhaps I should not have been astonished.

"Ah, here we are," said Hand. "Now to jam all five of us into that taxicab."

The taxi was built to accommodate five passengers, but not with much comfort. I did not, however, give that fact much thought as we drove to the alleyway leading to the laboratory. The inspector, it pained me to see, never relaxed his grip on the arm of Larry White. Even while the young man was unlocking the gate to the alleyway he clung to him. We trudged down the gloomy alley, finally emerging into the small court. Hand stopped and peered carefully round through the gloom.

"That," he said, indicating the rear of the building to our left, "should be the house where Jeremy Amesbury lived."

White, who was very crestfallen, glanced in the direction that Hand was pointing. Then he dropped his head once more.

"It is, Mr. Hand," he said, tonelessly.

"And where's this laboratory of yours?" asked Gerrity, gruffly.

He led us over to a small, rickety porch, approachable by four steep steps. The inspector still grasping his arm, White mounted them. A large padlock secured a blank wood door. White put out a hand to it.

"Do you want to go in?" he asked.

"I think it would be as well," replied Hand, whose eyes were darting about inspecting the building. "It seems to me that this is the building where we saw Mr. Blake and Mr. Anderson this evening."

"They live here," affirmed White, as he inserted a key into the padlock. "Mr. Blake got me this place for my laboratory. It used to be a store-room. They took the stores out at the front and made apartments out of them."

He opened the door and led us inside. A pull on a cord flooded the laboratory with brilliant light from a globe hanging in the center of the ceiling. A number of electrical appliances and a large work-bench were brought into sharp relief. Hand stood by the door, his eyes roving sharply over the room. Suddenly, with an exclamation, he bounded to his left and dropped to his knees. Quickly lifting his head, he gazed fixedly at a door in the wall before him.

"What is it?" cried Gerrity.

"On the floor here, Inspector, is a large drop of blood. What lies beyond that door, Mr. White?"

I glanced quickly at White. His eyes were staring wildly, and his face was ashen. Either he had not heard Hand's question or he was incapable of speech, for he remained silent, scarcely breathing.

Leaping to his feet, Hand reached the door with one quick stride. He twisted the knob and threw it open. A gasp of horror arose from us all. Huddled on the floor of a small closet lay the body of a man. He lay with his knees buckled under him, his arms outflung before him and his head sagging between them, almost in the attitude of abject prayer. Long, iron-gray hair fell below the collar of his coat.

"My uncle!" cried Amesbury. "My God, we have found him!"

Hand took the body by the shoulders and hauled it out of the closet. As the bearded face rolled into view, Amesbury cried out again.

"Heaven help us! That is not my uncle; that is Nick Haggerty!"

5

A PORTUGUESE

I was somewhat astonished that Amesbury had so quickly identified the body. The forehead of the dead man was crushed in, as though a mighty blow had been delivered it. I lifted my eyes from the blood-bespattered face, wondering how Amesbury had ever recognized it as one he had seen before.

"You are quite positive," asked Hand, "that this was your uncle's partner?"

"There is no doubt whatever!" replied Amesbury.

"How about you, Mr. White?" asked Hand. "Do you recognize this body?"

Larry White was nearing the breaking-point, or so he certainly appeared. He was half crouching, his hands, held forth, trembling as though the strong current of one of his own electrical appliances were coursing through them. His breath came rasping through his dry lips, and he glared as if fascinated at the awful face of the dead man. Finally he wrenched his eyes away and turned wildly to Hand.

"I didn't do it!" he screamed. "I tell you I didn't do it! I couldn't do this thing!"

Hand strode quickly over and stopped before White, obscuring his view of the corpse. For a moment he gazed steadily into the young man's terror-stricken eyes, holding them as if in a spell.

"Don't let yourself become hysterical," he cautioned, in a low-pitched, slow voice. "Calm yourself; there is no hurry."

White's breathing gradually slowed down to a normal cadence. He moistened his lips and for a moment closed his eyes. When he reopened them it was in a much saner fashion that he met Hand's steady glance.

"Feel better?" asked Hand.

White swallowed hard and nodded in the affirmative. Gerrity, I could see, all this while was in a state nearing the explosive from a self-thwarted desire. According to his methods, he should at the moment be verbally bludgeoning White, while the young man was in a state of distress, into making all sorts of foolish statements. But he knew, after a good deal of experience with Hand, that he would get much further by allowing him a free rein. He knew, also, that whatever credit might fall, Hand was only too glad to stand aside and let it descend snugly about the broad shoulders of Inspector Gerrity himself. Hence he contained himself in what patience he could muster, which was not much.

"Very well, Mr. White," said Hand. "Do you recognize that body over there on the floor?"

"Yes," replied White, in a steady voice. "It is Nick Haggerty."

"How did that body get into the closet of your laboratory?"

"I swear before God that I don't know!"

"Mr. White, that man was struck over the head with a hammer. The hammer lies in a small pool of blood on the floor of the closet. It is your hammer, for it has your initials carved on its handle."

"I have a hammer like that," admitted White, hoarsely. "But I tell you I never used it for any such terrible purpose as that!"

"Did you see that hammer when you came in here tonight with Nick Haggerty? Think carefully. If you did not see it, I can tell you that it will play an important part in your defence."

White dropped his eyes and cogitated. But then he flared up in anger.

"See here, what are you trying to do?" he cried. "I told you before that Nick Haggerty left me before I had so much as opened the door to this place. He was not in here with me, tonight or at any other time today. He walked away from me when I wanted him to come in here and talk, and that's the last I saw of him!"

"Very well," said Hand, quietly. "You have told us your story. If you do not see fit to alter it, why then, you will not."

"Through with him?" asked Gerrity, looking eagerly at Hand.

Hand shrugged his shoulders and slowly nodded his head. He was looking at a window near the entrance to the laboratory, as if he had lost all interest in Larry White.

Gerrity, who still held White by the arm, turned briskly to his prisoner. His other hand, disappearing for an instant beneath his coat, flashed forth holding a pair of handcuffs. With a deftness born of long experience, he snapped them fast. White started violently and gazed with dismay at his shackled wrists. His face paled; but he bit his lip, squared his shoulders, and uttered not a murmur.

"We'll see whether you'll change your story, young fellow," growled the inspector, moving over to a telephone that stood on a small desk. "I'll just get a wagon up here after you. Maybe by tomorrow you'll be singing a different tune. You can't get away with it, you know. Hello! Give me Spring 7-3100."

Gerrity ordered his patrol wagon. He also ordered all sorts of experts to be sent to the laboratory. He arranged matters so that, until he should reach there himself, several persons versed in such matters should interrogate Larry White at police headquarters.

I was watching Christopher Hand. The window over near the door, the only one in the laboratory, seemed to interest him tremendously. Amesbury likewise was watching him closely. The window was a large, ordinary frame affair, with quite dirty panes. Hand leaped lightly to the sill, balanced himself precariously there, and turned the beam of his torch on the lock. He snatched a glove from his pocket and pulled it on his right hand. Using his gloved fingers he unlocked the window, raising the sash an inch or two.

"Inspector," he called, over his shoulder, "this window has been opened recently by prying the lock. The scratches are quite plain on the metal."

Gerrity had finished telephoning. He moved over to the window, keeping a wary eye on the dejected figure of Larry White.

"Been opened, huh?" he said.

Hand dropped to the floor beside him.

"Yes," he said. "You might have your men look for finger-prints on the window and lock."

"All right," muttered Gerrity. "But I don't think it's worth it."

"Perhaps not," shrugged Hand.

"By thunder," exclaimed Amesbury, "I can't imagine how you discovered so quickly that the window had been pried open. Certainly you cannot see the scratches on the lock from the floor."

"I thought they might be there," explained Hand, shortly. "I was looking for them."

He had thrust the lower sash up, and now he was standing with his head and shoulders through the window. He played the light of his torch over the window-sill and the outside wall of the building near the window. Then he withdrew his head and, using his gloved hand, closed and locked the window.

"Was the window locked when you first looked at it?" inquired Gerrity.

"Securely."

"There, you see! If anyone had broken in here through that window tonight it would have been unlocked. The door was padlocked; he would have had to leave by the window. How could he have locked it from outside after he had passed through it and closed it after him?"

"It's a formidable question, Inspector. No other door to this place, except the one to that closet, and it appears that there is no way out of the closet with the exception of that door."

Just to make sure, he stepped back into the closet. Glancing in after him, I saw the murderous hammer. It was a short, heavy instrument, the thick, blunt end stained a deep crimson. It rested in a small pool of blood, and altogether I was glad to look away from it.

"No way to leave through the closet," announced Hand, stepping back into the laboratory. "Do you know of any other exit from this laboratory, Mr. White, besides the door and the window?"

The young man dully shook his head.

"You would do well to think carefully, Mr. White," counseled Hand. "If we could establish that this place has been broken into tonight it would not only aid us, but it would be distinctly in your favor."

"I suppose someone could get through that window," said White. "It's an old-fashioned catch, and I've thought before that someone might have broken in here."

"What made you think that?" asked Hand, quickly.

"Oh, just because I've been missing a few things. Nothing of importance; a few tools and some wire. Perhaps I just mislaid them. At any rate, I put the padlock on the door after that."

"Could anyone have got a key to that padlock? This is most important!"

White considered carefully. Gerrity watched him narrowly.

"Mr. Hand," said White, squaring his shoulders, "I am a God-fearing man, and I am bound to tell the truth! I have the only key to that padlock. It is on a chain attached to my belt. It has never been out of my possession, and there is no duplicate."

"Well," growled Gerrity, "that's that, then!"

Hand turned suddenly and disappeared through the outside door. Amesbury and I followed him as far as the little porch. Gerrity remained with his prisoner. Hand skipped down the steps and stood gazing down into the black pit of a sunken doorway under the porch. Stone steps at the side led down to it. Directly above them was the window to the laboratory. Hand played his torch on the wall beneath the window.

The window was about seven feet off the ground. It was too far away from the porch to be accessible from there. But half way between the window and the ground the brick wall was broken by a narrow ledge. Although the shutters had been removed from the window, the lugs for them still remained, providing an excellent grip for a climber. The outside window-ledge was quite wide. A man could have reached it without much trouble from the ground.

Next Hand became interested in the sunken doorway beneath the porch. Directing his light into the shallow pit, he quickly descended the steps. I leaped to the ground beside the steps and peered down at him. Amesbury joined me. Quite evidently the door below us had passed from use long before. The pit was filled with a litter of boxes, and the door itself was securely boarded up. Hand came up to where we were standing.

"What do you think of it, Clark?" he asked.

"Well, a man could have reached that window from out here, and it wouldn't have been much of a trick, either. If he missed his step, of course, he'd have taken a nasty tumble into this hole. But what are you supposing? Surely you don't think that Haggerty broke into the laboratory! And if he did, who could have killed him?"

"And then, the window itself," pointed out Amesbury, a note of excitement in his voice. "Inspector Gerrity, in my opinion, is absolutely right about that. If anybody broke in there through the window, how could he leave without failing to lock the window behind him? This is what it looks like to me. Several days ago somebody, boys, probably, broke in there by climbing up and manipulating the latch of the window with a knife-blade. They stole White's tools, and then they left through the window, leaving it unlocked. Since then, no doubt, White has locked the window without realizing that it had been unlocked. It's warm these days; I venture to say he has the window open every day. It would be easy, you see, for anything so trivial as an unlatched window to escape him. What do you think of that theory?"

"I find no flaws in it," said Hand. "It appears that our young friend Mr. White has got into a bad position, doesn't it?"

"I must say so," agreed Amesbury, with a shake of his head. "In spite of the fact that it must have been he who killed my uncle, I almost wish we could do something to help him. Perhaps I shouldn't say it, but I pity him. I pity him, indeed."

"We certainly cannot help him by standing here looking at that window," said Hand, briskly. "I doubt that we

can save him from jail, anyhow; that must be the bell of
the patrol wagon that I hear."

As we were retracing our steps to the porch, I also
heard the bell. It grew in volume until at last it stopped
at the end of the alleyway. Larry White, when he heard it,
raised his head and glared wildly about. His face flushed
as he fought and gained control of his emotions. That,
coupled with Gerrity's malicious manner, caused me for
the moment to abandon the background that I habitually
elect to keep myself in. I could not let the poor fellow go
off to jail without giving him some ray of hope. I stepped
up to him.

"Mr. White," I said, earnestly, "do you tell me on your
oath that you had nothing to do with the deaths of Jeremy
Amesbury and Nick Haggerty?"

White turned his brown eyes on me, eyes that looked
frankly into mine.

"I swear upon all that is holy," he solemnly replied,
"that I am as innocent of these ghastly murders as you are
yourself!"

"Then if you are telling the truth, don't for a minute
give up hope. My friend, Mr. Christopher Hand, let me remind you, has taken up this case, and I assure you that he
will not rest until the true facts of this dreadful business
have been uncovered!"

Gerrity scowled at my words. From past experience I
knew what he had in store for Larry White that night, and
for the young man to retain a shred of hope was not among
his schemes. He immediately set about to blunt the effect
of my efforts.

"And don't forget this," he growled at White. "You're
guilty as hell! You know it, and by morning I'll know
it, and so will Christopher Hand! Just wait until you
see who's coming in here. Detectives to search your past
just like putting water through a fine sieve. Men to take

microphotographs of the wounds on that dead man, and all the other evidence about here. Finger-print experts to get your finger-prints off that hammer-handle, the finger-prints you left on it when you beat that fellow's head in with it! The medical examiner to fix death at the exact hour that you admit you were with Haggerty. The district attorney to get the truth out of you! And don't forget this: I'm here too. I've got a few things to do first, but I'll see you down at police headquarters. I'll see you for a long time down at police headquarters, my boy. But there," went on Gerrity, changing his voice from the ferocious tone he had been snarling at White to one almost gentle, "I can do a lot for you, son. If you'll help me, I'll help you. Just because you killed a couple of men doesn't always mean the electric chair. I have influence, lots of it, and if you'll help me, why then, I'll help you. We can fix something up dead easy. You went temporarily insane; something like that. Come now, don't you want to tell me, before the others get here, that you went out of your head and had killed these fellows before you knew what you were doing?"

"No!" said White, vociferously. "I didn't do it! You can do anything you like to me, but you'll never get me to say that I did. I didn't do it, I tell you!"

"All right," growled Gerrity. "We'll see whether you'll admit it or not. You've lost your chance; here comes the crowd from headquarters. But I may give you another chance later on. Think it over."

Hand, all this while, had been prowling round the laboratory. Not until his eyes came into view could it be seen how alert he was. Otherwise he appeared lost in thought. As the headquarters men trooped in, creating a fearful hubbub in the place that had been so quiet, Hand leaned his tall body against the wall across from the door. He acknowledged with a nod the greetings that were called to him.

"Hello, Tim," I said to the old sergeant, who is never absent long from the side of Inspector Gerrity. "I expected to see you before this."

"'Tis me lumbago," he whispered in my ear. "I don't want no one to know about it, Mr. Clark. The Lord save us, they're only too anxious to retire me as it is."

"They couldn't afford to do it, Tim," I protested, in a voice most serious.

"Ah, yer a great feller, Mr. Clark," he grinned. "But it was me lumbago tonight. I was home with it, sure I was, it was that bad. But I can smell trouble, that I can! I wakes meself up, called up headquarters, found out what was up, and there I was at the office when the call come through from the boss. I come right up with the other boys. Sure the inspector can't hope to solve crime without me!"

"There you are," I said. "That's why they can't afford to get rid of you."

Gerrity had given rapid-fire orders to his men, and now they were scattered about the laboratory, attending to their several tasks. The fingers and thumbs of the dead man were inked, and impressions of them were made on printed forms. Soon the flash-light bulbs were blinking blindingly. Through the door I saw the reporters, held at bay by two bluecoats, over whose shoulders they were craning their necks. Presently they would be allowed to enter, and word pictures of the scene would appear in the early editions.

Through the crowd at the door a slight, business-like man carrying a small black bag forced his way. Dr. Richards, the police surgeon, had arrived. Hand immediately lost his careless air. He stepped briskly up to Dr. Richards.

"How do you do, Doctor?" he said.

"Oh, hello, Hand," said the physician. "You on this?"

"I don't suppose you'll examine this fellow here."

"No. Of course not! Take him to the morgue. Beast-ly nuisance this having to go round giving permission to remove bodies!"

"I looked him over, superficially, of course. I didn't see any other wounds on him except that one in his head."

"Um-m. Looks as if a safe dropped on him."

"And yet, I wonder whether it was something else that killed him."

Dr. Richards looked quizzically at Hand. Then he dropped quickly to one knee beside the corpse. He unbut-toned the dead man's coat and flipped it back. Instantly all eyes round him were riveted on the left shoulder of the corpse. Strapped to it was a shoulder holster, and in it was a large pistol.

"Ah, ha!" cried the doctor. "Didn't you search him, Gerrity?"

"Not yet," replied the inspector, in some confusion.

"I think," said Hand, "that you'll find a pipe in his right-hand coat pocket. A pouch of tobacco seems to be in the other coat pocket, together with a box of matches. In his right-hand trousers pocket there is a key and some silver, and in the other trousers pocket there is a roll of bills. Nothing at all in either hip pocket, and the inside coat pocket is likewise empty. No vest; so that's about all there is on him."

"How did you find all that out?" demanded Gerrity. "You didn't have a hand in one of his pockets; I was watch-ing you."

"Sometimes it is not necessary to be so meticulous. I felt all those articles through his clothing. Perhaps I am wrong about them."

Dr. Richards systematically emptied the contents of the pockets. Not only had Hand been correct about every article, but he had named its location on the person of the dead man. A murmur of admiration rose from the detectives, and Gerrity grinned and nodded to Hand.

"Well," said Dr. Richards, "he had over fifty dollars in his pocket, and it wasn't molested. Evidently he wasn't killed by a thief."

"Round his waist," said Hand, "there should be a money-belt with about twenty-five thousand dollars in it. It is gone. It appears certain that it was stolen from the body while it was in that closet."

"Ah," breathed Gerrity. "What makes you think that, Hand?"

"The clothing, you will notice, has been disarranged by the murderer when he removed the money-belt. In doing so he tore a button from the shirt. The button and a patch of cloth from the shirt are lying in that closet. I think you will have no trouble in matching it up with the tear."

Gerrity immediately dived into the closet, returning triumphantly a second later with the small piece of cloth, to which was sewed the button. He bent quickly over the corpse of Nick Haggerty.

"Fits into the tear perfectly!" he cried, with a malevolent glance at Larry White.

As soon as Gerrity had got out of the way, Dr. Richards went about giving the corpse a cursory examination. Finally he looked up at Hand.

"No other wound that I can find," he said. "May find something later. Looks to me as if that crack on the head did for him. Certainly didn't live after it, anyhow. Well, if you fellows are through with your pictures and what not, we'll put him on the stretcher and take him out to the ambulance. I'd like to get him to the morgue and get through with him. I'm tired."

The newspaper men at the doorway set up a clamor to be allowed to get pictures before the body was removed.

Gerrity gave the necessary permission. After the photographers had crowded in, the inspector took Larry White by
the arm.

"Come on, son," he said gruffly, starting the young
man for the door.

But before the patrol wagon engulfed him, poor White
was in for another ordeal. The newspaper men, with canny
foresight, had stationed a few of their photographers
outside by the porch. As the inspector and his prisoner
emerged the flash-light bulbs flickered brilliantly about
them. After the excitement was over, the plates would be
exchanged, each paper getting a picture of the murdered
man and one of the accused killer. Gerrity was not averse
to pose, but to White it must have been a torture.

Hand followed the inspector, and Amesbury and I followed him. The patrol wagon, as well as several police
cars, was parked at the curb near the entrance of the alley.

Several policemen took charge of White. While Gerrity
gave instructions to a sergeant in charge of them, I stole
up beside Larry White.

"Don't forget what I told you," I whispered into his ear.

He reached out his shackled hands and pressed one
of mine. Then, with a heavy sigh, he turned and quickly
entered the patrol wagon. A moment later Larry White was
on his way to police headquarters.

"Well, what's your next move?" asked Gerrity, turning
to Hand.

"The same as yours, I'll wager. I think we should finish
interviewing the rest of the stockholders."

"That's it. I've had pretty good luck interviewing them
so far. What I want to know now is the whereabouts of
Amesbury's body, but I have a notion the fellow I just
arrested can tell me where it is."

"Don't be too sure," I snapped.

Gerrity shook his head and laughed.

"Clark's softened up again," he said. "You've got to be hard-boiled if you expect to get anywhere in a criminal investigation. I feel sorry for the kid myself, but I also feel sorry for those poor fellows that he killed. And just think for a minute about those people he robbed. You begin to see him in a different light, Clark, when you do that."

"Well," I shrugged, "I'll keep my opinions to myself. You may have the laugh on me yet, to put it crudely, but I'd wager you won't."

"I say," broke in Amesbury, "if you fellows are going to traipse round all the rest of the night, I beg to be excused. I got to bed late last night, and I was up early this morning. Besides, I really can't stand seeing these poor people told that their fortunes have evaporated. I'll be blue for a week from what I've seen already."

"Your presence is not at all necessary," said Hand. "I should think you would be tired; why don't you go to your hotel?"

"I think I will, then," said Amesbury. "Good night, and—good luck."

He set off up the street in quest of a taxi. The rest of us walked away in the opposite direction, bent upon getting people out of their beds in order to darken the future for them. I did not blame Amesbury for wriggling out of that task; I should have liked nothing better myself. But I had never deserted Hand before, and I was not likely to do it then. Besides, I was anxious to see whether he could find anything that would extricate Larry White from his terrible position.

The result of our interviewing, from my point of view, held a measure of encouragement. At most places we merely wasted our time, but our last stop was worth our while, albeit he gave his information reluctantly. He was a wizened little fellow with small, close-set eyes. He came sleepily, clutching a bathrobe about his frail body, to let us in. Something about his long nose and small jaw reminded me of a bird. First he was shocked, then overwhelmed by the sense of his personal loss; and finally, when we told him about Larry White, he was filled with sadness. Hand had him marked on his list as Mr. Henderson Patcher.

"Why, Larry White is one of my teachers," he informed us, as if that absolved the young man of all guilt. "I am superintendent of the Sunday School at the Hendly Congregational Church, and Larry is one of my teachers. A splendid young man! You must be mistaken, of course."

"Perhaps we are," conceded the inspector. "But we happen to know that Mr. White was greatly in need of money."

"Yes, I know," said Mr. Patcher.

"You know?" asked Gerrity, quickly. "How do you know?"

Mr. Patcher seemed surprised that we did not know all about him.

"Why," he said, "I was over to Mr. Amesbury's this afternoon when Larry was trying to borrow money from him."

"Oh, you were, eh?" said Gerrity. "Did Amesbury lend him any?"

"No," replied Mr. Patcher, with a sad shake of his head. "I never saw either of them in quite such a bad humor. Mr. Amesbury actually invited Larry to leave. I got them to shake hands, and this evening they were the same old friends as ever. A little kind counsel, gentlemen, does much in this world of wickedness."

"Then," said the inspector, "Mr. White and Mr. Amesbury, although they couldn't see eye to eye, parted as friends this afternoon. That right?"

"Oh, yes," replied Mr. Patcher.

"All right, thanks," said Gerrity. "We'll let you get to bed now."

"Pardon me a moment," said Hand, as Mr. Patcher was sadly closing his door. "I understood you to say that you were visiting Mr. Amesbury at his room this afternoon."

Mr. Patcher opened the door a little wider and pulled his bathrobe more closely about him. He looked inquiringly at Hand.

"Why, yes," he said. "I visited Mr. Amesbury. That was all right, wasn't it?"

"It was most fortunate. Tell me, did Mr. Amesbury have any other visitor besides yourself and Mr. White?"

"No. But wait a minute! Yes, as I was leaving. Yes, of course."

"Ha! And who was he?"

"That I couldn't say."

"He was a stranger, then?"

"He was a stranger, and a most evil-looking one. As soon as he came in, I left. I am fond of spreading the Good Word, but not to a man with a face like that!"

"This is most interesting. You could describe this face?"

"He was a heathenish-looking fellow. I can still see his face. The fact is that I've been dreaming about it. I knew something would happen the moment I saw him. That man was possessed of the devil!"

"But the face. Please describe it as best you can."

"Why, why, let me see. He wore a thin, black mustache. I remember that. His mouth was thin and hard, too. That I'm sure of. He had beady little eyes—that's the expression, isn't it. It should be, for his eyes were black and shiny and looked no larger than two shoe buttons stuck on either side of his nose. And his nose; yes, that was bad, too. It was long and hooked and kind of thin. Very dark in the face, he was."

"Could this man have been a Portuguese?"

"Yes. Yes, he could have. He was a foreigner, all right."

"Did you notice his hair, particularly?"

"Yes. Very black and shiny. Plastered down on his head. His face was very thin. If he'd had a pair of horns to his head, I'd swear I saw the devil!"

"Did you overhear anything that went on between him and Mr. Amesbury?"

"Nothing to amount to anything. This fellow sort of glared at me when he came in. I left immediately. As I was going through the door this wicked-looking man spoke for the first time. His voice was sort of oily, if you know what I mean."

"What did he say? It's very important."

"Why, all he said was: 'So'—like that, questioningly."

"Did he say that as he came in, while all three of you were in the room, or just as you were leaving?"

Mr. Patcher, evidently, was not used to splitting hairs so finely. He regarded Hand in mild astonishment.

"It was as I was leaving," he replied.

"As I understand it," said Hand, "you left rather precipitately after this fellow arrived. That right?"

"I certainly did!"

"But surely there must have been something besides his evil appearance that drove you out so quickly."

"Well, his and Mr. Amesbury's."

"You mean that Mr. Amesbury suddenly became evil-looking too."

Mr. Patcher closed his mouth with a snap and regarded Hand coldly.

"Come, Mr. Patcher!" snapped Hand. "This may all seem irrelevant to you, but I assure you it is exceedingly interesting to us."

"I don't care to talk about a man," complained Mr. Patcher, "whose soul at this very minute may be standing at the gates of heaven."

"It is to determine whether his soul is still in his body that we are asking these questions. What was it about Mr.

Amesbury that startled you into leaving him so abruptly this afternoon?"

"Oh, dear! Well, all right. Mr. Amesbury got a very wicked glint in his eye when he saw this stranger. His face got very purple, and he put his hand under his coat at the left shoulder. I knew he carried a—a firearm there, and I left."

"I see. Did you overhear Mr. Amesbury say anything?"

"I have said enough about him. His soul is—"

Christopher Hand sighed.

"Mr. Patcher," he said, patiently, "we have the tremendous power of the law behind us. We can force you to answer our questions. But why place yourself in the category of a criminal? Believe me, it is far wiser for you to quietly answer them here in your own doorway."

"Yes, yes," agreed Mr. Patcher, hurriedly. "I hadn't thought. I didn't like to bear witness to what Mr. Amesbury said as I was leaving him this afternoon, because his only words were profane ones."

"He swore, did he! But surely his profanity merely enforced some statement that he made."

But Mr. Patcher raised his hands and directed a shocked glance to the heavens above.

"I tell you," he declared, "that I never heard such Godless words from the lips of a man before. He swore, and that's all he did. A terrible string of oaths followed me out of the door, and that's the last I heard Mr. Amesbury say this afternoon!"

"What time was that?"

"About five o'clock."

"Very well, Mr. Patcher," said Hand briskly. "You have provided us with more valuable information than perhaps you know."

We left him then, but first we had to give the customary assurance that we would immediately let him know should the funds of the Ajax Mining and Engineering Company come to light. Mr. Patcher timidly closed the door behind us.

"I wish," said Inspector Gerrity, glumly, "that I hadn't heard about that infernal Portuguese visitor."

"Complicates matters, doesn't it?" said Hand gleefully, to the inspector's astonishment. He rubbed his hands together and, in an almost nervous manner that he sometimes has, glanced quickly up and down the street. "Yes, Inspector, the deeper we go the more tortuous becomes the way. Really, the case is fast becoming more and more gratifyingly interesting."

"It's simple enough," grumbled Gerrity. "I've got the man I want, and by tomorrow morning I'll prove it!"

Once again I sighed for poor Larry White. But Hand was right, the case had become complicated. Somewhere in the city there lurked a dark, evil fellow. Could we but find him, I felt, we should be much nearer the solution of the mystery.

6

JUDITH BLAKE HELPS

We stood silent for a minute or two on the curb. Suddenly Gerrity hitched his shoulders and turned to Hand.

"What do you intend to do now?" he asked.

"I'm going home," replied Hand.

Both Gerrity and I regarded him skeptically. Neither of us were inclined to believe him. Gerrity laughed incredulously.

"Yes," smiled Hand. "When we are on an investigation, Clark refuses to leave my side, unless I entrust him with some mission. But I shall take him home, lest he miss a whole night's sleep."

"Then where will you go?" I demanded.

"Nowhere," he replied, with a shake of his head. "I plan to spend the remainder of the night at home."

Gerrity, I could see, was thoroughly unconvinced. He glanced petulantly at Hand, sure that something was being kept from him.

"All right," he muttered. "Let's leave this place, anyhow."

"And you, Inspector," said Hand, "will be at police headquarters all night?"

"What there is left of it, I suppose," affirmed Gerrity. "But I may get what I want before morning, you never can tell. Why don't you come along with me?"

Hand slowly shook his head. He had no faith in such inquisitions, I well knew. Gerrity shrugged.

"My car is round the corner, near the alley way," he said. "If you won't come to headquarters with me, I'll at least take you round to your rooms."

Hand nodded his acceptance of the offer. Silently we trudged along the lonely street, rounded the corner, and approached Gerrity's car. Beside the driver on the front seat sat Sergeant Tim.

"What are you doing here, Tim?" asked Gerrity.

"I was waitin', sir," replied Tim, with much dignity, "fer you to come back."

"I'm going to drop you off at your house," said Gerrity, severely. "And you're going to stay there. Don't come in tomorrow; you're not well."

"Yes, sir," replied Tim, quite dismally.

"He'll be at the office, bright and early, just the same," whispered Gerrity to me. "Well, let's get in. Take us to Mr. Hand's house first, Gilroy. Then we'll drop Tim off and go on over to headquarters."

During the short time that we rode with him, Gerrity kept stealing suspicious glances at Hand. But self-pride kept him from asking my friend what his thoughts were. Besides, he was secure in the knowledge that Hand would do nothing sensational without first informing him about it. We said good night before our door, and Gerrity was driven swiftly off.

"I'd hate to be in Larry White's shoes right now," I said, as I followed Hand up the stairs.

"Yes, he's sitting in an uncomfortable chair right this minute, with a brilliant light on him. He's been answering the same monotonous questions for over an hour, and he'll keep right on answering them until he cracks. Questions repeated time after time. When he falls asleep, they'll prop him up and go on with their questions. He's rather tired now, and he's terribly discouraged, anyway. I should say they'll get a confession out of him before noon. But if they don't they'll keep right on until they do."

"It won't amount to a thing, in my estimation!"

"Nor mine. But it will play its part in getting him indicted, nevertheless."

We entered the living-room. While I closed the door, Hand turned on the light and glanced quickly over toward his chair.

"Ah," he said, with satisfaction, "you didn't put any of my modeling equipment away. That is fortunate."

"You don't mean to say you are going to work at that bust?"

"Certainly. While you sleep, Clark, I shall ply my knife." He abruptly crossed the room and disappeared through the door to the bedrooms. I threw myself into my easy chair and waited. Presently he returned, tying the belt of his dressing gown. His eyes twinkled as his glance shot across the room at me.

"Formed any theories?" he asked.

"Only one," I gloomily replied. "And that one seems to spell doom for a young man I became rather fond of in a very short time."

Hand sat down in his Morris chair. Reaching out to the little table on which stood the uncompleted bust, he pulled it slowly to him. Finally he cocked an eye across the living-room table at me.

"You are feeling somewhat disappointed," he accused, "because I am not about getting evidence to clear young Mr. White."

"My dear fellow, I—"

"Yes you are. I remember that abominable hound dog you once inflicted upon us. He could look reproachful, Clark, but he was a mere novice compared to you."

"Well, I confess that I am a bit impatient to have you do something."

"There! But put a curb on your impatience, Clark. Before the light of day streams through that window, I shall travel far seeking just that very evidence that you crave. It is almost certain that I shall go to Alaska before morning."

"In spirit?"

"In spirit. My body will remain here in this chair, burning up innumerable cigarettes and fashioning the features of a man in this clay. But ere I ever return to it I shall have experienced several grotesque experiences, I assure you."

I forgot how sleepy I had been and leaned forward in my chair. Hand's long, sensitive fingers grasped the knife. He poised it for a moment; then he applied it to the lobe of the half-finished left ear of the bust.

"What do you expect to gain by these imaginative trips?"

"Much."

"This is a different procedure from that which you ordinarily employ. You usually stay hot on the trail, exhausting every possibility of a clue. I have seen you keep at it for seventy-two hours, incessantly."

He laid down his knife and glanced over at me. Then he sat back, placed a cigarette between his lips, and lighted it with something of a flourish, finishing by tossing the match to the floor. I made sure the thing was out and glanced up at him.

"I flatter myself," he said, blowing a great cloud of smoke round me, "that I do not become the creature of my systems. My systems are my creatures; I devise them, and I use them to suit my purpose. This case shows remarkable possibilities of becoming quite rarely unique. I do not say, Clark, that I see evidence of a mighty, cunning mind at work, and all that tosh! It does not take a man possessed of a mighty intellect to exterminate one of his fellows, nor does it take a very cunning man to do it quietly. A careful man, of course, will take pains to obliterate whatever evidence might lead to his being suspected."

"Unless the enormity of his deed shatters his self-possession."

"Precisely. But that we find, usually, in unpremeditated crimes. The passion that drove the murderer to kill quickly leaves him, for want of anything further to feed upon. We find our man overwhelmed by his act, with no plan to go forward upon, and too badly shaken to devise one. Such crimes rarely become a mystery. Ordinary police methods solve them quite easily."

"You are convinced, then, that this one was premeditated?"

"I have seen enough evidence to cause me to believe that it was. Quite carefully, too."

"I am relieved to hear you say that. I regard it as distinctly encouraging. White could have premeditated it, of course, but certainly he hadn't time to premeditate it carefully."

Hand smiled. Lazily he dropped his eyes to the cigarette in his fingers, rolling the little white, smoking cylinder dexterously between his thumb and forefinger.

"You have been pinning your hope on the Portuguese, I perceive," he drawled.

"But if it were carefully premeditated—" I cried.

"You go too fast, Clark," he sighed. "I shall never teach caution to either you or the inspector. There are a number of possibilities here; yet you and Gerrity devote all your attentions to one. By such unwise procedures the scope of the imagination, our most formidable weapon, is stunted and warped. The time for action, I tell you, is not here! I hold many fragments in my hands, but so far none has fallen into its proper place. They must be turned and fitted together from all angles. There is more evidence to be found, Clark, much more, but we shall know better in which direction to look for it after we have untangled the threads that we already hold."

"I fail to see what is to be gained in sitting here all night weaving hypotheses out of sheer fancy. I can deduce, you see, what you are going to do."

Hand chuckled. But then he glanced sharply at me.

"I don't know why you can't realize it," he said, a little irritably, "but I have not had my eyes tightly shut the whole time we have been on this case. We could go back over every step we have taken since we left these rooms, and I could find not one thing that I had not already noticed. Nothing escaped me! You say that I shall sit here all night weaving hypotheses out of sheer fancy. Nothing of the sort! From the evidence I have already collected I have eight embryonic solutions to this mystery. One of them, my boy, is the right one. I shall construct each one very carefully, ignoring no possible thread. Then, just as carefully as I put them together, I shall weigh one against the other. The strongest case shall win my adherence. By morning I should be well on my way to a solution."

"But I thought this case was singularly devoid of clues."

"On the contrary, there is a plethora of them. I must consider them all in different lights, thus separating the relevant from the irrelevant. For instance, Clark, I think it is a good wager that you attached no significance to the whiskey bottle that was standing on the table in Haggerty's room. Yet, I tell you, the whole mystery may turn on that one point. I grant you, there are more pieces of evidence to be found. Where is Amesbury's body? When we find it, if we ever do, we are sure to find additional evidence of the utmost importance. It is not inconceivable that I shall know where to look for it in the morning. I feel confident, at least, that I shall know where to look for further evidence that will shed new light on the case."

"I say, you won't go out looking for it without me?"

Hand laughed and once again picked up his knife.

"No, indeed. Go to bed, Clark. If your eyelids droop any lower I shall be able to understand why you don't see things."

"You'll call me if anything comes up?"

"Yes, I promise. Good night, old boy."

At the door to the bedrooms I looked back at him. With delicate care he was back at work again molding that ear. His gray eyes, set in his pale, thin face, reflected the light of the table-lamp brilliantly.

I had not thought I would sleep, but when I opened my eyes it was broad daylight. Something, I was conscious, had reached my ears that had sharply dispelled the slumber from my brain. What it was I had no idea, but I quickly determined not to lie there wondering. I leaped from the bed, pulled on my dressing gown and slippers, and crossed over to the door. As soon as I had opened it I heard a disquieting sound. Surely it was a woman weeping. That always disconcerts me. I heard Hand, who is thoroughly incapable of anything of the sort, trying to comfort someone. I hastened to the living-room.

In my easy chair, dabbing at her eyes with a tiny handkerchief, sat Judith Blake. Hand stood before her, looking most uncomfortable.

"Ha! Clark!" he cried, relief charging his voice. "I was just going after you. You—er—we saw her, you remember, last night."

"Yes, indeed," I said, hastening over to Miss Blake.

Hand hitched his shoulders and indulged in a sigh of relief. He thrust his hands deep into the pockets of his dressing gown and strode rapidly over to the other side of the room. There he stood looking at us askance.

"You poor child," I said, taking one of her hands. "You have heard, of course, what has happened. Please don't regard the situation so hopelessly; you can't help your fiancé by doing that."

All I got for that was a fresh burst of weeping. Hand's eyes rolled to the heavens.

"Come, now," I said, deeming that a little severity might help her. "This is no way to act. Your fiancé needs you now; he needs you now probably more than he ever will again. You must brace up."

She bravely struggled with her emotions. At length she had controlled her sobbing, and she turned to me with a pitiful smile.

"There now!" I cried. "That's much better. Mr. Hand is working very hard to prove that Mr. White is not guilty."

"He is not guilty," she said simply, as though the plain truth needed no amplification. "I know that it looks as though he were, but he is not."

"Might I ask who told you he had been arrested?" timidly inquired Hand, from across the room.

"Mr. Patcher told us. He came over first thing this morning. I came right over here to tell you that Larry couldn't have done this terrible thing, and to ask you to help me."

"Have you been to the police?"

"N-no."

"Then I wouldn't appeal to them. Try, by all means, to see your fiancé, but leave the police to me."

Miss Blake jumped to her feet and ran over to Hand, who seemed inclined to back away.

"You don't think Larry did it!" she cried, peering intently into his face. Thereupon Hand did back away.

"Now, now, Miss Blake."

"But you must tell me what you think! Father says you are the wisest man alive today. He says you know more than all the police put together, and he knows what he's talking about!"

"That is—hurrumph—that is very kind of your father."

"You don't believe Larry did it! Tell me!"

Hand glanced appealingly at me. Thoroughly in sympathy with the girl, I shrugged my shoulders and glanced out of the window. I could almost feel Hand's glance on the back of my head, branding me traitor.

"Tell me!" persisted Miss Blake, her voice vibrant with appeal.

"Miss Blake," said Hand, "I make a practice of never divulging my ideas until I am positive that I am right. I make no exceptions, not even my friend, Mr. Clark. Then, you see, unlike the police, I never have to admit that I am wrong. I am wrong, I frankly admit, many, many times, but nobody ever knows that. You see what you are asking me to do?"

I heard Miss Blake sob, and I turned squarely round.

"See here, Hand," I said sternly, at the same time winking an eye at him, "why don't you tell Miss Blake that you are positive her fiancé did not have anything to do with these crimes? You told me that just a few minutes ago."

Hand directed a glance at me such as Caesar in his last moments undoubtedly bestowed upon Brutus. Then he turned sadly to the girl.

"Miss Blake," he said, "I believe that your fiancé knows no more about those murders than I do myself."

"Oh!" she exclaimed, clasping her hands in her delight. "I'm so glad to hear you say it! I know you'll prove it, too. Oh, I just can't tell you what a relief it is to know that you are going to bring Larry back to me!"

"And now," said Hand, briskly, "won't you sit down and let me talk to you? As Clark says, your fiancé needs your help very badly right now. Perhaps you will be able to tell us something that will help."

The girl, who looked like a different person from the one I had first seen in my easy chair, skipped back to that same chair and sat down. Her big brown eyes were alight with excitement and hope. She looked earnestly up at the towering figure of Christopher Hand.

"I don't know what I can tell you," she said, "but I'll help you every bit I can. Oh, how I'll try to help you!"

"Very well," said Hand. "Understand, I have gone into every particular of this case very carefully. I have constructed theories that may be the solution to this mystery which surrounds us. Many links are missing, and until we have discovered them we cannot put anything to the final test."

"Yes," said the girl, breathlessly.

"What did Mr. Patcher tell you this morning?"

"Why, he told us everything. But we already knew from you and that police chief about everything except—except Larry. I mean, the finding of poor Mr. Haggerty's b-body in Larry's laboratory."

"And Mr. White's arrest?"

"Yes. He told us about that, too. It was cruel!"

"Did Mr. Patcher tell you about his having met Mr. White at Jeremy Amesbury's room yesterday afternoon?"

"Oh, no."

"Didn't mention that he had been visiting at Mr. Amesbury's room yesterday afternoon at all, did he?"

"Mr. Patcher? No."

"I thought not."

Miss Blake looked inquiringly over at me. The questions were puzzling her, but they were puzzling me too. I placed my finger to my lips.

"Now, Miss Blake," went on Hand, "has any stranger taken an interest lately in Mr. White's laboratory?"

"Did Larry tell you?" asked the girl, in surprise.

"Never mind. Will you please answer the question?"

"Why, yes, there was. There was a man who wanted to rent it from him."

"Ha! We are getting on. Was this recently?"

"Just the other day. It was Tuesday, I think. Yes, four days ago."

Hand became intent. He leaned over the girl, a disquieting gleam in his eyes. She looked up at him a trifle fearfully. I knew that he was close to some information of importance.

"Did you see this man?"

"Yes, I was in the laboratory when he came in. It was Tuesday afternoon. He offered to assume the lease and buy all the equipment. But, for some reason or other, he wanted to pay for it later. Larry needed money right away; so he wouldn't listen to the man."

"What did this stranger look like?"

"He—he didn't look reassuring. That's another reason that Larry didn't want to deal with him. He looked sneaky. You know the kind I mean."

"Not exactly. Please describe him to the best of your ability."

"Well, he wasn't very tall. He was about my own height, I should say, and rather slight. His face was dark and sleek. He had oily black hair slicked down on his head. Little black eyes, a thin, hooked nose and a small black mustache over a tight-lipped mouth. I remember him very clearly, because he frightened me. I mean, just by looking at him I became frightened. Actually he was very polite and quiet."

"That is a very good description. Did he speak good English?"

"No-o. He had an accent. I thought he was Spanish."

"Did he stay long?"

Miss Blake smiled and shook her head.

"If you mean too long, yes," she replied. "I don't suppose he stayed more than fifteen or twenty minutes. But as soon as Larry found out he didn't have any money he tried to get rid of him. The man still hung round, though, trying to make terms with Larry. He was very persistent. He even came back and tried again."

"Came back, did he? When was this?"

"The next day. He was in the laboratory waiting when Larry got back from lunch. Larry has lunch with mother and me. He found this man waiting for him in the laboratory when he went back there."

Hand took a turn up and down the room, scratching at the stubble on his cheek. Again he planted himself squarely before the girl.

"Are there any other laboratories, store-rooms or anything of the sort back there where Mr. White's laboratory is?"

"No. There used to be stores on the first floor of that building. About a year ago they were all torn out, and apartments were made there. Larry had a long lease on his laboratory. They offered him money to break it, but he wouldn't do it. It was so handy, you see. I could run in and see him most any time. We didn't have the money to get married, and we—we didn't want to give up our visits during the day."

At this point there came a loud rapping on our door. So abrupt was it that both the girl and I gave a start of surprise. Hand, with a quick, long stride, reached the door and flung it open. A buxom, florid-faced girl stood belligerently on the threshold, breathing heavily from the trip up the stairs.

"Oh!" she cried, rushing into the room. "There you are, you poor little darling! What are they doing, grilling you? I'll show them! You leave this poor little dear alone, you bullies! Shame!"

The newcomer had flung out her arms and enveloped Miss Blake. Over her shoulder she glared first at Hand and then at me. Miss Blake struggled to freedom and kissed the other girl on the cheek.

"Agnes!" she cried tearfully.

"There, there now, honey," cooed Agnes, stroking Miss Blake's head affectionately. "I won't let them at you any more. I should think you'd be ashamed of yourselves!" she said spitefully to Hand and me. "You, two grown men, grilling a poor defenseless girl!"

Hand sniffed. Miss Blake, once again at the mercy of her emotions, at last became articulate.

"They've been helping me, Agnes," she cried. "They are going to get Larry out of jail! Oh, you must apologize to Mr. Hand for talking that way. He's been awfully kind."

"Mean to say they haven't been tormenting you?" demanded Agnes, peering anxiously at her friend.

"Oh, no!" said Miss Blake. "No indeed!"

"Oh, well, then," said Agnes, a grin bisecting her face. "You mustn't mind me, Mr. Hand. Don't take what I said to heart. I'm that way—impulsive. You know, temperamental. But I'd do anything in the world for this little girl."

"Quite all right," conceded Hand, coldly.

"I'm answering some questions for Mr. Hand," said Miss Blake, proudly. "He says I am helping Larry by doing it. It makes me feel so much better, Agnes. What else can I do, Mr. Hand?"

"I think you have told me all that I wished to know," replied Hand, bowing with a smile. "You have been quite wonderful. One moment," he said, opening the table drawer and extracting a small pad and pencil. He scribbled a note and handed it to Miss Blake. "Go over to police headquarters," he directed. "Give this note to Inspector Gerrity, and he may let you see your fiancé."

Clasping the note between her two hands, Miss Blake leaped delightedly to her feet. She rushed over to Hand, threw her arms about his neck, and kissed him full on the cheek. For the first time in my life I saw my friend blush.

"Oh, how can I thank you?" cried Miss Blake. "You don't know how you've cheered me up. I love Larry so, and—and I can't bear to think of—"

She stopped and bit her lip. Agnes, with a bellow of compassion, rushed over and once more overwhelmed her. Then she leaped at Hand, kissed him noisily on the cheek, and leaped back again to Miss Blake's side. As the two girls moved over to the door, Hand backed away from them, stunned.

In the doorway Miss Blake turned back to us, once more master of her emotions.

"I will thank you some day," she smiled. "Some day I'll thank you properly."

7

THE APARTMENT HOUSE

When I had closed the door on our visitors I turned to Hand. He was making for the door to the bedrooms.

"Where are you going?" I demanded.

"My word," he replied, rubbing his fingers over his chin, "I want to get a shave."

"I doubt whether any more women come in," I grinned. "Young ones, anyhow, who are fond of kissing great big strong men with beards."

"Lord, I hope not!" he said, dismally. "I suppose, Clark, that you are fairly bursting with questions, too."

"I'll try to contain myself," I laughed. "Go ahead with your shave, but please don't take long with it; I am rather curious."

Hand looked at his watch, and slowly he moved over to his Morris chair.

"Seven o'clock," he muttered. "Just one detail I haven't gone over. I'll get it settled; then we can go ahead."

As he sank into his chair, save for the apparent tonsorial need, he looked as fresh as an athlete ready to go into a contest. A moment later the vitality had drained from his face, leaving it haggard, livid and strained. The luster left his eyes, and his whole form seemed to collapse. He slumped there in his chair, gazing at me with eyes that I knew did not see me. He scarcely breathed. Before he stirred the clock on the mantel advanced the day fifteen minutes.

I was ready, as he got slowly to his feet, to protest that he must give up and get some rest. The years when he could live on his nervous energy for days at a time quite apparently had passed. By degrees, as he slowly stood erect, an amazing change came over him. I stood gazing at him in amazement. Once again the electric, feline-like energy radiated from every line of him, once again his features were keen and sharp. The glance that his eyes darted at me told plainer than words how senseless it would be for me to urge sleep.

"Rest well last night, Clark?" he asked, casually.

"Much better than I thought. How have you progressed?"

"I've got on. I am treading on firmer ground now. By Jove, I all but finished that bust!"

"Well, yes, the bust. But I am more—hello! You've made a much older face out of that bust than it was when I went to bed!"

"Hum-m. So I have."

"Why, you've aged that face considerably. I thought you were going to make it a bust of that young fellow we saw at the opera. But how you were going to do it was beyond me; you gazed at the ceiling the whole time we were there."

"It's the same face, but, as you say, it is aged considerably. Simple enough to age a face. Ever try?"

"No!"

"Most interesting, Clark. You see, as one grows older the muscles of the face lose their strength—their elasticity. They allow the flesh to sag. It's most noticeable round the eyes, probably. Just step over to that mirror you have by the door to admire your hat. By the way, I've made excellent use of that mirror once or twice. As I sit in my easy chair with someone sitting before me it gives me a capital view of the back of his neck. Some people have remarkable control of their features, but their necks will swell when you have them in a tight place."

"Well, here I am at the mirror. What now, for heaven's sake?"

"Take the tips of your index fingers, Clark. Place them at the outside corners of your eyes and pull gently downward. That's it; look at yourself!"

I must confess that I was somewhat startled. By causing the flesh about the corners of my eyes to droop, I had imparted a haggard, aged appearance to my face. I jerked my fingers away, glanced sharply at my natural image in the mirror, and sighed with relief.

"A little transparent adhesive tape, covered with just the right make-up, would do just what your fingers did, Clark," chuckled Hand. "There are one or two other little devices that I could suggest. If you employed them all you'd get a pretty fair idea of how you will look thirty years hence."

"No thanks," I muttered. "It's bad enough to have old age in the foreground without trying to anticipate it."

"Well, that's what I've done to this poor chap," grinned Hand, indicating the bust. "He started out in life a handsome young fellow, and now over night, my heartless fingers have transformed him to the class of the aged and infirm. I had nothing to do with it; it was just a moment ago that I discovered what my fingers had done to him."

"Well," I said testily, "we get nowhere standing here talking about art. What are we going to do today?"

"First off we shall both shave, bathe, and then have some breakfast."

"How can you be so casual when the life of one man hangs in deadly peril and the fate of another stands shrouded in mystery?"

The amusement left Hand's eyes, and he turned somberly to me.

"Speed," said he, "is sometimes a desperate necessity, and at others it is an agency of destruction. We do well to hesitate, Clark. Come, you hop into your shower, and I'll hop into mine. By the way, I'm expecting a call from Dr. Richards, and a wire may come through at any moment from Alaska. If the phone should ring, and I shouldn't hear it, you skip out and answer it, will you, Clark?"

I quelled a desire to ask him what all this was about. I realized, too, that there was utterly no chance of his not hearing the telephone if it did ring. My one hope was that there should be no females in our living-room should the telephone ring while he was in the shower bath.

We met in the living-room, shaved and bathed. The telephone had not rung. Hand looked far fresher and more rested than did I. He stood just within the living-room, rubbing his hands together and peering about.

"I get no credit for anything round here," he suddenly and surprisingly announced; whereupon he fixed me with a haughty stare.

"What on earth are you talking about?"

"The newspapers."

"Newspapers?"

"Certainly. There they are, all piled neatly in the corner."

The newspaper situation, to be sure, had not entered my head. If it had I should have expected, when I first entered the living-room that morning, to find them scattered helter-skelter over the floor.

"But, Hand," I protested, "you never picked them up before!"

"Nevertheless," he sniffed, "I did this morning. I must have."

"My dear fellow!" I cried, in delight. "This is most encouraging. I can't tell you how much I appreciate it!"

"It's nothing, Clark, nothing. You deserve some consideration from me, after all. Glad I did it. Did you ring for Mrs. Flemming? I could do with some breakfast, and— By Jove, I hear her coming. That heavy, rolling footfall always sharpens my appetite."

Mrs. Flemming, puffing heavily from the exertion of the stairs, entered carrying our tray of breakfast.

"Good mornin't' both of yez, sors," she beamed, after her usual fashion. "Sure, I hope I didn't disturb yez, Mr. Hand."

"How's that?"

"When I picked up yer newspapers scattered all over the place. I sez t' meself: Is he dead, shlaypin', or hit over the head only? But then I see yez were workin' over that shticky shtuff on the little table there. I sez good mornin' t' yez, and never a word out of yez."

Hand caught my enlightened glance and quickly presented his back to me.

"I'm sorry, Mrs. Flemming," he cried. "Good morning. Good morning."

The living-room table also does duty as our breakfast table. As I slid into my chair across from Hand, I glanced amusedly at him.

"Sure I can't put a newspaper at your elbow?"

"No. No thank you, Clark."

"Well, anyhow, what was in them?"

"Quite a plenty. Gerrity was collared, undoubtedly, by the gentlemen of the press before ever he got to his office at headquarters. I'm afraid the inspector is going to make himself look a trifle foolish."

"Ah! You think he is on the wrong track, then?"

"I didn't say he was on the wrong track. I do say that he is on but one track, and he should be on several."

That was all I could get out of him. He devoured his breakfast and took to pacing the living-room, a streamer of cigarette smoke continuously passing over his shoulder. In spite of the fact that I had promised myself never again to let him give me indigestion, his impatient glances soon had me gulping my toast and coffee. As I was pushing my chair back from the table, there came a rapping at our door. Hand attended to it, and, before the knocking ceased, he had it open.

There stood Inspector Gerrity, his last energetic rap coming in contact with nothing but thin air. He gave a slight start and peered into the room.

"Oh, hello," he said. "Thought I'd drop in and see how you've made out."

"I see you have some finger-print photographs there," observed Hand, with satisfaction. "Come in, Inspector, come in and sit down."

Gerrity accepted the invitation. He laid his photographs on the table and, with a heavy sigh, seated himself in my easy chair.

"Quite a night," he said. "Looked like a pretty tough case, at first. I think you'll agree with me there, Hand. I don't believe I ever cleaned anything up so rapidly before."

"Ah," said Hand, lowering himself into his chair. "You have solved the mystery, Inspector?"

"If it could be called a mystery. It did present some puzzling features. I myself am surprised that I was able to get to the bottom of it so quickly."

"I take it, then, that you have solved this mystery by obtaining a confession from the murderer."

"Oh, yes. It was inevitable."

"I suppose it was. You have indeed worked swiftly. I had put the time for the confession at not before noon."

"Yes, I must say that I handled the situation pretty cleverly."

Hand lighted a fresh cigarette; then his eyes leaped back to Gerrity's face.

"Where is Amesbury's body?" he asked, suddenly.

"How?" said Gerrity, with a start. "Please, Hand, don't shoot questions at me like that. I've been up all night."

"Sorry. But, where is Amesbury's body?"

"Why, I—you see, I haven't found that yet."

"Dear, dear. What sort of confession did you get out of White, anyway? I trust that he hasn't forgotten where he put that body."

"He's still obstinate about one or two things. Fact is—"

"It begins to sound as if you hadn't found out where the money is, either."

"Well, that will come later. Can't expect everything at once. The important thing is that White has confessed to the killing."

"A clear-cut confession, I suppose, with all the details of the murder. Been over the actual ground with him, and he re-enacted the whole thing for you."

"Well—well, not exactly that. It was a virtual confession, though. I convinced him that probably he had gone a little out of his head, do you see?"

"Quite clever. Did his fiancée get to see him?"

"No. She had your note, but—well, I didn't think it a good idea. Perhaps in a day or so we'll let her see him."

"Yes, perhaps. You haven't told me about these finger-prints, Inspector. Let's just go over them. And how about that knife; was it human blood on it?"

Gerrity, who had begun to act reproachful, dropped his eyes to the pile of photographs and papers he had laid on the table. He picked up a report and glanced over it. Then he passed the photographs to Hand.

"The knife had human blood on it," he said. "We didn't find a finger-print on the latch of that window in the laboratory that wasn't left there by White. If the laboratory was broken into, he broke into it himself. So your theory about that is all smashed to smithereens."

"Too bad," murmured Hand. "I see that these finger-prints on the handle of the knife are all Amesbury's. At least, that's the notation on this picture of them."

"And it is correct. Whoever drove the knife into his heart wore gloves."

"Your own deduction, Inspector; I recognize your mind at work."

"Thank you, Hand. Now, those finger-prints on the hammer are mostly all White's. There is another set of a few, and they are Miss Blake's."

I was seized with an uncomfortable foreboding, and I glanced in astonishment at Gerrity. He smiled at me in a very superior fashion.

"I have Hand to thank for finding that out so quickly," he explained. "When Miss Blake was in my office this morning she laid her hand on the top of my desk near the visitor's chair. That portion of the desk is always kept highly polished. I had Saunders, after she had gone, compare the finger-prints she left there with those on the handle of the hammer that had not been accounted for. They were identical."

"Of course," I said quickly, "there is nothing surprising about her finger-prints being on the hammer. Miss Blake was in the laboratory a good deal; she could have picked up the hammer at almost any time."

Gerrity smiled and shook his head. Hand was watching him quite narrowly, and I was watching him quite fearfully.

"It would appear, I grant you," said the inspector, "that Miss Blake's finger-prints being on that hammer is not of much consequence. But we had already determined that the person who left the marks identified as hers was the last person to wield the hammer!"

Hand was scanning the photograph of Miss Blake's finger-prints on the hammer. Gerrity regarded him with haughty amusement.

"These marks of Miss Blake's, I see," said Hand, "are those of a person who had grasped the hammer rather tightly."

"They are," affirmed Gerrity. "They are the marks of a person who delivered a heavy blow with it. And," he said, leaning back with a satisfied smile, "perhaps she did deliver a heavy blow with it."

"I say, this is contemptible!" I cried. "You don't mean to tell me, Gerrity, that you are deliberately trying to incriminate that poor girl on any such evidence as that?"

Gerrity shot me a glance of annoyance. He hitched himself in the chair and glowered at the floor.

"My duty," he growled, "is to ferret out the guilty and bring them to justice. Some of the most atrocious crimes on record were committed by women. Ruth Snyder took the sash-weight from Judd Gray and finished off her husband with it. Why should I say this crime is dissimilar?"

"What did the autopsy show?" asked Hand.

"Just what our own inspection showed, of course," replied Gerrity. "Death was caused by a crushed skull. Instantaneous."

"Dr. Richards has completed his examination, of course."

"Sure. This case didn't give him much trouble."

"The body is at the morgue then? I suppose it will remain there for some time. By the way, has anybody claimed it?"

"Not that I know of. That minister, Mr. Bothwell, called me up this morning. He inquired about the disposition of the body. I suppose he'll do something about it. Someone should bury the poor old codger."

Hand rose abruptly and set off for the door to the bedrooms. As he was crossing the threshold, the telephone bell rang sharply.

"Ha!" he exclaimed, whirling about. "What now? A voice is waiting to come over that wire, and how will it

influence matters—perhaps the lives of men and women?
Answer that telephone, Clark."

I did so, as Hand stood tense in the doorway.

"Two telegrams for you," I said.

"Two! Either the telegraph company is holding up my
messages, or we have an odd coincidence here. Ask them—"

"They are both collect."

"All right. Tell them it is perfectly all right. Ask them
to give them to you, Clark, and copy them down as you get
them. I shall be right back."

He quickly disappeared through the door, and I turned
back to the telephone. As I was writing the messages down
on the pad, Gerrity was desperately trying to conceal his
desire to read them. I was a little astonished at them both.

The first one read: "Woodford Amesbury here 1:30 yesterday afternoon stop Showed credentials and received one
letter addressed to him stop Left immediately stop Only
description can give is clerk's who believed man was very
dark stop" It was signed: "P. S. Morgan, Mgr., Hotel Rich-
mond, Washington, D. C."

The second read: "Jeremy Amesbury and Nick Haggerty
filed gold claim here last May stop Nothing known about
trouble with Portuguese stop" It was signed: "Longstreet,"
and it came from St. Michael, Alaska.

Gerrity hummed a nonchalant air and took to parading
up and down the living-room. At each turn his humming
became indistinct and, with a short pause, he peered sharply over at the piece of paper on which I had scribbled the
telegrams. Then, with a renewal of his music, he hitched
his shoulders and paced on. After his trips back and forth
numbered a half dozen, Hand returned to the living-room.
I handed him the messages. With inscrutable countenance
he read them; then he handed them to Gerrity.

"Humph," grunted the inspector. "Checking up on your
own client?"

"I check up on everybody," replied Hand, with a shrug. "I've told you that before, Inspector. Once or twice in the past, as you know, I have found it of inestimable value."

Gerrity was scowling at the telegrams.

"Only description can give is clerk's who believed man was very dark," he read. "I don't call Amesbury very dark."

"He has black hair," pointed out Hand. "And besides, his face is very tanned. It doesn't take an elastic imagination to conceive of the man's calling him dark."

"It says very dark," corrected the inspector, poking his finger viciously at the piece of paper. "Amesbury has light eyes; they're gray."

"I believe they are," said Hand, casually. "Well, Inspector, I was about to go out. Do you want to accompany me?"

"What are we going to do?" asked the inspector.

"I am going to inquire into the construction of that building where we found Haggerty's body," replied Hand. "My theory about that laboratory's having been broken into may be smashed to smithereens, as you call it, but I satisfy myself about such things. I am not yet convinced that there is nothing to it. When I am, I'll let you know."

"I won't waste my time, then," smiled Gerrity, a trace of pity in his eyes. "I'll go down to the street with you, at least. I'm working on another matter now, and I'm working on it pretty energetically. When I've cleared it up, I'll let you know."

"Good of you, Inspector," murmured Hand, as he got his hat. "A word of advice, from one friend to another—let the newspapers cool their heels for a while; they've had quite enough news already."

Gerrity grinned and shook his head. In silence we descended the stairs to the street. There, with a self-satisfied chuckle, the inspector wished us good luck. We declined his offer for a lift, and he got into his car and was driven away. I turned impulsively to Hand.

"We've got to do something!" I cried. "Gerrity is surely going about incriminating that poor girl. He'll probably have arrested her by noon!"

"I shouldn't be surprised," said Hand, with a lingering glance at the inspector's retreating car.

"But we must stop him!"

"The inspector is too rash. Well, let us be going, Clark."

"Do you think there is any chance of thwarting him before it is too late?"

"Perhaps. Who knows?"

I had to be content with that. We walked quickly over to the house where Larry White's laboratory was located. There we hunted up the superintendent, a little man with a drooping, brown mustache.

"Mr. White's laboratory?" he said, in response to Hand's question. "Sure I know all about it. A nice young man; I never thought it of him."

"I am anxious to learn," said Hand, "whether there is any way of getting in or out of that laboratory other than through the door at the back and the window beside it. Can you tell me whether there is any way to get into the building itself through that laboratory?"

The superintendent pushed his hat over one ear and scratched his head. He peered suspiciously at Hand, and then he peered even more suspiciously at me.

"My name's Adolph Zinger," he said. "I like to know who I'm talkin' to."

"You shall," said Hand, displaying his badge of honorary membership in the New York police department. "My name is Christopher Hand, and this is my friend Mr. Ralph Clark."

"Oh!" said Adolph Zinger, quickly pulling his hat straight and squaring his shoulders. "Oh. I'll tell ya all I know, Mr. Hand, and that, I guess, is all there is to know.

There ain't no way in or out of that laboratory 'ceptin' through the door to it or the winder."

"How are you so sure of that?"

"That's the way it was done. The boss wanted it that way. This building was remodeled a little while ago. We put apartments in the first floor instead o' the stores that was there. Couldn't rent 'em. Mr. White wouldn't give up his lease, ya see."

"I think I see. But you might explain a little more clearly."

"Well, the boss was sore at 'im because he wouldn't give up his lease, ya see. Mr. White has his lunch with the Blakes, and he wanted a door left in the back o' the laboratory so's he could get through to their apartment. The boss bein' sore, he wouldn't do it. He tells the contractors, instead, to close the laboratory up as tight as a drum. And that's what they done, too, Mr. Hand. I seen 'em do it. A mouse couldn't get out o' that place 'ceptin' through the door or the winder!"

"So, in order for Mr. White to have luncheon with the Blakes, he had to leave his laboratory and go all the way round the block to get there, even though his laboratory and the Blakes' apartment are in the same building. Quite a nuisance."

"That's what the boss figgered it'd be. He was sore, like I told ya. Yes, sir, he was good and sore."

"Now, Mr. Zinger, can you tell me the name of the contractor who altered this building?"

"Sure. Thomas Higgins. Here's his card; he left a bunch of 'em with me, and this is the first chance I've had to pass one along."

"Very much obliged, Mr. Zinger. Good day."

We left the building and went in quest of Mr. Thomas Higgins. We found him, after first being given directions at his office, up to his neck in work making alterations to a grocery store. Hand asked to speak with him. After giving a few vociferous orders to his men, he followed us inquiringly to one side.

"Mr. Higgins," said Hand, "have you read of the murder of Nick Haggerty by Larry White?"

"Yeah," replied Mr. Higgins. "It was on the front page of the *Herald* this morning. I knew that guy White."

"I thought you must. I believe you did some work on the building where he had his electrical laboratory."

"I sure did. Nice young fella, but very stubborn. They tried to get him out o' there, but he wouldn't budge."

"So I understood. I also understood that you had instructions to leave no doors in that laboratory leading to the interior of the building."

"That's right. The old guy that owns the building was madder'n a wet cat at him for not getting out. It wasn't up to me. When we got through there the only way he could get out was through the back door."

"And the window."

"Well, yeah, and the window. But what in time would he wanta hop out the window for? Oh, I get you; in connection with the murder, eh?"

"I am following up a lead in that direction."

"You from the police?"

"I am making an investigation in conjunction with the police. You are quite sure, are you, that it would be impossible for a person to leave that laboratory except through the door or the window?"

"Well, he might bust a hole through the wall. But not unless'n he did that."

"You know that building pretty well, I imagine. What surrounds that laboratory?"

"Kitchens on all three sides. I'm going back to the shop for some things; I was figgering to go when you come in.

If you want to go back with me, I'll let you see a blue print of the first floor of the building."

Hand readily accepted the offer, and we climbed into the contractor's car. At his shop he rummaged through an old desk and produced the blue prints. Hand studied them intently.

"The apartment in front of the laboratory," pointed out Mr. Higgins, "we had to make a three roomer. That's why the owner was het up. We planned it so's we could convert it into a four roomer as soon as White got out of his laboratory. But you see, the laboratory is surrounded by kitchens."

"So it appears," mused Hand. "It certainly does not seem that a secret door could be built in any of the laboratory walls."

Mr. Higgins smiled and shook his head dubiously. Hand thanked him, and we immediately departed.

"Where to now?" I asked.

"Too bad to run you round like this, Clark, but I want to leave no stone unturned. We now go back for another interview with Mr. Zinger."

"You are not satisfied, then, that no one broke into the laboratory last night and left it by some secret means of egress?"

"Not yet."

Back we went in search of Mr. Zinger. We found him standing on the sidewalk, gazing enraptured at a powerful roadster drawn up at the curb. Hand stepped quietly up to him.

"Beautiful car, Mr. Zinger."

"Eh! Oh, you back again, Mr. Hand?"

"Yes. You know, Mr. Zinger, that automobile probably belongs to someone very much interested in the murder."

"No!"

"I feel quite sure of it. Have you noticed the license plates?"

"Well, no, I ain't."

"They are Texas registration plates. This is a beautiful car."

Hand stepped up to it and inspected it carefully. A moment later he swung quickly round to face Mr. Zinger, who had crowded up behind him. The superintendent quickly fell back a step. He cleared his throat nervously and seemed undecided into which pockets to put his hands.

"All the apartments rented on the first floor?" demanded Hand.

"Huh—what? Oh, yes, all of 'em. Every one."

"Hum-m. What is over that laboratory?"

"The second floor."

"Indeed? I presume that it would be safe to say that the second floor is used for something?"

"Sure it is. Sure thing, Mr. Hand. We got apartments up there."

"And there is one directly above the laboratory?"

"Well, no, not exactly that. There's the kitchen of one, though."

"That apartment is occupied?"

"Yes, sir. We're very lucky here. But then, we do have an awful nice place, if—"

"Now tell me, Mr. Zinger, are the people in the apartments on the first floor all new tenants? I am interested only in those surrounding the laboratory."

Mr. Zinger walked over close to Hand and looked earnestly up at him.

"Mr. Hand," he said, concernedly, "I don't want you to get all mixed up about this. The only parts of apartments round that there laboratory is kitchens. There's kitchens round it, and there's a kitchen on top of it. Not apartments. Course the kitchens do belong to apartments."

Hand solemnly stroked his chin.

"I think I understand," he said. "While Mr. White did things with electricity, his neighbors on three sides of him and one on top of him did things with frying-pans. But tell me, were these neighbors of his old tenants of yours?"

"Every one of 'em. We keep people. The Blakes, them that lives upstairs over the laboratory, have been here eight years. Think o' that, eight years! Then in the three apartments downstairs round that laboratory there's the Maddens and the Cranes—course they moved down after the apartments on the first floor was built. But they been with us over five years, both of 'em. Then there's Mr.— hold on! What did you ask me, Mr. Hand?"

"I asked you whether there were any new tenants in those apartments."

A half-frightened gleam came into Mr. Zinger's eyes. His mustache seemed to droop lower than was its natural habit.

"Why—why," he stammered, "why no, they ain't all old tenants."

"I understand, then, that in one of the apartments on the first floor adjoining the laboratory there is a newcomer."

"Y-yes, sir."

Hand leaned intently toward the little man.

"What's his name?" he snapped. "How long has he been here?"

"I—I—oh dear!" wailed Mr. Zinger. "The house is gonna be ruined, I can see it! Dead bodies lyin' round and that feller; I knowed somethin' would happen with him here! Why didn't I tell him we didn't have no apartments on the first floor! Now look! What did ya ask me, Mr. Hand?"

"What is this newcomer's name, and how long has he been here?"

"His name is—lemme think. It's Brown. No, that's the name he gimme first. It's Smith, that's what it is. I wrote it on the lease."

"Do you mean to tell me that he changed his name right before your face?"

"Well," cried Mr. Zinger, wildly, "he give me two names. First he said it was Brown, and then, after I'd rented him the apartment, he gimme his name as Smith to put on the lease. A. B. Smith, it was. He paid a month's rent in advance—cash."

"When did he rent this apartment?"

Mr. Zinger placed his finger alongside his nose and gazed thoughtfully at the heavens. By the way he nodded his head he seemed to be counting. At length he turned triumphantly to Hand.

"Wednesday!" he cried. "Wednesday o' this week."

"Has he moved in?" asked Hand.

"Not yet. He keeps comin' round, though. I seen him three or four times goin' in or comin' out o' his apartment. Said he was gettin' ready to move."

"Mr. Zinger, give me a careful description of this Mr. A. B. Smith."

Once again Mr. Zinger placed his forefinger alongside his nose.

"He was kind o' dapper. Dressed pretty elegant. Had black hair that I guess was combed down with shoe polish. Very dark, he was, with a wicked pair o' little eyes and a foolish sort of a little black mustache."

"Could he have been a Portuguese?"

"A Portugee? I don't believe I'd know a Portugee if I seen one."

"Well, then, could he have been a Spaniard?"

Mr. Zinger started so violently that he nearly poked his finger into his eye. His underlip fell down below his mustache, and he regarded Hand with a startled expression in his eyes.

"Mr. Hand," he said, "that's just what I thought that feller was—a Spaniard."

8

AN EYE-WITNESS

Hand bustled the superintendent into the house. He ordered him to direct us to the mysterious Mr. Smith's apartment, and when we stood before the door, he bade him open it. Mr. Zinger's hand, when he applied the key to the lock, was shaking so badly that I doubted whether he would ever get the thing inserted. He finally did, however, and, giving the door a push, he stepped quickly back out of the way.

We looked into a room as bare as any could be. Hand strode to the center of the room. I followed in after him.

"Get away from that!" snapped Hand, suddenly.

I glanced round in time to see Mr. Zinger recoiling from the door.

"W-what?" he stammered.

"Don't touch that door-knob; I want it."

"You—you want it! You want that there door-knob? But, Mr. Hand, it belongs to the house!"

Hand turned his back on the superintendent. To our left was a small dining-room. Beyond it was a kitchen. As all the doors stood ajar, we could look right through. Hand passed through the dining-room to the kitchen, glancing sharply all about as he moved.

In the kitchen were two windows, overlooking the court at the back. Before one of them Hand stopped. Here a box had been drawn up to the window, and all about it on the floor were scattered cigarette stubs, ashes, burnt matches and four empty, crumpled cigarette packages.

"You see what has been going on here, Clark," said Hand. "Rather an expensive look-out point. He's been spying on Amesbury and Haggerty. You see that building right across there? The second story window in the left corner is Haggerty's window."

Next he turned quickly to the wall separating the kitchen from the laboratory. Here a sink, a gas stove and a kitchen cabinet were set up against the wall. Hand tried to peer behind them.

"Is this cabinet fast to the wall?" he asked, darting a glance at Mr. Zinger, who had followed us apprehensively into the kitchen.

"Yes. Yes, sir," replied Mr. Zinger, quickly. "They're all fast to the wall, even the stove. You ain't gonna tear 'em loose!"

Hand was tugging mightily on the cabinet. It refused to yield, greatly to the relief of Mr. Zinger. The stove and the sink seemed just as solidly attached. Hand bounded to a door beside the one we had passed through to enter the kitchen. He yanked it open, revealing a shallow closet, one wall of which formed part of the laboratory wall. He stepped inside and examined it carefully. Then he knocked his knuckles against the wall from top to bottom. That completed, he shrugged his shoulders and stepped into the kitchen.

"We may be wrong," he said, "but I don't believe there is any way of getting into the laboratory from this room. What do you say, Clark?"

"If you didn't notice it, I'm satisfied that there is none."

"Don't be too sure; I've been wrong before."

Apparently satisfied, however, he returned to the room we had first entered. Here he took out the little kit of finely-wrought, tempered steel tools that he carries. First covering the inside knob of the entrance door with a hand-kerchief, he set about detaching the knob. Mr. Zinger was plainly distressed.

"Ya ain't gonna take nothin' else off, are ya?" he timidly asked. "I'm responsible for this buildin', Mr. Hand, and while I ain't standin' in your way none, I sure would appreciate it if you leave as much as possible."

"This is all I want," grunted Hand. "There we are."

He slipped the knob off, wrapped his handkerchief carefully about it, and dropped it into his pocket. Then he strode out of the apartment.

"You may lock that apartment, Mr. Zinger," he said. "Just accompany us out to the back, if you don't mind. I want to look over that laboratory again."

Mr. Zinger seemed half thrilled at being with us and half apprehensive about being drawn into the sinister business. He took Hand's orders, however, and carried them out with no objection whatever. He knew of a way to get to the back court without the necessity of going all the way round the block. To do it we had to go to the basement. Rough boarding formed a narrow corridor extending from the stairs to the back of the building. Half-way down it an unshaded electric light bulb vainly strove to illuminate the corridor properly. Toward the rear the corridor ended at a door with two glass panels. Before we reached it, Mr. Zinger indicated a door in the side wall to our right.

"That there is my apartment," he said, a note of pride in his voice.

"Ha!" exclaimed Hand. "You live there, do you? Were you at home, by any chance, about ten thirty last night?"

Mr. Zinger appeared dismayed. He glanced at the door as if he blamed it for his having mentioned it. Then he glanced sidewise at Hand.

"I ain't had nothin' to do with this here murder, honest!" he protested. "I was here in my apartment when poor Mr. Haggerty was beat to death, right over my head, you might say."

"Did you hear anything that attracted your interest?"

"Not one thing!"

"Have you a wife?"

"No, more's the pity. I'm a natural born family man, I am, Mr. Hand. I got a very kind heart, and all. Why, I even keep a cat. I've had my chances at weddinglock, but every time I got right down to askin' the question I got all cold inside and yammered and blammered round without gettin' nowhere! One of 'em is still waitin' for me, out in Pennsylvania. Poor Huldah! But I just can't get up my nerve!"

"Fortunate," muttered Hand, absently. He had been standing, hands on hips, peering intently over the corridor. "Your apartment doesn't take up the entire basement other than this corridor, does it?" he shot at Mr. Zinger.

The superintendent had been lost in melancholy contemplation of his unfulfilled matrimonial dreams. Hand's question brought him up with something of a snap.

"No. Yes. What?" he said, with a start.

"I said, your apartment doesn't take up all the basement with the exception of this corridor, does it?"

"Oh, no, sir. I only got a bedroom and a kitchen. This corridor, ya see, runs down the side o' the basement. There's lots o' room out on this side besides my apartment. My apartment's right nice, though; wanta see it, Mr. Hand?"

"Not just yet. Is it directly under the laboratory?"

"No, praise be!"

"Then what is directly under the laboratory?"

"Nothin'. I mean, just an empty cellar. It ain't used for nothin'. The storekeepers, them we had, used to keep boxes and things down there."

Hand nodded and strode briskly on to the outside door. We had to go up three cement steps to reach the ground level. Outside, Hand glanced over two windows flush with the ground level between the door and the small porch outside the laboratory.

"Them's my winders," explained Mr. Zinger. "One's the kitchen and the other's my bedroom. It's very nice."

A policeman stood on the laboratory porch. He swung about to regard us suspiciously. Recognizing Hand, something of relief came into his bearing. But he said nothing as we climbed up the steps to join him. Hand shot a glance at the laboratory door, which was tightly closed and locked with the padlock.

"Have you a key for that?" asked Hand.

"I have, Mr. Hand," replied the policeman, patting his coat pocket.

"Well, would you mind opening that door with it?"

The policeman evidently found himself in a dilemma.

He scratched his head and seemed uncomfortably perplexed.

"I ain't just sure, Mr. Hand," he said. "Inspector Gerrity give me this key, and he told me not to let nobody in with it unless I got orders to do it from headquarters. I know he wouldn't mind if I let you in, but orders is orders, you know. Can't you call him up, or somethin'?"

"You say the inspector told you not to let anybody in the laboratory with that key?"

"That's it, sir. It's the only key there is; we got it off of White."

"But if I had a key to fit that lock, I don't suppose your orders would cover that. The inspector said nothing against my using a key of my own, did he?"

I turned quickly away from the harassed policeman, lest my face should betray my friend. For I had seen Hand, with the deftness of a professional, shamelessly pick the pocket of one of Gerrity's most trusted minions, and I knew that the key to Larry White's laboratory was no longer in the possession of the law. The policeman continued to summon inspiration by the expedient of scratching his head. Finally he had it.

"I suppose if you did have a key, Mr. Hand," he said, brightening, "you could go ahead and use it. But of course you ain't, because I got the only one."

"Well, I have one here that I'd like to try," said Hand, grasping the lock. "It won't hurt to try it, anyhow. Ha! It worked."

"Well, I'll be—" muttered the policeman, uncomfortably.

Hand pushed the door open. He stood on the threshold, peering in.

"Nothing seems to have been disturbed," he observed.

"No," agreed the policeman, but in rather a doubtful manner. "Nothin' does look like it was disturbed. But I was disturbed plenty a couple o' minutes ago! There's a ghost or somethin' in that dam' place!"

"You don't say so? Did you see it?"

"No, but I heard it. A kind o' knockin'. I let meself in; the inspector didn't say nothin' about my usin' the key to let meself in."

Mr. Zinger showed signs of wishing to depart. I took him by the elbow and shook my head at him. He rolled his eyes and muttered something that sounded religious.

"What did you see when you came in here?" Hand asked the policeman.

"Nothin'! But no sooner'n I'd stepped out and locked the door again than the knockin' started all over again. Sounded like somebody thumpin' against that wall over there."

"Hum-m. There's the kitchen of an empty apartment on the other side of that wall. I happen to know that."

"I'm gonna report it!" said the policeman, firmly.

"I should," agreed Hand, with a twinkle in his eye. "It should give Inspector Gerrity food for thought."

Suddenly Hand peered at the padlock, hanging on the staple outside the door. He shook his head and glanced at me.

"We slipped up there, Clark."

"I don't understand."

"That padlock should have been examined for fingerprints. No doubt it's so full of them by now that nothing under the sun could be learned from it. The inspector would never have done it, of course; he does not incline toward the theory I advanced last night. Perhaps we should have gained nothing by it, anyhow. Well, let's see what we can find in here."

We all entered the laboratory. Hand first examined the wall that separated the laboratory from the kitchen we had just been in. The closet where Haggerty's body had been found was set in this wall. After a careful scrutiny of this wall, Hand went into the closet. Very shortly he stepped back into the laboratory.

"That's settled, Clark," he said. "Nothing in that wall to give access to the apartment next door. I'll swear to that."

He next subjected the floor to a most careful examination. Once he paused long over a spot near the center. I was paying keen attention to his proceedings. The floorboards were wide. Hand bent over the end of the heavy work-bench and peered intently at the floor.

"Let's all take hold of this," he said, "and see whether we can move it."

Even the policeman got rather excited. He grasped the bench along with the rest of us. With our combined strength we dragged it aside a few feet.

I could see no evidence of a trap-door where the bench had stood. Hand picked up a heavy wrench and commenced hammering lightly about on the floor with it. Every one of the floor-boards seemed securely nailed down, as nearly as could be told from the sound of his hammering. I suddenly thought I had seen something significant, a break in one of the floor-boards. But I quickly saw that it was merely the indentation made by the edge of the bench where it had rested upon it.

Hand, too, seemed satisfied that he could find nothing. He gruffly suggested that we put the bench back where it originally had stood. This second task was somewhat harder, because the policeman did not deign to help us. He appeared to be getting tired of us, and to be wishing that we would leave before one of his superior officers discovered us there. But suddenly, as he was leading us over to the door, he started violently and cried out.

"What's the trouble?" I asked, quickly.

"My key!" he cried. "By golly, I've gone and lost it!"

"Are you sure?" asked Hand, concernedly.

"Sure," cried the policeman, wildly. "I had it right here in me pocket. It ain't there now, I tell ya! I'll get hauled up on charges for this!"

"By Jove!" exclaimed Hand. "Now how did that key get there?"

"Where?" demanded the policeman, glaring all about.

"Right in your shoe," said Hand. He reached quickly down to the policeman's right foot, and when he straightened he held the key in his fingers. "There you are," he said.

"Hey! No!" protested the policeman. "How could it get there? I never put it there. It ain't possible!"

"It was there, just the same," shrugged Hand. "I should keep it in my pocket, if I were you. A policeman's pocket is a pretty safe place for things, you know."

"I did have it in me pocket," muttered the policeman, as he locked the door after us. "I wish to Gawd they'd relieve me; I'm gettin' sick and tired of this job!"

Next we returned to the basement. Hand asked to be shown to the unoccupied part, and Mr. Zinger led us to a door beyond his in the corridor. We entered a place as black and dank as a subterranean chamber could be. Hand got out his torch, directing me to get mine in use also. Battered stone walls divided the basement into narrow compartments. Toward the rear of the building the walls had been removed completely, to allow for the construction of Mr. Zinger's apartment.

"How long since was your apartment built, Mr. Zinger?" asked Hand.

"Just a couple o' months. They built it after they got through puttin' in the new apartments upstairs."

"That is why these walls are broken down at the back?"

"Yes, sir. The boss didn't care so much how they busted these walls out, just so long as they could build my apartment in. Each one o' the stores used to have a cellar of its own, ya see. It don't look so nice in here now, but nobody sees it. No sense o' spendin' money on a place that ain't gonna be used for nothin'."

We picked our way round Mr. Zinger's apartment. Hand led us to a spot at the rear that I reasoned was directly under the laboratory. Here Hand directed his light on the ceiling.

"Do you happen to have a step-ladder?" he asked Mr. Zinger.

"Yes, sir," replied the man, looking nervously about the basement. "It's right in a closet at the bottom of the stairs. It's awful dark back there where we come from, ain't it?"

His glance at it told me that he coveted my torch. I gave it to him, and he made his way back among the broken walls. Hand was moving slowly along the floor, keeping his light on the ceiling.

"Still looking for a trap door?" I asked.

"Clark," he replied, "I don't think we are going to find a trap door."

I felt quite miserable over it. If only we could find some manner of leaving the laboratory besides the door and the window! If we could only establish that such a thing were possible, I felt, we should have Larry White out of jail in no time. It was beginning to appear that we could never prove the young man's innocence. Perhaps he was guilty, after all.

Mr. Zinger came struggling back with the ladder. He seemed to be bothered a good deal by a conviction that he should continually inspect the territory to his rear. At every step he twisted himself about, knocking the ladder into things and getting his feet mixed up in it, in order to send the beam of the torch circling about him. I walked over and took the ladder from him. Deeming it an act of human kindness to let him retain the torch, I neglected to ask him for it.

Hand snatched the ladder from me and set it up. Then he climbed quickly to the top of it. He had picked up a loose stone from the floor, and with it he commenced knocking against the boards over his head. I could imagine our policeman outside having another attack of the jitters.

It was tedious work. Hand would cover as much space as he could from the top of the ladder; then he would leap down, I would push it along, and he would bound back up to the top of it. Every board that he thumped upon seemed to be as securely nailed down as could be. At length he had covered the whole area of the laboratory floor.

"It's like I told ya," said Mr. Zinger, with a shake of his head. "A mouse even couldn't get out o' that laboratory 'ceptin' through the door or the winder. That place was closed up, and it was closed up tight!"

"It most certainly appears so," said Hand. "Well, let's get out of here; I am satisfied on this point."

Mr. Zinger needed no further urging to lead us forth. But he kept my light, which he still retained, sweeping back and forth. Once or twice he turned his white face over his shoulder to see that we were with him.

"See here," said Hand, suddenly, "you've taken us the wrong way. This is not the direction that the door to the corridor lies in."

"Oh! Oh! Oh!" wailed Mr. Zinger. "We're lost! We'll never get out alive! I'm a goner!"

Hand turned and, quickly retracing his steps, passed round the broken end of the wall. Mr. Zinger, his breath hissing through his teeth, also turned quickly to retrace his steps. In doing so he banged my torch against the stone wall. It went out, and the darkness engulfed us.

"Oh," said Mr. Zinger, tremulously. "Now I lay me down to sleep, I pray—"

"What's the matter?" I demanded.

"It's th-the only prayer I—I know."

"Well, come on. Hand is waiting for us; see, he's shooting his light back to guide us."

I led Mr. Zinger quaking round the broken wall. Hand's light came into full view, and a moment later we were standing in the corridor.

"I never knowed what a terrible place that was!" declared Mr. Zinger, with feeling. "Nothin' could get me to go back there!"

Hand was intently examining the door-knob on the inside of the door to the basement. Mr. Zinger's practical nature superseded his agitation.

"You gonna take that one too?" he demanded. "I hope the boss don't come round till you bring them knobs back. But I busted your friend's light; go ahead and take it."

"No, I don't want it," said Hand. "You notice, Clark, the knob is covered with a thick coating of dust. Nobody has opened this door from the inside for quite a while. Is there any other way out of that portion of the basement, Mr. Zinger, besides through this door?"

"No, there ain't. Wait a minute, there is, too. There's an old door at the back, but it's all boarded up."

"That's the one under the porch outside the laboratory?"

"Yes, sir. That's the only one there is."

Hand grunted and turned to the stairs. We went up to the front entrance hall. There Hand turned to Mr. Zinger.

"I want to thank you very much," he said. "You have been most helpful. But I want to ask a further favor of you. If you should encounter Mr. A. B. Smith, either here or on the street, will you let me know at once? If you see him on the street you might follow him to see where he goes. But if he comes here, call me right away. Here's my card. I'm afraid, however, that you have seen the last of Mr. Smith."

"All right, Mr. Hand," agreed Mr. Zinger, dubiously. "But I'm a-scared of that feller; he gives me the creeps."

"I don't think he'll hurt you, but if you'll call me, I won't let him. I see that the roadster is still parked outside. Come on, Clark, we are now going to call on the Blakes."

We went up to the second floor and knocked on the Blakes' door. I presumed that Hand wanted to inspect the floor of the kitchen above the laboratory.

Judith Blake admitted us. She seemed quite cheerful, in spite of Gerrity's refusing to allow her to see her fiancé.

"Oh, Mr. Hand!" she cried. "Come right in. And Mr. Clark, too. What have you to tell us? Have you cleared Larry of this dreadful thing?"

"Don't be in too much of a hurry, Miss Blake," smiled Hand. "We have found one or two significant details this morning. Perhaps they will help, but I can't say anything about them yet."

I wondered whether he was talking just to hearten her, or whether he really meant what he said. Nothing that we had discovered that morning seemed to me likely to help, so far as Larry White was concerned.

Miss Blake ushered us into the living-room. There we found her mother and Woodford Amesbury. I was not surprised to see him, for I had divined that it was his roadster we had seen parked at the front. Amesbury walked eagerly over to Hand. He was quite elegantly dressed, in contrast to the ill-fitting suit he had worn the night before. In his lapel he wore a gardenia.

"Well, well," he greeted us, "I stopped over at your house, but you were out. What's the good word, Mr. Hand; are we clearing White?"

"I have hopes of doing it," replied Hand.

The expression of eager expectancy on the face of little Mrs. Blake faded to one of disappointment. She sat back in her chair and folded her hands.

"I did so hope you'd have some definite word for us, Mr. Hand," she sighed.

Only Judith Blake seemed undismayed. But I sensed that her tranquility was rather forced. I admired her for it, however.

"Mr. Hand is going to succeed for us," she said. "I feel that he is! But he is right, we mustn't be in too much of a hurry."

"I must urge you to bend every effort to that end, Mr. Hand," said Amesbury, pompously. "I have been trying in my poor way to cheer Miss Blake, but something concrete from you would, I know, be far more effective. I want nothing more."

Hand strode over and gazed out the window.

"You've heard no word from your uncle?" he asked, without turning round to his client.

"Why—but how could I?" protested Amesbury. "I am relying upon you, Mr. Hand, to find out what frightful fate has overtaken my uncle."

"Yes; but I wanted to make sure you had not heard anything yourself."

"Then you don't think he is dead?"

Hand shrugged his shoulders.

"So long as his body remains undiscovered," he said, "we can always hope for the best. Only when we have seen him dead can we be sure that he is."

"But that landlady of his saw him dead!"

"That's what she said. Miss Blake, have you been out anywhere this morning except to my house and police headquarters?"

"No," she replied. "After they wouldn't let me see Larry I came right home. I felt awfully blue, but Mr. Amesbury has cheered me up. You've been most kind," she said, clasping her hands and turning gratefully to Amesbury.

"Believe me," he said, looking earnestly into her beautiful eyes, "had I the power to do it, I'd make you happy again though it cost me my life!"

She blushed and dropped her eyes. Then, giving him a rather startled glance, she moved over beside her mother.

"Thank you," she said, quite timidly. "You—you've been very kind to me."

"And I shall not cease to be," cried Amesbury. "Mr. Hand, let me urge you again to redouble your efforts to exonerate Mr. White. I am more interested in that, now, than I am in finding my uncle's slayer. After all, the living deserve our help far more than the dead. I ask you to confine your efforts to this end, and if you are successful I promise you a very liberal fee."

"The amount of my fee is a fixture," coldly retorted Hand. "You may rest assured, however, that every phase of this case will be gone into most thoroughly. But, Mr. Amesbury, I came in here to ask you a question."

"How in thunder did you know that I was here at all?"

"I judged that it was your car that I saw standing out at the front. Tell me, did your uncle ever settle in one place for any appreciable length of time?"

"I can't say. I believe, from different things he has said, that he resided in the West for some years. But I don't know where it was, nor do I know how long he lived there."

"I should like, if possible, to trace the path of his life. Sometimes very significant details can be picked up in that way. Can you give me any help whatever in going about that?"

"I'm afraid none. My uncle was very much of a rolling stone. So am I, but our paths rarely crossed."

We stood in silence after that, Hand thoughtfully stroking his chin. All at once there came an energetic rapping at the door. With a feeling of uneasiness, my thoughts turned to Gerrity. His would be just such a rap. Judith Blake started for the door. I imagine Hand's mind had run in much the same channel as my own, for he put out an arm to restrain the girl. With a puzzled expression on her face, she stepped aside. Hand quickly strode for the door, and I followed him. If it were Gerrity, I wished to say a word or two to him.

Gerrity it was, and, as Hand opened the door for him, he stepped belligerently into the small hallway. He was a little startled at seeing Hand. Also he was, I could see, a little chagrined.

"You here?" he said, trying to appear casual. "Anything new?"

Hand's reply filled me with astonishment.

"Yes, Inspector, I have an eye-witness."

"No! Bring him to me, Hand. Where is he?"

"That I don't know."

"You don't know! Well, for the love of—say, what's the idea?"

"I have every reason to suppose that this man can be found. That he witnessed the crime I am certain, and, given a little time, I think I can apprehend him. I should like to show you on just what I base my opinion."

Gerrity waxed a little uncomfortable. He glanced into the room where the others were standing; then he turned uneasily to Hand, tracing with his toe the line of the rug.

"I have some men outside," he said, "if you'll just give me a few—"

"You don't mean to say you've brought a squad of men along with you to arrest that poor girl?" I chided, in a low voice. "Couldn't you have done it all alone, Inspector? She doesn't appear to be a very dangerous person to me."

I glanced into the living-room. We had all spoken in low tones, and I was relieved to see that Judith Blake apparently had not heard us. She was talking earnestly to Amesbury. I glanced back to behold Inspector Gerrity getting rather crimson round the collar, which is usually a sign that he is about to do something foolish. But at that moment there was a mild commotion in the hall outside.

"Mr. Hand's in there, I tell ya," a familiar voice insisted. "I got to see him, and I got to see him right now! There's somethin' funny goin' on."

Hand quickly opened the door. Just outside the door, with plainclothesmen towering over him, stood Mr. Zinger in heated argument.

"I know Mr. Hand, I tell ya!" he was vociferating. "Him and me are just like—there he is! Mr. Hand! Mr. Hand! As sure as my name's Adolph Zinger there's somethin' or somebody movin' round in the cellar underneath the laboratory!"

9

FRAUD

I could almost have hugged Mr. Zinger. His pronounce-ment, delivered with a vigorous upheaval of his arms, had the effect of driving all previous intentions from Inspector Gerrity's head. At once the inspector went into action on this new development. He grasped Mr. Zinger roughly by the arm.

"You're the janitor of this house?" he cried.

"I ain't," retorted Mr. Zinger, with great hauteur. "I'm the superintendent! And leggo my arm, Mister, please; you're stoppin' my circulation."

"You are the janitor, blast it! I know you. What's all this about somebody being underneath the laboratory?"

"I think, Inspector," interrupted Hand, quietly, "we shall find out with the greatest dispatch if we go there to investigate. I don't think Mr. Zinger has done more than obtain the evidence of his ears. Come, and please try to be quiet about it."

"I guess Mr. Hand knows a thing or two!" said little Mr. Zinger, exultingly.

Gerrity, after an instant to glower at the superinten-dent, turned quickly and followed Hand down the stairs. I followed close after him, and the inspector's men crowded after me. Mr. Zinger strutted down the stairs after them.

Pausing at the basement door, Hand placed his ear to it. Gerrity hitched his broad shoulders impatiently. He stood immediately behind Hand, squinting at the door. After the manner of an apparition, Hand slowly opened the door and faded through it. The inspector and I followed after him. It was not the first time we had followed him into such inkiness. We both are convinced that Hand, like a cat, can see in the dark. This, of course, is not true. But Hand, once having seen a place, retains such a perfect image of it that later he can get about in it quite as well in the dark as he can aided by light.

I put out my hand and grasped the inspector by the shoulder, perfectly certain that he was following Hand in the same manner. Thus we moved slowly, noiselessly along. I felt the inspector stop, and I likewise halted. Scarcely breathing, I stood motionless in the dark. The unwholesome dankness of the place seemed to creep into the marrow of my bones, and momentarily I expected something frightful to happen. Instead, from the blackness to our right, I heard a soft thud and a low cry of pain. The inspector started moving on, and I followed after. Soon a faint brilliance dimly outlined the edge of a broken stone wall. We advanced toward it, presently rounding the wall.

Holding a small electric torch, a tall, thin, stoop-shouldered man stood with his back to us. The place where he stood was directly beneath the laboratory. All we could see, as he moved slowly along keeping his light on the floor, was his black outline. He seemed to be looking for something.

"Put up your hands!" called Gerrity, roughly. "And keep 'em up!"

Upon the prowler of the basement the effect of the order was galvanic. He shot straight up into the air, and his light, released from his fingers, shot straight down to destruction. Darkness swallowed him up, leaving me with the impression of his angular, dark form suspended in mid-air.

Another light beam, powerful and unwavering, split through the darkness and fell upon our fellow. Crouched, white of face and glaring through his spectacles with eyes filled with terror, stood the Reverend Mr. Bothwell, pastor of the Hendly Congregational Church. With pitiless deliberation, Hand held the light on him several moments before he spoke.

"Well, well, Mr. Bothwell," he said, "this is a most unusual place to find a clergyman."

Mr. Bothwell seemed mightily relieved to find that the devil himself was not about to attack him. He straightened and heaved a great sigh.

"My soul and body!" he exclaimed, producing from his coat sleeve a handkerchief with which he vigorously mopped his brow. "You frightened me. You frightened me most abominably. Who are you, anyway?"

"There are a number of us," replied Hand, speaking out of the darkness behind his torch. "I am Mr. Christopher Hand. Here also are Inspector Gerrity, Mr. Clark and a number of the police."

Mr. Bothwell continued to shake from the fright he had received.

"I met you gentlemen last night, I believe," he observed. "I really wish that you would illuminate yourselves; I can't tell you how spooky it is talking to nothing, as I am, but a glare of light."

We walked toward him then, Hand directing his light at the ceiling. Thus that portion of the basement was suffused with a soft light. Mr. Bothwell appeared grateful at not being the only one with any brilliance about him. Gerrity walked pugnaciously up to him.

"What're you doing here?" he demanded. "I don't like to get rough with a minister of the Gospel, but you've got to explain your business here, and you've got to do it satisfactorily!"

"I can do that very easily," said Mr. Bothwell, calmly.

"Well, go ahead and do it," invited Gerrity.

"It is my duty," pointed out Mr. Bothwell, quite spiritedly, "to look out for my flock. You have gone ahead on little or no evidence and incarcerated one of the members of my church. It is shameful! His name is being bruited about, and the police are bearing false witness against him in the newspapers. He is a young man of great promise and excellent character, and he contemplates holy wedlock with a lovely young woman, whose spiritual advisor I also am. She called upon me this morning and told me that you have even become so ruthless that you actually refused to allow her to see him!"

"That's my business," growled Gerrity. "You haven't told me yet what you were doing down here when we found you just now."

"I have taken it upon myself," said Mr. Bothwell, "to straighten out this frightful mistake. If the police have not the wit to discover this wicked brother of Cain, then I, with the grace of heaven, will endeavor to do it. You may rant at me all you please, Mr. Inspector, but you will find it difficult to prevent me from carrying out what I conceive to be my duty. Now I was investigating down here. Evidently nobody has taken the trouble to do that. You base your suspicions of Mr. White, I believe, on the finding of poor Mr. Haggerty's body in his laboratory. Has it not occurred to you that the murderer might have deposited the body there and then escaped by dropping through the floor to the basement?"

"The police still have a few brains," snapped Gerrity. "That floor has been carefully examined, and so has everything else in that laboratory. Every board in that laboratory floor is tightly nailed down. There is no trap door. Isn't that right, Hand?"

"If there is a trap door there," replied Hand, with a shrug of his shoulders, "I haven't been able to find it. For your information, Mr. Bothwell, I have made a careful examination of the floor, both from above and from the underside down here."

"Then," said Mr. Bothwell, with finality, "I shall not have the impertinence to continue my investigation here. But I warn you, Mr. Inspector, I shall continue my investigations elsewhere."

"Go to it," offered Gerrity, gruffly. "But I have work to do; see you later, Hand. Come on, you fellows."

"Just a moment, Inspector," said Hand, quickly. "May I have a word with you?"

Gerrity regarded Hand for a moment; then he allowed himself to be drawn aside. I thought I knew the purpose of this conference; so I walked over to the corner where they had gone. I wanted to add my plea to Christopher Hand's.

"Well, what now?" growled the inspector. "You can't stop me, Hand. I've got a clear case against those two, and I'm going to prove it!"

"I don't disagree with any effort to clear up this case. What I do deplore, Inspector, is seeing you placing all your eggs into one basket. Suppose your case falls down; where are you then?"

"I don't see just what you mean."

"You have seized upon a theory, and you are devoting all your energies to advancing it. Why not try to round out the case? You are disregarding a good many significant details. In your rather hectic pursuit of weaving a net about that boy and that girl you are utterly ignoring a great many possibilities. I warn you, Inspector, you can't afford to do it. You are going to find yourself in an assailable position if you are not careful."

"Well, what am I supposed to do? If you've got a theory, why don't you tell me about it?"

Hand's head snapped back, and even in the soft light about us I could see the gleam of his eyes.

"Because," he snapped, "I am not yet ready to prove it. I am not positive that I could prove it. I have already disproved one hypothesis that I had begun to trust. Suppose I had gone ahead on that theory, announced my convictions, and caused an arrest; and then the whole case had collapsed about my ears. I don't say that your theory is not correct, Inspector, but I do most certainly say that you cannot prove it to be!"

"If I get them both down to headquarters, I'll get the truth out of them!"

"Perhaps, but I doubt it. Inspector, if my hypothesis leads me to the solution of this mystery, you will be the first to know about it. If I prove this boy you have locked up and that girl upstairs guilty, I will tell you at once and give you all the material to convict them. You know me well enough for that. I'll do the same no matter what my investigation leads to. But don't arrest that girl now, Inspector, don't arrest her now."

Gerrity considered in silence for several moments.

"I suppose," he sulked, "you want me to turn that fellow loose, too."

"I refuse to advise you on that. You've already acted there, and you will have to be guided by yourself. Now, I've told you that I have discovered evidence to show that there was an eye-witness to this crime. Will you come have a look at it? You are exceedingly unwise if you don't, and I do not intend to waste any more time over it!"

"All right, all right. Where is it, Hand?"

For answer Hand turned on his heel and left the basement. We all crowded out into the corridor. Mr. Zinger, who in spite of his valiant efforts to gain the van had been left in the rear, skipped out and shut the door after us. We proceeded on up the stairs to the first floor.

"I don't think we shall need all your men, Inspector," said Hand. "Let them stay out in the hall."

Mr. Zinger unlocked the door of Mr. A. B. Smith's apartment. Mr. Bothwell paused long enough to peer suspiciously at us through his heavy eyeglasses; then he quickly departed. The superintendent accompanied us into the apartment and out to the kitchen. He stood circumspectly aside as Hand strode up to the window.

"This apartment," said Hand, "was rented Wednesday of this week by a man who gave his name as A. B. Smith. Fictitious, of course. His description is identical with that given by Mr. Patcher last night of the Spanish-appearing gentleman who called upon Mr. Jeremy Amesbury yesterday afternoon. I have determined that a man bearing the same appearance attempted to rent the laboratory where the body of Nick Haggerty was found."

"Hum-m," mused Gerrity. "That's significant, isn't it?"

"I would say so. Particularly after having viewed the evidence left behind him in this apartment."

"Evidence? Let's see. Smoked a lot of cigarettes, didn't he? Sat on that box and looked out the window. What makes you think he was doing it when the murders were committed?"

Hand motioned us away from the window. Then he knelt beside the box, with his long index finger pointing out the evidence scattered on the floor.

"First of all, Inspector," said he, "we must assume that from this window our man witnessed at least one episode of the crime we are investigating. Having assumed that, we shall begin from that assumption to reconstruct his actions. When we have finished, you yourself may judge whether my deductions are logical."

"Go ahead," invited Gerrity, gruffly.

"To begin with, this litter on the floor was not dropped at one sitting. Whereas there are four empty cigarette

packages here, there are but forty-four cigarette stubs—
just a little over half the number originally contained in
the packages. Therefore, thirty-six of the cigarettes were
smoked elsewhere. He visited this apartment no fewer than
four times, Inspector."

"How do you know?"

"Because there are forty-four cigarette stubs on the
floor, but there are only forty burnt matches. Four times
he came in carrying a lighted cigarette."

"But he might have carried lighted cigarettes out with
him, too."

"I have not overlooked that. If he carried lighted cigarettes out with him, the match that lit them must be here.
In that event he visited this apartment more than four
times. I said that he visited it no fewer than four times.
The calculation is a simple one."

Gerrity drew a long breath.

"I guess you're absolutely right, Hand," he said. "But
what do we care how many times he visited this blasted
apartment?"

"It forms the basis of a deduction that this fellow rented the apartment in order to keep a systematic watch over
Nick Haggerty and Jeremy Amesbury. Although he could
not see Amesbury's room from here, he could look right
into Haggerty's bedroom window."

"Yes; I noticed that. But what makes you think that he
was here at this window when the murders were committed?"

"Because the evidence I have found here bears out the
assumption. Let me show you. He sat well over at the side
of the window, you see. His cigarette stubs are all in a pile
at the side of his box. But he flicked the ashes out before
him. Fortunately, he was careful not to pass in front of the
window. The ashes, you see, lie scattered beneath it prac-
tically unmolested. But there are four foot-prints in the

ashes, two with the toes toward the window, and two with the toes pointing away from it. Look at these two nearest his box, Inspector. They, you notice, are the two with the toes pointing in the direction of the window. Obviously he got quickly to his feet and stepped to the window. Would he have exposed himself in that fashion had it been daylight? I don't think so. Notice over there under the stove. There you see the ashes of almost a whole cigarette that has burned itself out. It was tossed there by an agitated person, who let it burn up and scorch the floor unheeded. Moreover, it is the only one that was not put out. I can see him rising in his excitement from that box, tossing his cigarette aside, and advancing to the window."

"Go on, Hand, for heaven's sake don't stop!"

"He was watching something, Inspector, watching something that was sending the blood pounding through his veins. He gripped the window-sill and pressed his face to the pane."

"How on earth do you know that?"

"Look at the gloss on that fresh paint on the windowsill. The prints of both hands are in it. You can't see them unless you look carefully, but your experts will get them. Look closely at the window-pane. Don't you see the print of a man's face, left there when he pressed it against the glass?"

"Yes, yes, I see. What else, Hand?"

"He stood there for several moments, straining to see. He pulled his face back toward the window-casement to see the better off to his left. Don't you see the marks he left on the window-pane? Inspector, he was trying with all his might to see on the laboratory porch!"

Gerrity's eyes were kindled with excitement. He wet his lips.

"I believe you're right," he said, quickly. "I believe you're right, Hand. He's an eye-witness, no doubt of it. What else have you deduced?"

"Somebody went into the laboratory, Inspector. I don't think this fellow could quite see that, but unquestionably he could see enough to know what was going on. After the man he was watching disappeared, he opened his kitchen window and climbed out into the courtyard."

"You know that he did!"

"I deduce that he did. In swinging his feet over the sill he dropped particles of the cigarette ash that had clung to his shoes on this inside sill. More than that, he ground them into the brick ledge outside the window. I have inspected the earth beneath this window. I did not even bother to inspect it closely; the marks of his feet when he dropped can be plainly seen from that porch outside the laboratory. I tell you, he climbed out of this window!"

"But surely you don't know what he did then!"

"I believe I have deduced it correctly. By means of the ledge in the back wall of this building, he climbed up to the laboratory window and peered in. A little while later he climbed back through this window, shutting and lock-ing it after himself. He left particles of dirt on the ledge, both below this window and the one to the laboratory. The marks of his hands as he climbed in are also plain on this window-sill. Look at this foot-print in the ashes below the window, Inspector. It is badly scuffled, you see. He stood on the ball of his foot and swung himself round to close the window. No doubt he braced his other knee against the window-sill as he drew the window down and secured it. Then he swung himself round again, brought his other foot down beside the one that was already on the floor, and walked away from the window. Is it plain to you?"

"Yes, yes, I agree with you. I must get the Bertillon men up here to get pictures of these finger-prints. I'll do it at once."

Hand took out of his pocket the knob he had taken from the entrance door of the apartment. He held it out to the inspector.

"Give them this, too," he said. "The prints you find on this should match those on the window-sill. I think probably you will find some in Jeremy Amesbury's room that will check with them. And, Inspector, we must find this man!"

"But how are we going to do it? The fellow is probably a thousand miles off now! If he's that Portuguese he's probably headed back for Alaska. What a fool we were not to inspect this building at once; now he's got through our fingers!"

"I have an idea he is still in the city, Inspector. And I think further that the chances of finding him are excellent. But, Inspector, I have a favor to ask of you."

Hand glanced narrowly at Gerrity, who glanced eagerly back at him.

"All right, all right, but for heaven's sake tell me how we are going to find that Portuguese!"

"I have a plan to do it, but publicity on what I have just shown you is not part of it."

"I'll say nothing about it! But how are we going to find this fellow, will you tell me?"

But Hand shrugged his shoulders and turned away from the inspector.

"By watchful waiting," was all he would say. "I don't think it will take long. You might station a couple of detectives in here, but I have very little hope that they will accomplish anything. I'll let you know, Inspector, if my plan works out. In the mean time, keep that laboratory closed up, and don't let anyone disturb the evidence in here."

Hand turned abruptly and started for the door. Gerrity, looking very much astonished, went quickly after him. He caught Hand by the sleeve and stopped him.

"What are you going to do now?" he demanded.

"I have a few things left to determine," replied Hand, stiffly. "If I come across anything else of interest, Inspector,

I will let you know at once. Better get working on those finger-prints."

Hand walked out of the apartment, and I turned to the bewildered inspector. I wanted to assure myself that Miss Blake was in no immediate danger of arrest.

"You are not going to take action against Miss Blake?" I asked.

Gerrity spread his hands in exasperation.

"Not just yet," he growled. "I'd like to, and I should; but what with Hand against it, and with all this fresh evidence he's dug up, I've got to give more thought to it. By thunder, I'd like to know what he's got in his head!"

I ran out in time to see Hand's tall figure descending the steps outside. As I caught up with him on the sidewalk, I saw that Amesbury's roadster was still parked at the curb. With a glance at my watch I surmised that the client was going to take Larry White's place at the Blake's luncheon table.

"Where are we going now?" I asked.

"Over to Jeremy Amesbury's room," he informed me, as he swung along.

"I thought you were satisfied with your investigation there."

"When we were last there I did not know so much about the case as I do now. I sincerely hope we do not find another of Gerrity's men there in possession of a key."

At the foot of the stairs we came upon Mrs. Ackner. She came from the direction of her own quarters. She was dressed to go out, and under her arm she carried a market basket.

"Good morning," said Hand, pleasantly. "Out for a little marketing, Mrs. Ackner?"

"Oh, yes," she replied, with a little flurry of pleasure. "I'm so glad, now, that you gentlemen stopped in last

night. My husband has talked of nothing else but having
met you, Mr. Hand. He's read about you."

"That's your work, Clark," remarked Hand, gloomily.
"I hope your husband is well, Mrs. Ackner."

The woman shook her head dismally.

"He's never well," she said. "Being tied up in an invalid
chair like he is gets onto his nerves some days. But he's
been awful good since you come in last night. He's been
almost happy today."

"And I am happy to hear it!" cried Hand. "But we are
taking your time, Mrs. Ackner. Very glad to have seen you."

Mrs. Ackner smiled and went out through the door.
Hand and I quickly mounted the stairs. A policeman stood
outside Jeremy Amesbury's door. He turned sharply about
as we rounded the corner of the hall.

"Hello," Hand accosted him. "They've given you special duty."

"Yep, Mr. Hand," smiled the officer. "It's kinda lonesome now, but when I first come on the people in the
house all come round askin' questions. I had lots o' company then."

I recognized him instantly. He was Felty, whose regular
beat is patrolling our neighborhood at night. Hand is a
great favorite of his.

"Look here, Felty," said Hand, "you must be the officer
whom Mrs. Ackner called in last night after she had found
this man Amesbury murdered."

"That I was, sir," affirmed Felty. "It was a funny business, too."

"I believe the inspector said that you saw an automobile parked in front of this house when you ran in here
last night."

"There was, Mr. Hand. I been doin' some deduction
like yourself, I have. That car was what took this poor

feller's body away with it. Now why didn't I think o' that last night? I'd o' got meself a promotion, I would."

"Too bad. But maybe you can get that promotion yet. What sort of car was it that you saw parked out in front?"

Felty removed his hat and scratched his head. I wondered whether that was something they learned at the police college.

"It was—it was an automobile," said Felty, at length.

"Yes, but what kind?" insisted Hand. "Was it a touring car, a coupe, sedan, roadster, or what?"

"It was a big car, but it was small!" exclaimed Felty, as if this impossibility had just filtered through from some dark recess of his head.

"Ah, it was a big roadster, then," said Hand.

"Or a coupe," supplemented Felty.

"You're not sure which? Think!"

"Um-m, no. I ain't sure, and that's a fact, Mr. Hand. You see, I only seen it once, and then I was runnin' fit to bust me lungs. It didn't do me one bit o' good to run, because when I got here I remembered that I'd forgot to ask Mrs. Ackner what room this here feller was killt in. I had to wait until she got here. When I come out, this here car had gone and took the body away with it. You see, I didn't get much chance to inspect it."

"But you're prepared to say that it was either a big coupe or a big roadster?"

"Yes, sir. It was one or the other, and I'll say so, too, if I go on the witness stand. I make a very good witness, Mr. Hand."

"I shouldn't wonder. Did you notice the license plates on this car?"

Officer Felty smiled tolerantly and shook his head.

"I was goin' so fast, Mr. Hand," he explained. "I didn't take no time off to go jottin' down license numbers."

"I didn't mean that exactly," pursued Hand. "Did you notice whether the car bore New York license plates, or the plates from a different state?"

Once again Felty resorted to scratching his head.

"Mr. Hand," he said, "I don't believe I saw them license plates at all. Probably had plates, but I didn't see 'em whatever."

"Very well, Felty; I suppose it is all right for me to go in."

Felty speedily took to scratching his head again. Finally his blue eyes twinkled and he turned chuckling to Hand.

"Me orders," he said, "is to let no one in. No *one;* do you get it, sir? Now if you and Mr. Clark was to both go in, I ain't lettin' no *one* in."

Hand laughed, twisted the knob of the door, and strode into the room where Mrs. Ackner had seen Jeremy Amesbury stretched dead. As I passed Felty I lost possession of a handful of cigars. He put them into his cap and turned his back squarely upon us. I walked into the room and closed the door.

Hand was yanking open the drawers of the little table in the far corner of the room. I glanced round. Everything seemed to be as I had seen it the night before. Even the scattered contents of the duffle-bag lying about on the floor had not been disturbed. The broken coffee cups, that had been dropped by Mrs. Ackner, still littered the rug over near the door.

I walked over to watch Hand, who by then was at the chest of drawers. He pulled one open after another, carefully scrutinizing their interiors. They all seemed to be perfectly empty. After closing the last one, he rested his elbow on the top of the chest, cupped his chin in his hand, and stood for several moments gazing motionless at the floor. All at once he bounded over to the bed and threw it open. There he stood, peering down at the sheets and

pillow case. He reached quickly out and turned the pillow
over. After carefully inspecting it, he swung round to stare
blankly at the opposite wall, pulling slowly at his under lip.

"Make that bed up again, will you, Clark?" he asked,
still staring at the wall.

I am not much good as a chambermaid, and I did not
fancy the job then. But it was my own fault that I was
there, and I made the best of the situation as well as the
bed. Hand, meanwhile, strode back to the chest of drawers. He opened all the drawers again, banging them shut in
turn, with a low mutter of frustration in his throat. Finally he straightened once more, and his eyes darted quickly
over all portions of the room. I straightened from my task
at the bed.

"Not a vestige of it," he muttered.

"Of what?"

"Let's get out of here."

Dutifully I followed him to Haggerty's room. Felty regarded this intrusion as also quite in order. Here Hand
subjected the place to the same careful search that he had
Jeremy Amesbury's room. Finally, with a growl of dissat-
isfaction, he walked over to the small table in the corner.
There sat the whiskey bottle, almost empty, and beside it
a glass tumbler.

Hand had taken from his pocket the light pair of cot-
ton gloves that he always carries. He put them on; then he
took from his vest pocket a small glass phial with a metal
stopper. Reaching quickly forth, he picked up the glass
tumbler and carried it over to the window. I had thought
the thing was empty, but when he tipped it up I saw that
it contained a small amount of amber liquid, certainly not
more than a teaspoonful. Of this he poured about half into
his phial. Then he put the glass back on the table.

As he was tucking the phial back into his pocket, I
went over and sniffed at the tumbler. I sensed a faint odor

of whiskey. When I glanced back, Hand was peeling off his gloves and stuffing them into his pocket.

We immediately left Haggerty's room. Hand led the way down the hallway, passing Felty with a nod. We quickly descended the stairs. I thought we were going to leave the building, but instead Hand went back to the door of the closet under the stairway. He popped inside, and I could see that he was using his electric torch. Presently he rejoined me.

"Well, Clark," he said, "I guess we—what was that?"

I did not know what it was, but I had heard it. Somewhere toward the rear of the house something heavy had fallen over. Hand, in three cat-like strides, had gained a door to the rear. I recognized it as the door that led into the Ackners' quarters. As I joined him he stood tense, his ear held to the panel of the door. His long, sensitive fingers sought the door-knob, and slowly, noiselessly he turned it. A second later he was slowly opening the door.

When the door had opened wider, I was able to hear unmistakable sounds of industry beyond it. Hand peered cautiously round the edge of the door. Then, with a quick stride, he passed through it. I followed after him.

There was no one at all in the Ackners' living-room. This, in itself, was not surprising. But the invalid's chair, standing over in the corner where we had seen it the night before, was empty. A door to our left stood ajar, and through it the mysterious sounds were coming. Noiselessly I followed Hand over to the center of the room. Over his shoulder I peered through the door into the bedroom it opened into. No one was in sight. But that someone was in the room outside our range of vision was clearly told by the sounds that we heard. Thus we stood, waiting for something to materialize from our illicit adventure.

Presently there came to our ears the sound of a rather sharp snap, and with it the sounds from within ceased abruptly. A tall, raw-boned man came into view. He was holding something to his chest, so that his head and shoulders were hunched over. He was walking across the room, and his back was half presented to us. But as he reached the center of the room he raised his head, giving us a glimpse of his profile. The man was Mr. Ackner, and he was walking as well as man ever learned to do it!

10

GERRITY MOVES AGAIN

Mr. Ackner strode rapidly across the room to a table set up against the wall. Here he relieved himself of the burden he had been clasping to his chest. I saw, then, that it was a tin box about six inches square. This he laid on the table.

Hand quickly drew me back so that the door-jamb shielded us. It was well that he did, for I had seen Ackner start to glance furtively over his shoulder. A moment later we glanced back into the bedroom. Quite evidently Ackner had not seen us. With his lascivious face hanging over the box, he raised trembling hands and thrust them into it.

In my excitement a low gasp escaped me as Ackner withdrew his hands from the box. Cupped in the palms of his two hands lay a pile of glittering gold coins! He poured them out on the table-top. After gloating over them for a moment, he commenced to arrange them in piles. This done, he filled his hands again with gold from the box.

So intent was I in Ackner's proceedings that I failed to notice Hand move from in front of me. The pressure of his hand on my arm caused me to look round at him. He jerked his head in the direction of the door to the hallway, and I followed him over to it. After leaving the living-room, Hand closed the door quite as noiselessly as he had opened it.

"Aren't you going to confront that villain?" I whispered.

"Not just yet, Clark. Come, let's be going."

I said no more until we stood on the sidewalk. Then, as Hand struck off up the street, I turned excitedly to him.

"What does all this mean?" I cried. "That fellow is an old fraud! Where did he get that gold? There must have been an immense amount of it in that box."

"Bills, also, Clark. I'm positive I heard the crackle of them as he lifted the gold pieces out of the box."

"Do you suppose he's just a deceitful old miser?"

Hand turned and glanced significantly at me.

"Did you notice that treasure box, Clark?"

"Yes. Yes, of course I did."

"What did you notice about it?"

"Why—why, it was tin. Looked like an old cracker box."

"Old? I'm afraid you are wrong there, my boy. It was a new box. Surely you noticed how shiny it was. Not the least bit oxidized. Looked as if the paper had just been removed from it. I should say that he has kept the money in that box no longer than a few days at the most. Is it not possible that he has kept the money in it less than twenty-four hours?"

That was food for thought. We continued on in silence as far as the corner. There Hand hailed a cab, and I, without invitation, followed him into it.

"To police headquarters," said Hand to the driver.

On the way over he sat all hunched up in one corner, staring vacantly at the back of the driver's neck. I stared out the window, trying to piece together what clues were in my possession. There seemed an abundance of people to suspect. And yet, turning the matter over in my mind, I realized that there were the barest details to connect anyone with the crime. I was forced to admit that the strongest case seemed to be against Larry White, but there too

only the flimsiest sort of circumstantial evidence could
be marshalled. I felt quite confident that a clever lawyer
could tear Gerrity's case to rags. In the end I was reduced
to pinning my faith upon Hand's eye-witness. But for the
life of me, I could not see how he was to be discovered.

At police headquarters Hand bounded out of the cab,
leaving me to settle with the driver. I quickly followed him
into the building. He went directly to Gerrity's office. In
the outer office we encountered Sergeant Tim, who from
behind his little desk smiled broadly at us.

"I thought you were home in bed, Tim," I said, in astonishment.

"Sure I was," he grinned, "for what was left of last
night. But if the inspector thinks he can coop me up when
somethin' like this here is doin', then I give him one more
think. I told him so, too."

"Is the inspector in?" asked Hand.

"He is," affirmed Tim. "He's in there alone, and he's
sore as blazes at the world in general. Here, let me open
the door for you."

We found that Tim had not exaggerated. Gerrity was
pacing irritably up and down his office, leaving a heavy
trail of cigar smoke behind him. He turned as we entered
and favored us with a glowering frown. But the moment
he recognized us he swung round and looked expectantly,
eagerly at Hand.

"I told you, Inspector," said Hand, "that as soon as
anything new turned up I would let you know of it."

"And something has?" cried Gerrity, some of the creases
smoothing out of his brow.

"Sit down," invited Hand, "and I'll tell you all about it."

Gerrity quickly sought his swivel chair behind the desk.
Hand and I seated ourselves at either side of the desk, and
the inspector leaned expectantly forward.

"You remember Mr. Ackner, don't you?" asked Hand.

"Of course. The fellow with the rheumatism. Wife is Amesbury's and Haggerty's landlady."

"Your mental picture of him, no doubt, is that of an invalid sitting helpless in a wheel-chair. What would you think if I told you that actually he has no more need for that wheel-chair than you have?"

Gerrity lifted himself half out of his chair. Leaning over the desk he stared excitedly at Hand. Then he slowly sat down again.

"Go on," he said, grimly.

Hand gave the inspector a minute account of what we had just witnessed at the Ackners' apartment. Gerrity got more and more fidgety as the account went on.

"I'm going to arrest him!" he snapped, when Hand had finished. "We'll catch him red-handed with the goods, by thunder!"

"But that is precisely what I don't want you to do," protested Hand.

The cigar fell from Gerrity's lips to the table-top.

"What?" he said, weakly. "You don't want me to arrest him? Blast it all! What do you want me to do, give him the keys to the city?"

"Not exactly. My case is shaping up, Inspector. I am not asking your indulgence just to see whether you will give it. I know you will indulge me, because you are aware that it is a wise thing to do."

Gerrity got to his feet, glared at Hand for a moment, and then resumed his angry pacing. Finally he stopped belligerently before Hand's chair.

"No arrests!" he fumed. "Every time I get a chance to make an arrest and pin something on somebody, why, you won't hear of it!"

"I think," retorted Hand, calmly, "that in the past when I have asked you to make an arrest you have found that you had the right man."

Gerrity quieted down a little and walked over to his chair.

"Well," he growled, "why don't you ask me to make an arrest now instead of asking me not to?"

"Because I don't know whom to ask you to arrest. I have a habit, when I ask you to make an arrest, of putting enough evidence in your hands to be sure of a conviction. I haven't that much evidence."

"Well, all right. But I warn you, I'm going to put a man on Ackner!"

"Do so by all means. See that he makes no escape. And now, Inspector, I have another favor to ask of you."

Gerrity glanced up suspiciously.

"What is it?"

"I want to interview Mr. Larry White at the Tombs."

"I've interviewed him pretty carefully, Hand. If there's anything you'd like to know about him, I think I could tell you."

"I don't think you could," said Hand, unfeelingly. He got abruptly to his feet and clapped his hat on his head. "Will you come with us?" he asked.

"I will," replied Inspector Gerrity, with determination.

We were driven to the Tombs in Gerrity's car. Soon we stood outside Larry White's cell. The young man lay on his cot, apparently sound asleep. The jailer unlocked the door and stirred up his prisoner. White rubbed his eyes sleepily and struggled to a sitting posture. We entered his cell and grouped ourselves round his cot. Suddenly he gazed wildly about. Finally, as realization of his plight dawned on him, he sank back dejectedly on his elbow. Then he turned languidly and stared up at us, a gleam of resentment kindling his brown eyes.

"How are you?" grunted Hand.

"Oh, all right," replied White, turning his gaze boldly upon the inspector. "This is the first time I've ever been in jail; I'm not used to it yet."

"I hope you never do get used to it," I said. "I don't think you will, either. Is there anything you'd like me to tell Miss Blake for you?"

White sat up and looked eagerly at me.

"How is she?" he asked, quickly.

"She's splendid!" I warmly assured him. "She tried to get in here to see you this morning, but—but you were asleep. She believes implicitly that you are innocent, and she thinks that anyone who thinks you aren't is quite silly."

White laughed almost gayly.

"Then if you will," he cried, "tell her that I'm crazier than ever about her. And also," he added, becoming concerned, "tell her not to worry about me. I'll get out of this pickle—somehow."

"Of course you will," I assured him. "You don't seem to have been treated very badly. Did you remember what I told you last night?"

"We won't go into that," interrupted Gerrity, gruffly. "I remember what he told me last night. And don't you forget it, either, young fellow! I assure you that I won't!"

"What did I tell you?" asked White. "I got all muddled up. Questions coming at me from all sides, one on top of the other! You—"

"Never mind!" snapped Gerrity. "Go on, Hand, ask him what you were going to, and let's get out of here."

"I haven't much that I want to ask," said Hand. "Mr. White, you told us last night that you had been missing some tools from your laboratory. I have an idea what they were. Was one a file?"

"Yes, sir," replied White, who seemed a little startled.

"And the other was a hammer?"

"Yes. Yes, the other was a hammer."

"No other tools?"

"No, sir. No other tools, but I thought a coil of wire was taken."

"That is all I wanted to know, Inspector," said Hand, turning briskly to Gerrity. "If you are anxious to leave, I have no objection."

They turned to leave the cell. I grasped White by the shoulder and looked reassuringly into his eyes. He put out his hand, and I grasped it.

"Don't worry," I said. "I'll have Judith Blake here opening the door of your cell before you know it."

"Thanks," said Larry White, huskily.

As I passed before him, Gerrity stood outside the cell and looked coldly at me. I glanced back at him, just as coldly. The inspector followed Hand and me as we made our way up the cell block. Presently I heard him chuckling.

"Poor old Clark," he said. "You get all sticky the minute you lay your eyes on two love-birds."

"Well," I flared, "I get no pleasure from tearing them apart, I can tell you that! I'd rather get them back together again."

Gerrity patted me on the shoulder.

"You're all right, Clark," he said, and his voice was by no means so harsh as it customarily is. "I get no fun out of tearing them apart, either. It's my job, sometimes. I suppose I've got pretty tough about it; you do, you know. Damned young fools! If they could only wait to get married. But no, they've got to get their hands on money right away, even though it means murder to do it! Then we have the girls coming to our offices and crying their eyes out, trying to get us to let the kids off. What can we do? And don't think it doesn't tear the soul out of me sometimes. I've got kids of my own! It's not fun, Clark, to send somebody else's kid to the chair."

"I'm sorry, Gerrity," I said, with feeling. "You know perfectly well that I don't consider you diabolical about these things. You are doing your duty, of course, and you deserve all the more credit for it because you aren't devoid of feeling. But I tell you I do hope you are on the wrong track now!"

"Clark," he said, with a heavy sigh, "I hope so too. I'll take the criticisms if White's really innocent. And I'll be glad of it, too. But if that kid's guilty, I'll send him to the chair!"

We left the Tombs and got back into Gerrity's car. The inspector turned to Hand.

"Where do you want to go?" he asked, gruffly.

"Police headquarters will do for us."

We sat in silence for a minute or two, the three of us, as we were driven along. Gerrity was fidgety. Finally he turned once more to Hand.

"How the devil did you know a hammer and file were taken from that laboratory?" he demanded.

"It seemed logical," was all that Hand would say.

We said good-bye to Gerrity at police headquarters. After walking a short distance, Hand hailed a cab. He directed the driver to take us to the parsonage of the Hendly Congregational Church. It was not long after that I was paying the driver off before the parsonage itself. A small lawn separated the house from the sidewalk, and round it was a low iron fence. The grass was unkempt, and a lilac bush at either side of the short walk to the vestibule endeavored to give the place a note of distinction. As we waited for Hand's ring to be answered, I glanced across the street. A suspicious-looking chap was loitering there. With his back to us, he was idly glancing up at the building across the way.

"There's something familiar about that fellow over there," I said to Hand. "I noticed when we got out of the cab he turned about, and he's been hiding his face from us ever since."

"Odd," mused Hand, giving the bell-button another push.

"Rough-looking chap," I observed.

The same colossal woman who had admitted us the night before did a like service for us again. She informed us rather icily that Mr. Bothwell was in his study; whereupon Mr. Bothwell emerged from it and invited us in. He preceded us and lowered himself into his chair behind the table. Hand hung back, more or less forcing me to enter the study before him.

"How are you making out?" inquired Mr. Bothwell.

"I might ask you the same question," countered Hand, with a smile.

Mr. Bothwell made a helpless gesture with his hands.

"I am completely baffled," he said. "I'm afraid this business is too complex for my poor intellect. But we take heart with you on the case, Mr. Hand. Miss Blake, particularly, seems to have invested an enormous amount of faith in you. I repeat, how are you progressing?"

"I have run across one or two interesting facts. You know, Mr. Bothwell, it would be interesting could we trace Mr. Jeremy Amesbury's life a few years back. It is just possible that in his past we might come across something that would shed some light on his fate.

Mr. Bothwell pursed his lips and slowly shook his head. "Mr. Haggerty knew his past," he said, slowly, "but Mr. Haggerty is no more. I could tell you of his youth, but I assure you there is nothing in that which might shed light on this tragedy. I could, also, repeat for you various tales he told about himself. But I'm afraid there would be nothing in them that you could anchor to, because he never mentioned, to my recollection, any specific localities in which these adventures took place."

"Then you know nothing concrete concerning his life during the lapse of time during which you were separated?"

"No, nothing concrete. A careful investigation might bring something to light."

"Undoubtedly. But here is something concerning which you may have some information. I refer to the cash which Mr. Amesbury and Mr. Haggerty carried in their money-belts. Do you know whether it was in gold pieces or in bills?"

Mr. Bothwell glanced sharply over my shoulder at Hand, who was standing behind me. I stepped aside so that they could confront each other.

"Have you found the money?" asked Mr. Bothwell, sharply.

"I can't say," replied Hand. "But it would help if you could tell me in what form they carried it. Do you happen to know?"

"Yes, I know. You see, I am the treasurer of the Ajax Mining and Engineering Company, and I was with Mr. Amesbury when he drew the money. It was in both gold and bank-notes. In some parts of Alaska, he told me, they would deal with certain individuals who would accept nothing but gold. For that reason they were going to take some along."

"This is very interesting. Do you happen to know just how much was in gold and how much in bank-notes? It would help, too, if you could tell us the denominations of the notes and the gold pieces."

Mr. Bothwell considered carefully.

"There was two thousand dollars in gold," he said, at length. "Mostly fifty-dollar pieces, but they varied in amount. The remainder of the amount was in bills, but I'm afraid I can't tell you just what denominations they were."

"Well, we have something, anyway. What can you tell us about the character of this young man Larry White?"

Mr. Bothwell became about as incensed as I imagine was possible with him. He sat up and leaned across the table, his eyes shining behind the thick lenses of his spectacles. His hands tightly gripped the table.

"This is a grievous mistake the police have made," he solemnly declared. "Mr. White is a sterling young man. It is preposterous to think that he has been guilty of such wickedness! I am sure that he will be exonerated, and I am just as sure that I shall publicly condemn the police after they have been forced to release him."

"Hum-m. Well, the police do their duty as they see it. We won't bother you any further, Mr. Bothwell. The information that you have given us is very valuable, I assure you."

As we left the room, Mr. Bothwell sat pensive behind his table. We let ourselves out of the house, and on the sidewalk I turned excitedly to Hand.

"If we were to seize old Ackner's treasure box," I said, "and it contained two thousand dollars in gold and forty-eight thousand in bank-notes, it would be what you might call a significant fact, don't you think?"

"Yes, indeed. We may do that, too, Clark."

"Let's get hold of Gerrity then, and go do it."

Hand chuckled and walked straight on.

"You are becoming quite as impetuous as the inspector," he said. "Before we do anything else, I want to see whether that roadster with the Texas license plates is still parked outside the Blakes' apartment house."

We rounded the corner, and a glance up the street showed us that the roadster was gone. Hand quickened his pace and entered the apartment house. Quickly we mounted the stairs to the second floor. Hand rapped on the Blakes' door. A moment later, getting no answer, he rapped again.

Suddenly Hand turned about and glanced over toward the stairs. Following his example, I beheld Mr. Zinger advancing down the corridor toward us, a worried light in his eyes.

"Hello, Mr. Hand," he said. "I seen ya come in. Lookin' for the Blakes?"

"We are."

Mr. Zinger shook his head sadly.

"Well, they're gone," he said. "That inspector feller that was with ya this mornin' come a few minutes ago and took 'em off. He had a lot o' cops with him, and he took both Mrs. Blake and her daughter."

I turned indignantly to Hand.

"Gerrity said he wouldn't do this," I cried, angrily. "It's contemptible!"

Hand shrugged his shoulders and turned to Mr. Zinger.

"You are sure it was the inspector?"

"Well, it certainly looked like him."

Hand, to my dismay, seemed quite excited.

"We should make sure," he said, quickly. "There is a dangerous criminal who looks almost exactly like Inspector Gerrity. He often impersonates him. Frequently he carries women and children away from their homes. Always has his men with him. This sounds very much as if it were he who has just taken the Blakes away!"

"Oh, my goodness!" wailed Mr. Zinger, wringing his hands.

"Here, open this door," commanded Hand, sternly. "I can tell in a minute whether the inspector has been here, or whether it was this criminal."

Mr. Zinger's trembling hands finally managed to unlock the Blakes' door. As we entered the apartment he stood on the threshold, craning his neck after us. Then he timidly followed us in.

Hand darted from room to room. Mr. Zinger stood for a moment in the small hallway, wringing his hands worse than ever. Then he rushed into the living-room, catching up to me as I was about to follow Hand into one of the bedrooms.

"Don't leave me!" cried Mr. Zinger. "Please don't leave me!"

"You're safe enough," I said, turning back to him. "There's no one in this apartment but ourselves. Besides, we are armed; we'll protect you."

Deeming it wise to give Hand a free rein in whatever he was up to, I kept Mr. Zinger in the living-room, talking reassuringly to him. Hand was gone several minutes, but finally he briskly rejoined us.

"It was the inspector, all right," he announced. "Nothing whatever to worry about."

"Th—then the Blakes are—are all right?" chattered Mr. Zinger.

"I fancy they are safe enough. Well, Clark, let's be going."

Mr. Zinger, with many a troubled shake of his head, accompanied us until we had left the building. Hand immediately struck off in the direction of our rooms.

"What was all that business about the criminal?" I demanded. "You've reduced poor Mr. Zinger to a pretty state. He's as nervous as a witch."

"Yes, I've observed that he is."

"But why all that nonsense about the criminal?"

"Merely wanted a chance to do a little looking round."

"Oh. But what for?"

"If Miss Blake, as Gerrity is disposed to think, actually wielded the hammer that killed Nick Haggerty, it would be quite possible that blood would have scattered on her dress. It was worth investigating."

"You found no such evidence, I hope!"

"None. I hardly thought that I should. The dress she was wearing when we saw her last night has no such stains on it. She probably wore that dress all of last evening. Easy thing to determine that. It should be equally as easy to determine whether she absented herself from her home after Nick Haggerty left it. Probably has a rock-bound alibi. But Gerrity is working on that phase of the case.

He's very thorough about such things, you know. We can rely upon him to get all the information concerning Miss Blake."

We walked along in silence for a way. I was busy with troubled thoughts. Finally I turned resolutely to Hand.

"I admit that you can baffle me," I said. "I cannot penetrate you. But there are some things that do not escape me. I didn't like the way you were rubbing your hands together when you returned to Mr. Zinger and me in the Blakes'

living-room. I assume that you had just come from Miss Blake's room. What did you find in there that furnished you food for thought?"

Hand turned to me and smiled, his eyes twinkling.

"Jove, Clark, you are certainly getting on," he cried. "I did come across something interesting there. It was a make-up box."

"A make-up box? What is that?"

"You are so fond of the theatre that I should think you would know. It is a box of materials for altering or accentuating the features. Face-paint, rouge, powder, false hair and so on. There were two wigs there, also."

"Well, I don't see what harm there is in a girl's having a thing of that sort. She probably has dramatic aspirations; she's pretty enough."

"Precisely."

We continued on in silence as far as the rooms. There Hand snatched up the telephone and gave a number. A few seconds later he was asking to speak with Mr. Woodford Amesbury."

"Hello," he said, after a short wait. "This is Christopher Hand. I just thought I'd let you know that I'm leaving the city for a few hours." He listened a moment; then he said: "Yes, it's on business concerning the case. If anything turns up I'll let you know. There is nothing new at the present. Good-bye."

"Where are you going?" I demanded, as he hung up.

"Nowhere," he replied, turning to get a cigarette. "I told him I was going away, Clark, so that he would not come over here. I want you to do some work. I called him to locate him. He's in his room at the Skelton, Clark."

"Well?"

"I want you to go over to Amesbury's hotel. Sit in the lobby and watch the elevators. If Amesbury goes out, you follow him. But above all be careful of one thing—don't let Amesbury see you!"

11

FILIPO

I was not so astonished by my mission as perhaps it seems I should have been. Of my own free will I choose to mix myself up in Hand's cases. He is, in his peculiar way, delighted to have me observe him at work. Were I to question everything that he asks me to do, or to demand an explanation for everything he does himself, he would not be so delighted. I go about, therefore, in a complete fog of ignorance. It is not until a mystery has been solved, if indeed it ever is, that I learn the meaning of what I have been doing.

As I left the rooms Hand was getting into his dressing-gown. I engaged a cab, and soon I was entering the lobby of the Skelton. Selecting a high-backed chair whence I could observe the elevators, I slipped into it and commenced my vigil. While I waited I wondered how I was going to explain my presence to Amesbury if he did see me. I gave it up, deciding that, if such a misfortune should befall me, I should let the spur of the moment be my prompter.

There I sat for fully an hour. For all I had seen I might just as well have been home at the rooms. Then things began to occur. Glancing casually over my shoulder, I was suddenly startled by the sight of Miss Blake crossing the lobby. She was evidently headed for the desk, but in order to reach it she had to cross directly in front of my chair. I

leaned over at once and commenced fussing with my shoe-
lace.

"Why, Mr. Clark!" I heard directly over my head. At
the same time, with a feeling of defeat, I saw two trim
little feet stop directly in front of me.

Actually, I was not sorry to see her. It was indeed a
relief to find that she was out of Gerrity's clutches. I did,
however, feel distinctly uneasy about her discovering me
there. I felt that it was going to be quite as difficult to
explain my presence to her as it would have been to Amesbury. Besides, I could imagine that whatever my plot had
been, it was now frustrated. But I managed a cry of delight
and jumped to my feet.

"Miss Blake!" I said, seizing her hands. "You don't
know how glad I am to see you. It was not so long ago that
I was told you had been spirited away by several misguided
policemen."

"I've come to find out," she smiled, "that they are not
so terrible, after all. In fact, after my ordeal at police
headquarters, I have become considerably heartened.
They just asked mother and me a few questions, and then
Inspector Gerrity told me that I could see Larry tomorrow.
Better than that, he told me that it might be for keeps.
I'm beginning to think that Inspector Gerrity is really
human."

She finished with a rippling little laugh, in which,
however, I detected a note of nervousness.

"That's fine!" I beamed. "It will be only a matter of
time before they discover their mistake. If they don't find
it pretty soon, then Christopher Hand will show it to
them. I think he's getting very close to the solution of this
ghastly riddle."

"Oh, I hope so," said Miss Blake, earnestly. "Are you
waiting for Mr. Amesbury?"

FOOL'S GOLD   191

"I—ahem—I—no," I stammered, the spur of the moment, in the final test, doing me utterly no good. "I was just—well—by the way, what are you doing here?"

"Why, I just came over to see Mr. Amesbury. I was just going over to the desk to find out whether he is in. But now I won't have to; you can tell me."

"No, no, he isn't in. You see, I wasn't waiting for him to come down from his room; I was waiting for him to return to the hotel."

Miss Blake, to my despair, slipped into a chair beside the one in which I had been sitting. There was something of a disquieting twinkle in her eye as she looked up at me.

"I'm awfully glad I saw you," she said. "Now we can wait together, and neither one of us will be lonesome."

My mind seems to have a habit, sometimes, of going completely out of gear. Now if Christopher Hand had been in my predicament, he undoubtedly would have done something clever about it. All I could do, however, was to seat myself dismally beside her. Worse than that, when I glanced over at her, I found that she was regarding me with a distinctly mischievous light in her brown eyes. Was she aware of just how guilty I felt? Such a thing was impossible.

"Don't you think you should go back to your mother?" I asked, hopefully. "It seems to me that she must be rather upset, after having been subjected to a questioning at police headquarters, and all that. I think she must need you. And I'm quite certain that Mr. Amesbury may not be back here for hours."

"Oh, Father is with her," she brightly replied. "He'll take better care of her than I could."

"But I thought your father was at work!"

"He was, but they brought him to police headquarters too. He didn't go back to the office afterwards."

"What do you want to see Mr. Amesbury for, anyway?"

At the sound of my voice, which, I am afraid, was a trifle irritable, Miss Blake looked her astonishment. But then she smiled and shook her head.

"Mr. Amesbury has been so kind," she said. "At first I was going over to tell you and Mr. Hand about our experience with Inspector Gerrity; but I knocked at your door, and nobody answered. Your landlady came out of somewhere and told me that she thought Mr. Hand was out with a client. Then I decided to come over here and tell Mr. Amesbury. You see, before he left us this morning he said he wanted to do all he could to help get Larry out of jail."

"Yes, yes, of course."

I was still desperately trying to conceive of some adroit means of getting her to leave. I knew Hand was at the rooms, and I reflected bitterly that he could just as well have let her in. He has a periscopic arrangement concealed in the wall by the door. By means of it he can see who it is that seeks to be admitted. If he does not wish to see the potential caller, he ignores the knocking.

I was startled out of my gloomy reverie by Miss Blake, who, with a glad little cry, had jumped to her feet. I glanced quickly round. Amesbury stood over near the elevators, talking to the bell captain. Quickly reaching up, I grasped Miss Blake by the arm and pulled her back into her chair.

"Why, Mr. Clark!" she exclaimed, in astonishment. "Whatever—"

I pulled my chair round so that the back of it protected both Miss Blake and me from Amesbury's vision.

"Listen!" I hissed. "I don't wish Mr. Amesbury to see me. I can't explain anything, but he must not see me!"

"Why not?" demanded Miss Blake, in spite of the fact that I had just assured her that I could not explain. Her eyes were now flashing at me a little angrily.

"You must take my word for it. I am going to follow Amesbury, and it is for a very vital reason. Perhaps it will result in Larry White's being set at liberty. Now you must go home, but wait until after we have left."

As I talked I peered covertly round the side of the chair, keeping Amesbury constantly in sight. He walked swiftly across the lobby, in a direction that would take him to one of the side entrances. I reached out and patted Miss Blake reassuringly on the arm. Then I rose to follow my man. But I was not to get away so easily. Miss Blake clutched at my sleeve. I turned impatiently to her.

"You must tell me what this is all about!" she insisted, speaking lowly but intently. A quick glance showed me that Amesbury was leaving the lobby.

"Please don't delay me," I pleaded. "I must keep him in sight. Go home, now, and promise me that you will say nothing about what you have seen. If you do you may complicate our endeavors to free Larry White. I must leave you; good-bye."

I turned quickly and strode across the lobby. I burst out to the sidewalk in time to see Amesbury climbing into his roadster across the street. By good fortune, a taxicab was standing at the curb beside the hotel, headed in the same direction as Amesbury's car. I walked over beside it, putting it between Amesbury and me, and hastily spoke to the driver.

"Do you see that roadster across the street?"

"Sure."

"I want you to follow it! There's five dollars in it for you if you don't let it get out of sight. Are you willing?"

"Get in, boss. I could follow the Graf Zeppelin in this crate for five bucks."

Turning to get into the cab, I was astonished to find that the door had mysteriously opened. My astonishment, however, was as nothing to my dismay when I beheld

Judith Blake sitting with the greatest complacence inside my cab, powdering her nose. The driver was letting in his gears, and Amesbury was starting up across the street. With a mutter of exasperation I leaped into the cab, slamming the door shut after me. We set off in pursuit of Amesbury.

Holding her tiny mirror and powder puff before her face, Miss Blake turned her big eyes innocently upon me.

"Were you swearing, Mr. Clark?" she asked.

"Certainly not!" I replied, stiffly. "I merely said—ah—I said hang it, or something like that."

"Flattering," she murmured, once more applying the powder puff.

"See here," I said, warmly, "this has got to stop! You are deliberately ruining my plans. I can't get anywhere with you along; it's fatal!"

"Is that so?" she sniffed. After a few dabs at her pert little nose with the powder puff, she stowed that indispensable object and the mirror away in her handbag. Then, settling herself comfortably back, she turned to me. With a feeling of alarm I saw that a smile was lurking at her lips, and her eyes were positively laughing at me. I concentrated deeply upon becoming stern.

"You don't realize the seriousness of the situation," I lectured. "I am engaged on a mission of the utmost importance. As I said before, perhaps the very life of your fiancé depends upon the success of it. And here you are, deliberately endeavoring to foil me. I am disappointed in you."

I paused and glanced sharply at her, hoping to detect that my words had had the desired effect. But Miss Blake merely sighed gently and continued to look steadily at me in that half amused, half mischievous and wholly devastating manner.

"Go on," she invited.

"You cannot possibly help me," I continued, desperately. "What can you do, anyway? You will just be in the way, and there may be danger, for all I know. If you would only—oh, well, I suppose there is nothing that I can say!"

With an impulsive little movement, she put out her hand and laid it on my sleeve. All at once the smile faded from her lips, and she became exceedingly serious.

"I know that you think I am just meddling," she cried. "But I'm not! I'll go mad if this dreadful thing isn't cleared up soon! Please, Mr. Clark, please don't try to make me give up. And," she added, with an uptilt of her little chin, "you can't, anyway!"

"But there may be danger!"

"I don't care. Nobody tells me what is going on. Nobody is more desperately concerned about what is being done than I, and yet I am kept completely in the dark. I am going to find out for myself! Tell me what it is you are going to do, and then perhaps I'll agree to let you alone."

As I replied I shook my head miserably, and Miss Blake regarded me in astonishment.

"But I don't know myself," I said. "I haven't the faintest idea why I am following Woodford Amesbury. All that I know is that I was told to go to Amesbury's hotel and keep a watch-out for him. If he went out, I was to follow him, and I was to observe all that he did. But I must not be seen. You see how difficult it is going to be for me to remain inconspicuous with you along, don't you?"

"You don't know why you are spying upon Mr. Amesbury!"

"I haven't the faintest idea. I was merely given my orders; they were not explained."

"I can't see any likelihood of danger in that. Mr. Amesbury is a perfect gentleman. I'm sure following him about won't run us into danger. Sorry, Mr. Clark, but I've decided that you can't get rid of me."

From the determined way in which she said it, I knew perfectly well that indeed I had no chance of getting rid of her. But I could not help turning to her with a smile, in which there was something of embarrassment.

"Well, then," I said, "I'm really proud of you. I said I was disappointed in you, but I guess I'm not. I realize just how terribly concerned you are. But if it should appear that we are running into danger, you will leave me and go straight home, won't you? Promise me that you will."

"Yes," she complied, with a return of the smile. "But, remember, it is still up to me to decide whether there is any danger or not."

Sighing disconsolately, I settled back to keep my eyes on Amesbury. The man drove with an abandon that, emulated perforce by the cab driver, was more than a little disconcerting. I had not noticed it, particularly, while I had been pleading with Miss Blake, but now I found my heart constantly in my throat. I glanced anxiously at my companion. She had braced herself, but she looked as if she were actually enjoying the experience. Even the driver was incapable of that. I caught a glimpse of his face in the mirror on the windshield, and he looked tense and worried. I leaned forward to him.

"Keep going," I encouraged him. "If you get a ticket, I'll pay the fine."

"I ain't worried about no ticket, boss," he replied, over his shoulder. "Alls I'm worried about is gettin' a trolley car in the lap. Cheese, that guy must think this here burg's nothin' but one grand race track. You ain't forgot that five bucks, have you?"

"I have it right here in my hand, and it's over and above what your meter will read. We must not lose sight of that car."

The driver grimly nodded his head. A feeling of uneasiness stole over me. Perhaps Amesbury knew that he was being followed. Perhaps he was driving so wildly in order to lose us. Suddenly he swung out and almost skidded to a stop alongside a traffic officer. The policeman skeptically regarded his sudden visitor.

The taxi-driver pulled over to the curb and waited. I wondered whether Amesbury was about to put into effect some scheme to have the policeman delay us. He put his head out of the car and spoke to the officer. Apparently he had merely asked directions. The policeman pointed on ahead, spoke briefly to Amesbury, and turned back to his job. Amesbury started up with a jerk and was soon speeding on down the street, still pursued by our cab.

Finally he spun round a corner, narrowly avoiding the destruction of a push-cart. The proprietor of the portable business, loud in his bitter imprecations, heeded us not at all. He pushed his worldly goods right in front of us; whereupon the taxicab nearly stood up on its front end. But the push-cart business went angrily on its way, miraculously saved twice from being demolished within the space of ten seconds.

The incident was not without its value to us. Turning my attention back to Amesbury, I perceived that he was stopped just round the corner. Had we continued on, he surely would have discovered that we were following him. As it had turned out, our taxi had not yet rounded the corner.

Amesbury craned his neck out of the roadster. He appeared to be scanning the street numbers across from him. Finally he started up and proceeded slowly down the street. At the risk of losing him altogether, I ordered the driver to pull over to the curb. Amesbury, at length, brought his car to a halt before a dingy-looking restaurant in the middle of the block. I got out of the cab and paid the driver his promised reward.

Miss Blake skipped out and stood excitedly beside me.

"Won't you get back into the cab," I pleaded, "and let this man drive you home? Your being here makes me most uncomfortable."

"But surely," she protested, "there is no danger here!"

"I know, but this is not the best neighborhood in the world."

"Let's not waste any more time, Mr. Clark. Look, Mr. Amesbury is going into that restaurant. Come on, we must follow him!"

Resignedly I took her arm, and we set swiftly off for the restaurant. By the time we had neared it, Amesbury had disappeared through its door. We quickly entered the place. The door admitted us to a small hallway. Miss Blake was acting like a hound on a fresh scent. I was forced to take her by the arm and hold her back in the hallway. I edged over to a door and peered cautiously into the restaurant proper. Amesbury was standing a few feet inside, glancing inquiringly about.

I thought surely he would see us, and I censured myself for having entered so rashly. But at that moment Amesbury was accosted. The fellow who came smiling up to him was dark, and, in a sleek, unwholesome way, his face was rather handsome. The corners of his mouth, rather than curling upward when he smiled, curled down, imparting a sort of sneer to his features. A little, black mustache accentuated the extreme whiteness of his teeth.

I felt Miss Blake clutch my arm. Amesbury's companion, smiling and bowing ingratiatingly, ushered him to a table set in an alcove across the room. There was one that I had my eyes on directly behind it. Miss Blake tugged at my sleeve. I looked down into her eyes, and in them I saw a frightened expression.

"That is the man who tried to rent Larry's laboratory!" she whispered.

I had begun to suspect that it was. I nodded to her and spoke rapidly in an undertone.

"I don't like the looks of this place. There are a number of rough-looking men sitting round in there. Please go home, and I will tell you later exactly what I have found out."

But she shook her head and looked more determined than ever. And then I felt myself being guided into the restaurant by my courageous little companion. I took charge then, and we went directly to the alcove behind the one in which Amesbury and his strange companion were sitting.

An uncouth waiter sauntered immediately over to us. Taking a chance, I boldly but quietly ordered two glasses of beer. The fellow, after glancing narrowly at us for a moment, nodded in a surly way and moved off. I turned my attention whole-heartedly to trying to catch the conversation in the next alcove.

Amesbury, evidently, was sitting on the side of the alcove farthest from me. His remarks were not so clear. But those of his companion, who, I judged, was sitting directly on the other side of the partition from me, I could hear quite distinctly. He was speaking.

"So," he said, in a soft, slurring speech, "Mucker Amesbury does not know hees old pal, eh? Ah, you no fool me, my frien'. You are clevair, yes?"

Amesbury mumbled something, evidently in protest, that I could not catch.

"Let us undairstan' each other," suggested his companion. "You do not know Filipo, eh? That ees what you call very reech, eh? But Filipo know you, my frien'. And more too, Filipo know what hees old pal Mucker is doing."

"Cut out the monkey-business," said Amesbury, so sharply that I could hear him quite easily. "What did you want to see me about?"

"You are in so much hurry, Mucker. You have not change so much, my frien'. It ees as you weesh. Filipo has had what you call bad luck, much bad luck. Filipo is poor. He has been very seek. Maybe you will help heem, yes? Filipo is good man to have your frien'."

"See here, if you—"

"Not so loud, my frien', pleese," cautioned Filipo. "It would be mos' too bad eef somebody hear, eh? Let us talk quiet, pleese."

They dropped their voices, and strain my ears as I would, I could overhear nothing more. To further embarrass me, the waiter arrived with our glasses of beer. I tried to appear nonchalant, but a thrill of apprehension coursed through me as the waiter failed to move away after setting down our glasses. He remained beside me, instead, looking coldly down at me. I endeavored not to notice him.

"Aren't you going to pay him?" asked Miss Blake, quietly.

"Oh! Oh, yes."

I gave him a two-dollar bill and waved him away. The fellow gave me an uncertain glance as he moved off.

Once more I strained my ears to listen. The pair on the other side of the partition, however, had dropped their voices so low that I could hear nothing but a mumble. Occasionally Amesbury would raise his voice, but before he had said more than a word or two, Filipo would caution him to quiet down. They talked for fully twenty minutes. Finally I heard the scrape of a chair in the other alcove. Then Amesbury's angry voice was borne to my ears.

"Very well," said he, "if you are going to threaten me with that, I suppose I'll have to come across. I think you're lying, though. It's five hundred, and not one cent more! I'll see you tonight."

"Theenk well, my frien'," said Filipo, insidiously. "I know what I know. I do not forget that you nearly keeled me once. Perhaps you have tol' me the truth, but I do not believe you. I want to see you tonight!"

"You'll see me tonight," grumbled Amesbury. "You dirty crook!"

Filipo laughed softly, so softly that I could scarcely hear him.

"You weel breeng the money, eh?" he said. "Five hundred may do—for now. But you are not going to get away, my frien'. You are watched! Eef you try to cheat poor Filipo, the leetle note will go off to the police. The newspapers too, eh? Don' forget, right here tonight at ten."

I heard someone, with an angry growl, walk out of the alcove. It was Amesbury, and he stalked right by without a glance to right or to left. His face was flushed, and he was scowling blackly. I was glad that I was not in his path just then. He walked out of the restaurant and slammed the door after him. Again I heard that soft laugh coming from the other side of the alcove. Filipo, evidently, was holding a trump.

12

ANOTHER TRAIL ENDS

What my next course of action should be was giving me trouble. Clearly, it seemed to me, the thing to do was to get Filipo arrested. Hand and Gerrity both believed the man had witnessed the murders. I was now in contact with him, but if I should let him slip through my fingers we might never see him again. And there he sat, not three feet from me.

On the other hand, I had every reason to believe that he would be right there again at ten that evening. Might it not be better to let matters take their course? I was wishing that Christopher Hand had taken charge of that part of the investigation himself. Miss Blake was watching me expectantly.

"What are you going to do?" she asked.

I leaned across the table to her and whispered.

"I am going to get back to the rooms as quickly as possible. I want to report this interview to Christopher Hand at once."

"All right, but what are we going to do about this beer?"

"Don't worry about that; it's paid for many times over."

"I know, but won't they think it strange if we don't drink it?"

"Hum-m, I suppose they would. It's probably the very worst kind of beer. I don't want to drink it, and I forbid you to."

"I can't," she said, a little piteously. "I tried it, and it tastes perfectly horrid!"

"Well, there's nothing for it," I said, grimly. "I shall have to drink them both. Then we must get out of here as quickly as we can."

I downed the beer, which more than fulfilled my expectations. As I set Miss Blake's glass down, after gulping the last of her beer, I was attracted by a man walking casually across the floor. It was Filipo. He stopped to talk to the waiter, who was standing over near the door. The waiter, I noticed with consternation, was eyeing Miss Blake and me. Filipo was immediately addressed by the waiter, who accompanied his remarks with a nod in our direction. I feigned not to notice them, but I was aware that Filipo had turned his black eyes upon us. Out of the tail of my eye I saw that sinister smile grow on his face.

Filipo turned and walked briskly toward the rear of the restaurant, out of our line of vision. I nodded to Miss Blake and quickly got to my feet. Together we crossed the restaurant. But at the door to the little entrance hallway the waiter stepped squarely in front of us. His face was twisted into an ugly scowl, and he put out a hand to stop me. I glanced back at him as coldly as I could.

"How about payin' for them beers?" he growled.

"Why, I did pay for them. Rather than argue about it, however, I'll pay again. How much is it?"

"I ain't so sure you ain't a couple o' dicks. Just step back inside again, and we'll look you over. You don't look right to me."

"I have no intention of staying here any longer. Step aside, fellow, and let us get by. If you don't—"

The sight of four or five ruffians who had stepped up beside us gave me pause. I turned resolutely to the waiter.

"See here," I said, "if you have any doubts about me, all well and good. I think I shall have no difficulty in satisfy-

ing you that I am all right. But I ask you not to embarrass
this young lady. Let her go, and I'll stay as long as you
like."

But the waiter shook his head. He planted his hands
on his hips and stood even more solidly before us. Miss
Blake, I was relieved to see, was quietly adjusting her hat.
She looked altogether bored. I was glad that she did not
realize the seriousness of the situation. I had it in mind
to draw my pistol and hold the men at bay until we could
make our escape. But with a young girl as my companion
the risk was too great.

"Step into the back room," ordered the waiter.

I was for protesting further, but Miss Blake took me
by the arm and shook her head at me. Disconsolately I
allowed us to be herded to the rear of the restaurant. We
were taken into a wretched little room at the back. The
waiter closed the door and, stepping belligerently forth,
stopped towering before me.

"Well," he snarled, "what was you up to?"

I maintained a sullen silence, while Miss Blake regarded the men, who had crowded into the room with us, quite
disgustedly. The waiter barked at me again and again, with
no effect upon either me or Miss Blake. This seemed to be
the limit of his resources for such a situation, for after that
he just stood and glared at us. One of his mates, whose
appearance betokened a somewhat higher intelligence than
the rest, took the waiter aside and spoke earnestly to him.

"Stay where you are," growled the waiter, although it
was not apparent what else we could do. "Stay where you
are, both of you. I'll be right back; don't try nothin'!"

The waiter and his counselor withdrew and closed the
door after them. As we waited for eventualities, the men
who were left to guard us looked fiercely at me and ad-
miringly at Miss Blake. I could have choked the life out
of every one of them. I was wishing I had abandoned the

attempt in the first place and taken Miss Blake straight home from Amesbury's hotel.

All at once there was a commotion outside in the restaurant. The men who had been left to guard us became distinctly nervous. They glanced quickly at one another, and complete understanding seemed to prevail among them. They left. Their departure was made precipitously through a rear door. Miss Blake and I were left alone in the room. She looked at me and smiled.

But I was far from satisfied with the situation. Pulling my companion over into a corner, so that we were out of line with the door leading to the restaurant, I drew my pistol and waited. Then I heard a familiar voice calling my name.

"Mr. Clark," it said. "Mr. Clark, where are you?"

"Right here, Leonard. This little room at the back."

Detective Sergeant Fred Leonard of police headquarters walked quickly through the door. He glanced sharply at us; then he leaped over and opened the door at the back. Three other headquarters men filed into the room.

"Where's the proprietor of this joint, Mr. Clark?" asked Leonard.

"He went out into the restaurant a moment ago," I quickly replied. "Perhaps he wasn't the proprietor, but he was surely in charge. Several other fellows went out that back door as you came in."

Leonard nodded and, distributing his men, proceeded to search the place. I took Miss Blake out into the restaurant. There we waited until Leonard rejoined us. He looked disgruntled.

"Got away," he grumbled. "Beat it through the back entrance."

"By Jove, Leonard," I said, warmly, "you arrived in the nick of time. I don't think those fellows would have tried anything desperate, but they certainly had us in a helpless position. I gathered that they didn't quite know what to do with us, but a crowd of rough-necks like that are not nice people to have holding the upper hand on you. Who sent you to this place, anyway?"

"Inspector Gerrity. We were doin' the same thing you were."

"How's that?"

"Followin' Amesbury. We trailed him here, right behind you. I don't know how you got in, but the bouncer spotted our fellas and kept 'em out. Lieutenant Dockery, who's in charge of our party, sent Daniels beatin' it round to Judge Dillon's to get a search warrant in a hurry. But he ain't even back yet. When he gets here I'm gonna go through this place from top to bottom, and I ain't gonna miss nothin', either!"

"How is it that you came in here before the warrant arrived?"

"Well, when Amesbury come out of here, the lieutenant and a couple of fellas followed him. He left me here with these other fellas to see that you and the young lady come out all right. When you didn't come out, I figgered somethin' was on the hoof and busted in. Wish I'd been a little earlier."

"I wish you had, Leonard. But that doesn't detract from my appreciation. Sergeant Leonard, meet Miss Blake. I think she is just as grateful to you as I am myself. I hope you get that waiter, too; he got a dollar a glass from me for some very inferior beer. I had to drink it, too! But see here. What about Filipo; did you get him?"

"Filipo? Who the heck is Filipo?"

"A dark, medium-sized fellow with black eyes and a small, black mustache. He was the first to leave the place, I think."

"We didn't see him," said Leonard. "What's he got to do with it?"

If Gerrity wanted to know the part Filipo had played in the restaurant, I was perfectly disposed to tell him, and I knew that Hand would wish it so. But I decided not to divulge my information to one of the inspector's minions, no matter how far I was in his debt.

"Sorry, Leonard," I said, "but I don't know just what he has to do with this. Of course I did find out something about him, but I think I had better tell the inspector himself about it."

"I get you, Mr. Clark," said Leonard, readily. "If you don't want to wait here, there's no reason for it. But I'm gonna stay here and clean up this joint!"

"All right, Leonard," I said, guiding Miss Blake over to the door. "And it is going to give me a great deal of pleasure to tell the inspector how commendably you have acted this afternoon."

"I'm going to, too," declared Miss Blake. "And besides that, I'm going to write a letter to the chief himself and tell him about it."

"There ain't no chief, Lady," grinned Leonard. "But if you want to write to the commissioner, I ain't got no objections."

I hailed a cab and told the driver to take us to the Blakes' address. As we started up-town I turned smilingly to my pretty little companion.

"How did you like that experience?" I asked.

"Well," she confessed, wrinkling her brow, "it was fun at first, but I didn't like the ending. Did I look scared, Mr. Clark?"

"You most certainly did not! I am prouder than ever of you. Were you frightened?"

"I've never been so scared in all my life!" she said. I chuckled.

I left Miss Blake at her home, first exacting a solemn promise from her that she would tell no one what she had seen or heard. Then I had the driver take me over to our rooms. I bounded up the stairs and, unlocking the door, burst into the living-room. Hand sat in his easy chair, once again fussing with the clay head on the little table before him. He glanced up as I entered and laid away his work. Picking up a cigarette that was charring the living-room table, he sat back and fixed me with a sharp glance of inquiry. I tossed my hat on the table and dropped into my chair. Then, excitedly, I commenced my recital.

"Hand, I think I've solved the case! I never could have done it without your directing me, but I've run down the solution to this business!"

His eyebrows raised almost imperceptibly.

"Hum-m. You don't say so."

I told my story, from beginning to end, as I had seen and heard it. But I waited to the last to inform him that Judith Blake had also figured in it. At last I reluctantly began my admission.

"I'm afraid you won't like it," I said, "but I was not alone when I trailed Amesbury to his incriminating appointment."

"Yes; so I gathered."

"So you gathered! How the deuce did you gather that?"

"You gave it away, Clark. Although your story was generously sprinkled with the pronoun *I*, occasionally you slipped and said *we*. Miss Blake, wasn't it?"

I sat up and regarded him in astonishment. But then, in a moment, my astonishment had given way to bitterness.

"Surely I deserve better than this, Hand," I reproached him. "To think that you would entrust me with a mission, and then deliberately spy upon me. Am I not to be trusted, after all?"

"My dear fellow, you have jumped to a fearfully erroneous conclusion."

"But Miss Blake! How can you explain—"

"Perfectly simple deduction, Clark, and partly guess-work. From your story, I judged that you were not alone. Miss Blake uses a delicate brand of perfume—jasmine. Decidedly I had an inescapable opportunity to notice it when she—ah—saluted me on the cheek this morning. A faint aroma of just such perfume you have brought into the room with you. Others use it, no doubt, but the field from which to choose your companion was materially cut down."

I sniffed quite violently, but the only odor I could detect was the stale tobacco smoke with which he had filled the room. Besides, Hand was sitting a good four feet from me. I looked resignedly at him and sighed.

"I should hate to be a raccoon trying to get away from you."

"You have neglected to tell me just why Miss Blake accompanied you while you shadowed Amesbury for me."

I flushed, and plunged into a detailed account of my embarrassment in the lobby of Amesbury's hotel. Hand, the while, regarded me coldly.

"What else could I have done?" I cried, when I had finished.

"You might have excused yourself from Miss Blake the moment she saw you, and then returned to watch them both from a vantage point. You might, by now, have a great deal more to tell me. But I don't censure you, Clark. You have done a splendid job, my boy, and what you have learned helps me immeasurably."

"Then you think Amesbury is the man?"

He smiled and slowly rose from his chair.

"I don't recall," he said, "having mentioned what I think. It is too early, Clark, to make any rash statements."

"If it is Amesbury," I pointed out, "you will surely lose your fee. I can't imagine anything more foolish than his paying you when the evidence you uncover may send him to the electric chair. But then, I know only too well that you care little or nothing for fees."

"Don't put your hat away, Clark," he said, as I started for the closet with it. "The inspector just phoned that he would be over presently, and I think we shall have to go out. He'll want to hear your story, of course."

He disappeared into the bedrooms, stripping off his dressing-gown as he went. I laid my hat back on the table and moved over to inspect the bust he had been working on. I found to my astonishment that the face had once again been altered. The clay features once more were those of a man in his early maturity.

I shook my head dubiously and returned to my chair. I was there, engrossed in thought, when there came a lusty rap at the door. At the same instant Hand rejoined me in the living-room.

"One moment," I said, as he started for the door. "Do you want me to tell Gerrity about Miss Blake, or shall I keep it from him?"

"Small good your keeping it from him. You introduced her to Leonard, so you said. He probably knows all about her by now."

I reproached myself bitterly for having given her name away. Hand opened the door, and the inspector stalked in. He muttered a greeting and dropped into a chair. Hand moved his modeling table aside and sat quietly down across from Gerrity. The inspector looked sharply up at me.

"Well, Clark," he said, "I hear you've been up to something."

"I have," I affirmed, importantly. "I think I've just about the most significant information that has yet come to light. But I should never have got it, of course, had it not been for Hand."

"You put one over on my fellows, all right," admitted Gerrity. "Leonard said you found out something. What is it?"

I went over the story again, concluding with Leonard's rescue of us at the restaurant. Gerrity hammered his fist on the arm of the chair.

"Amesbury!" he cried. "By thunder, I'm going to arrest him!"

Hand laughed softly.

"The first thing you know, Clark," he said, "the inspector will be clapping us in the Tombs. We are about the only ones left who haven't been threatened with it. It's a wonder to me, Inspector, that you haven't the place overflowing."

"I know he's your client," snapped Gerrity, "but just the same, you can't make me believe that he's so innocent after what Clark has just told us."

"But my dear Inspector," protested Hand, with a chuckle, "I haven't tried to make you believe a thing. I leave it to Clark."

"Well," growled Gerrity, "you intimated that I'm on the wrong track."

"Nothing of the kind," objected Hand, as he languidly lighted a cigarette. "Neither am I intimating anything when I remind you that on other cases you have suspected my clients. I remember one in particular—the case which Clark has taken the liberty of calling *Sinister Cargo*. What a ghastly error that would have been, Inspector. Caution is an exceedingly valuable trait."

"But this fellow must be guilty!" insisted Gerrity.

Hand leaned lazily back and blew a large cloud of smoke at the ceiling.

"It would be interesting," he said, "to hear your theory concerning Mr. Woodford Amesbury."

"Very well," snapped Gerrity. "I'll tell you what it is, and it's a mighty clever stunt, if I must say so. There haven't been two murderers; there's been only one! Woodford Amesbury disguised himself and took the part of his uncle, who is dead, like as not. He got his hands on twenty-five thousand dollars, and his partner had another twenty-five thousand. Then Amesbury killed Haggerty, stole the money, dropped his disguise, and has been hobnobbing round with us ever since as the nephew of the man who is supposed to be dead. A clever stunt, but we caught him at it!"

"That is rather a clever hypothesis," admitted Hand. "You haven't backed it up very concretely, though. You would have to defend it in court, you know."

"What's the matter with it?" demanded Gerrity, in an injured tone.

"Well, in the first place, how do you account for Mrs. Ackner's having seen Amesbury stretched dead on the floor of his room?"

"It was probably Haggerty, don't you see! Both men had beards, and she could easily have made the mistake."

"I don't fully agree with you. Mrs. Ackner knew both men quite well. But I grant you that, in a moment of terror, she might have jumped to the conclusion that the body at her feet was that of Jeremy Amesbury, since it was lying in Amesbury's room. But the body she saw had a knife in its heart. You found the knife yourself, all covered with blood. Haggerty's body had no knife wound in the heart, Inspector."

Gerrity leaped to his feet, clasped his hands behind his back, and commenced pacing irritably up and down the room. Finally he whirled about to face Hand.

"I can't explain that," he growled. "But, never fear, I'll think of something that will explain it. What else do you find the trouble with my theory?"

"That's easy," shrugged Hand. "How do you account for Haggerty's body being found stowed away in the closet of Larry White's laboratory?"

Gerrity puckered his brows for a moment.

"Amesbury had a key to the place!" he suddenly exclaimed. "He carried the body out there, put it in the laboratory to throw suspicion on White, and then he locked the place up again and beat it."

"That's my version of it, too," I cried, glad that Gerrity had at last seen the light. Gerrity bestowed a glance of acknowledgment upon me.

"Assuming that you are correct," said Hand, "and that Amesbury did beat it, as you say, why, then, didn't he do a good job of beating it? What purpose can he have in lingering in New York, taking a vast chance of being detected? It doesn't seem sensible for him to stay on here."

"I think I can explain that," I said, leaning over the table to Hand. "Although your eyes have a habit of seeing a great deal more than mine, nevertheless mine do see some things that yours overlook. I think that Amesbury, while masquerading as his uncle, found himself becoming infatuated with Judith Blake. His reason for wishing to throw the guilt of his crime upon Larry White was twofold. In the first place he wanted to clear himself, and in the second place he wanted to eliminate Larry as a rival for Miss Blake. Since the crime he has been most attentive to her, and as for his protesting that he is mostly concerned with clearing Larry White, that is all put on. He wants Larry White put out of the way, and then he wants that poor girl for his wife!"

"That's it!" cried Gerrity, smiting the table. "You've put your finger right on it, Clark. Good for you! I'm going to arrest him!"

Hand smiled serenely at us both.

"My poor client," he sighed, in mock sadness. "You fellows have as good as got him in the electric chair. So he was Jeremy Amesbury all the time. My, my!"

"Come on, Hand," chided Gerrity, "admit I'm right, for once."

"But I haven't said that you are not. As a matter of fact, I have paid some attention already to the theory you are now clinging to. I looked very carefully in Jeremy Amesbury's room for some evidence that he had been using disguises. It is extremely difficult, Inspector, to use the materials for a disguise without leaving some trace of them. Powder, for instance, gets into the most unlikely places, and paint adheres tenaciously to whatever it comes into contact. Glue is always dropping about and hardening to things. I looked very carefully for such evidence in Amesbury's room, but I found none. I thought for a brief period that I had discovered something of importance in Miss Blake's room. It was a box of just those very materials that Amesbury might have used to disguise himself with. But I have since learned that she is an amateur Thespian. Has quite a following among the congregation of the Hendly Congregational Church, where the plays she takes the lead in are given. I thought at first, you see, that she and Woodford Amesbury might possibly be in league."

"But the result of your work is purely negative. You found nothing to support the theory, but I still feel that something can be found. I'll arrest Amesbury, I tell you, and get the truth out of him!"

"Very well, Inspector," said Hand. "But before you go to hurl my client into a dungeon, I should like to have your company for a few moments. Your car is outside? Good! Come on, then."

Gerrity, as we followed Hand down the stairs, glanced apprehensively at me. Then he moved over and put his lips close to my ear.

"I'm on the right track this time," he assured me, and thereby, no doubt, bolstered up his own assurance. "I feel it! This will be the greatest thing in my career."

We got into the inspector's car, and Hand asked to be driven over to the building where Nick Haggerty's body

had been found. The Blakes lived there, I reminded myself, and I began to feel a trifle nervous about what he was
up to. But I felt confident that Gerrity and I had struck
upon the real solution. The only confusing thing about
the case was that Amesbury had cleverly reversed the age-
old idea of disguise. Instead of assuming a character to
avoid detection after the crime, he had played an assumed
role before it. Jeremy Amesbury was more than dead; he
had evaporated into thin air.

We climbed out of the inspector's car in front of the
Blakes' apartment house. Hand immediately led us inside.
With a feeling of relief, I followed Hand and the inspector
right by the stairs to the second floor. Evidently we were
not to call upon the Blakes. Instead we descended at once
to the basement. Hand stopped before the door leading
into the unused portion of the basement. He opened the
door and stepped quickly inside.

As I entered after Hand and the inspector, the unwholesome atmosphere of the dreary place sent a shiver up my
spine. Shadows from Hand's torch swallowed themselves
up as we advanced upon them. The broken stone walls of
the basement crowded dimly beside us, and to the rear the
darkness followed us, like an evil presence approaching as
close as it dared. Here the throb and hum of the city was
stilled, and all about was the quiet of an age-old tomb.

Hand turned the corner of a broken wall. The inspector
slipped on a loose stone and swore softly. Something on
the floor glistened. I recognized the fragments of the lens
from my torch, broken by Mr. Zinger against the wall.
Hand's tall dark figure, like a shadow moving behind the
light, pressed slowly on. I crowded up behind him in order
to be near the torch. Gerrity, walking beside me, cast an
uneasy glance over his shoulder.

Ahead of us the light streamed brilliantly on the floor
and along the somber walls. Ten feet ahead yawned a black

rectangle in the hard dirt of the floor, like a huge open grave. As we approached its brink the rays of the torch slanted into the pit. Suddenly Hand shot the light straight down into it. Sprawled on the shallow floor of the hole below us, brought into piteous relief, lay the grotesque, twisted form of a man! He lay on his face, with his arms doubled up under him.

Hand extended his long right arm. The shadow of his white hand fell squarely between the shoulders of the corpse.

"There," he said, solemnly, "lies the body of Jeremy Amesbury."

13

A COLD PIECE

For several moments after this dreadful announcement, we stood dumbly gazing down at the dead man below us. A bewildered mutter escaped Inspector Gerrity. Then he turned quickly to Hand.

"My God!" he said, almost in a whisper. "When did you find this, Hand?"

"Not long ago," replied my friend, holding the light unwaveringly on the corpse. "Identification has not been made, of course, but I think you will agree with me that it is Amesbury's body. Jeremy Amesbury, not Woodford."

"I can't tell; his head is buckled under him."

"But you can take a look at it."

Gerrity crouched down and peered intently into the pit. But suddenly he straightened and turned almost resentfully to Hand.

"See here," he demanded, "how in blazes did you find this fellow? I believe the spirits of dead men guide you to their bodies!"

"A process of reasoning guides me to their bodies," corrected Hand. "The theory that Woodford Amesbury had been impersonating his uncle did not deter me from putting other theories to the test. I felt that this basement should be thoroughly searched, and this is what I found."

"I seemed to have made such a clear-cut case against Woodford Amesbury," admitted Gerrity, dismally, "that I didn't bother with any others."

"Inspector," said Christopher Hand, "the great tragedy in being wrong lies in not being able to admit it."

"Even to yourself; that's right. Well, maybe my first theory concerning Woodford Amesbury is all shot full of holes, but I still have my eye on him! I'm not so sure yet that I'm not going to arrest him."

"First you might examine this body."

Gerrity leaped resolutely into the hole. Grasping the body by the shoulders, he rolled it over on its back. The bearded face of the dead man was horribly contorted, as though the agony of death had implanted itself forever upon his features. I had no doubt that the man was Jeremy Amesbury. The descriptions I had had of him tallied precisely with the appearance of the dead man, even to the iron gray hair that grew long on his head. Though bearded and horrible in death, the face that stared blankly up into the rays of the torch bore a remarkable resemblance to that of Hand's client.

"Stiff," muttered Gerrity. "Must have lain here a good while."

"I fix his death," said Hand, "at approximately the time that Mrs. Ackner saw him lying on the floor of his bedroom. Dr. Richards might differ with me."

"No, I think you're right."

The left breast of Amesbury's tightly-buttoned coat bore a dark stain, and his left hand, upon which he had been lying, was covered with congealed blood. Gerrity quickly unbuttoned the coat and threw it back.

"Stabbed through the heart," he observed, "just as the landlady said he was."

"Except to determine that the money-belt has been stolen from it," said Hand, "I haven't examined this body yet. I thought that you should see it first, Inspector. Have you any objections to my examining it now?"

"None at all."

Hand leaped into the pit. He stood beside the corpse, holding his light on it. He dropped to his knee and pointed to the bloody left hand.

"Deep gash on the palm of this left hand, Inspector," he said.

Gerrity peered sharply at the injured hand of the corpse.

"So there is," he said, with a shake of his head. "The poor devil tried to ward off the knife-thrust. You're sure the money-belt is gone?"

"Yes; this body has been robbed, too. That was the first thing I determined when I discovered it."

Hand was paying a good deal of attention to that pitiful injury he had just discovered. Suddenly he glanced up at Gerrity.

"He has a slight wound on his wrist, Inspector."

He had rolled back the shirt-cuff from the left wrist. Gerrity and I peered intently at it. The wound in the wrist was very small, hardly more than a half inch in length.

"That didn't kill him," growled Gerrity. "Got that trying to defend himself. It was the thrust to his heart that did for him."

"Yes, indeed. Just let me see—"

Hand's voice trailed off. With careful fingers he unbuttoned the shirt at the throat and laid it back. Taking out his knife, he slit the undershirt, revealing the fatal wound over the heart. He regarded it carefully for a moment; then he prodded the wound with the blade of his knife. To my astonishment I heard a metallic click.

"This is most peculiar, Inspector," said Hand. "The blade of the dagger still seems to be in the wound."

"Impossible!" cried Gerrity. "I have the knife that killed him at headquarters, blade and all. You must be mistaken, Hand."

"Well, see for yourself," invited Hand, offering the inspector his knife. After an investigation of his own, Gerrity looked up in vexation.

"Now what the devil!" he growled. "Nothing turns up that isn't more confusing than the last thing we've discovered. The more we work on this blasted case, the farther we seem to get from the solution of it!"

Jeremy Amesbury still wore his pistol in its shoulder-holster. Hand, as the inspector ranted against his bad fortune, examined the weapon carefully. He donned his gloves and extracted it from the holster. Gerrity took interest and craned his neck to watch him. When Hand had broken the piece we saw that, although fully loaded, the pistol had not been fired.

"Much good it did Amesbury and Haggerty to carry their guns," muttered Gerrity. "Neither one of them had a chance to draw them."

Hand placed the pistol back into the holster and got to his feet. He flashed his light all about the pit, his eyes swiftly following its course. Finally he put the light back on the corpse. Gerrity stood and looked inquiringly at him.

The inspector seemed more than ever to resent the course events had taken. He looked rather aggrieved.

"Quite upsetting, isn't it, Inspector?" said Hand.

"Awful!" agreed Gerrity, vehemently. "How in blazes do you suppose this hole in the cellar floor ever got here, anyway?"

"I think it was once the foundation for a furnace. This building is now supplied with steam from an outside source. Its own heating plant has been dismantled, and I think this is where the furnace stood."

"Guess that's it. Wonder where the handle of that knife got to."

"I think you'll look in vain for it here. I have just looked round this pit without seeing it. It may be, of course, that it was thrown into some other part of the basement. But it is my opinion that you won't find it here."

Gerrity once more dropped to his knee beside the corpse. He went through all the pockets, without producing anything to which significance could be attached. Then he rose and placed his hands on his hips, glaring down at the dead man.

"How do you suppose the murderer got the body in here?" he asked.

"Through the door at the end of Mr. Zinger's corridor," I cried. "Maybe we can find blood-stains, or some other clue out there!"

"I've looked very carefully out there," said Hand. "Of course that is the apparent way that the body was brought in here, but I found nothing to prove it."

"Well," said Gerrity, "the thing to do is to call Dr. Richards, have him come over and order the removal of this body to the morgue, and then determine definitely whether there really is the blade of a knife through the heart."

Hand switched the light full on Gerrity's face, causing him to squint painfully.

"Inspector, do you suppose we can keep the discovery of this body secret for a little while? I think it is very important that we do."

"Hum-m, we can try. What's the idea?"

"I think, if it becomes known that this second murder has been established, that it will effect to our detriment the movements of certain people that we are interested in. It can do no harm, at least, to say nothing for the present of the discovery of this second body. What do you think about it?"

"I'm perfectly willing. Of course I can't be responsible for what the newspaper boys find out. They're hot over this story."

"We'll take a chance on them. Get Dr. Richards and the morgue wagon. We'll do the whole thing as unostentatiously as possible."

Gerrity went quickly off in quest of a telephone booth. Hand and I commenced a search of the basement, looking for the handle of a knife. My own light being out of commission, I was able merely to follow Hand about. I found him taciturn and silent. Soon Gerrity rejoined us, and, using his light as well as Hand's, we combed the basement from one end to the other. Gerrity got quite excited over the pieces of my torch-lens on the floor. We explained, to his disappointment, Mr. Zinger's unfortunate experience in the basement that morning.

We saw nothing of the knife-handle, but Hand pointed out to us something that excited the inspector's optimism. It was a button, of black bone, lying on the floor not far from the pit in which lay the body. The light of the torch glinted on its ebony surface.

"That button has lain there but a short while," said Hand. "Otherwise it would be covered with dust, just as everything else down here is."

"It's the button from a man's coat," gloated Gerrity. "It's not from Jeremy Amesbury's coat, because all those buttons are sewed fast to it. Pretty slim clue, but if we can find a man with a button missing from his coat ten to one we lay our hands on the criminal. Blast it all, why can't I remember whether White has a button missing from his coat!"

At last we gave up the search.

"Well, the murderer took the knife-handle away with him," averred Gerrity. "That is, assuming that the blade is still in the body."

Gerrity, taking the button by its edges between his thumb and forefinger, picked it up from the floor and glanced critically at it. At the sound of someone entering the basement, he dropped the button into his vest pocket. The newcomer was Dr. Richards. He was accompanied by Mr. Zinger, who was palpably upset.

"Mr. Hand!" cried the little superintendent. "You here too? You ain't goin' to take nothin' else off the buildin'?"

"No, Mr. Zinger," replied Hand. "Have you anything to do upstairs?"

"Yes, sir," replied Mr. Zinger. "I'm moppin' the third floor. I just come down to get my pipe and tobacco, and this here gentleman asked me how to get to the cellar. What's goin' on now; found somethin' else about the murder?"

"No, nothing," lied Hand. "I think you might as well get back to your mopping."

"Yes, sir," complied Mr. Zinger, willingly. "I get the creeps in here. Mind puttin' your light over there toward the door? I can see's far as the wall then, and when I get round it I can see the door. I left it open. Thanks."

Mr. Zinger made his hasty departure. No sooner had he disappeared, however, when Gerrity clutched Hand excitedly by the arm.

"That janitor has lost a button from his coat!" he said tensely.

"Yes," agreed Hand. "But his coat is gray, and so are its buttons. That button we found is black."

"I'm going to have him watched!" snapped Gerrity. "If I find anything funny about him, by thunder I'll arrest him!"

Dr. Richards was becoming impatient.

"Where is this body?" he demanded.

He followed us over to the furnace pit, where we stood looking down for a moment at the body of Jeremy Amesbury.

Then Dr. Richards leaped into the hole and bent over the body, putting out his hand to it.

"This fellow has been here quite a while," he announced.

"How long do you think he's been dead?" asked Gerrity, quickly.

"Hum-m, that other murder was committed about ten thirty last night, wasn't it? I should say this fellow was killed about the same time."

"There's something devilish peculiar about this case, Doctor. I guess you know that this man was seen stabbed to death about ten thirty last night. You know, too, that I found a blood-stained knife that I thought was the one used to stab him. Well, there seems to be a knife-blade in his heart right now! I'm very anxious to have that determined without delay."

Dr. Richards quickly probed the wound with a small instrument that he took from his pocket. Then he got quickly to his feet and turned to us.

"Something in there; no doubt of it," he said. "Better get him to the morgue right away. I can't tell what it is until I've extracted it."

"I can't understand," said I, "how a knife-blade could be left in a man's body like that. Surely the thing must have had a handle!"

"Easy, Clark, easy," said Dr. Richards. "I've come across lots of them. The blade probably struck a rib when it was thrust into the body. From the position of the wound, I'd say that's what happened. Blade broke off at the handle, d'you see? The murderer had no way to get the blade out, of course."

"I say, Doctor," said Hand, "did the inspector tell you that we are anxious to keep the discovery of this body a private matter?"

"Yes," replied Dr. Richards, with a grin. "You fellows are up to something again, I suppose. It's all right with me; I won't say anything."

"Thanks," said Hand, shortly. "Now, I think the best way to take the body out is through the basement door at the back. They can carry it out through the alley to the street. Get them to pull the morgue wagon over to the entrance of that alleyway, Inspector, and have them work swiftly."

Gerrity left us, soon to return with three fellows carrying a stretcher. All that remained of Jeremy Amesbury was carried away, and we left the basement. We went out to the front of the building. As Dr. Richards prepared to enter his car, Gerrity stepped up to him.

"Give me a report as quickly as possible, Doctor," he requested. "There may be something on that knife-blade, if you find it, that would lead to the identification of the owner."

Promising a speedy report, the doctor got into his car. As he was about to drive off, Hand strode over and thrust his head and shoulders into the car. Gerrity and I stood apart looking at them, but what Hand had to say to the doctor we could not hear. Dr. Richards seemed to be regarding Hand in astonishment. He nodded his head, Hand stepped back, and the doctor drove off.

As Hand walked up to us a police car careened round the corner and quickly pulled over to the curb before us. Stanton, one of the headquarters detectives, jumped out and ran up to us.

"Inspector," he cried. "Just found out from headquarters where you were. I think I've come across something pretty important. You said to bring all tips to you; so I haven't investigated it yet. Looks good, though!"

Gerrity gripped Stanton by the shoulders and looked intently into his face.

"What is it?"

"I've found a guy that saw White shortly after the murder last night. He went into a little jewelry store in his neighborhood and gave the proprietor a gold coin! A gold coin, get it? This guy seen it."

Gerrity cast a swift glance of triumph at Christopher Hand.

"What time was this, Stanton?" he snapped.

"About eleven o'clock last night. This guy I got over at headquarters was shootin' his mouth off about it to some fellas on the corner up there. I was moseyin' round, like you ordered, and I heard him. When I pulled the tin on him he tried to back down, but I took him down to headquarters, and then he come clean. He was in the store, and he seen White slip this guy a gold piece."

Gerrity smiled expansively and turned to Hand.

"Do you want to come with me," he asked, "while I put the hooks into Mr. Larry White? Maybe the confession I got out of him before doesn't amount to much, but wait until you hear what I get out of him now. Want to come?"

"I think it would be illuminating," replied Hand, stepping into the inspector's car.

We drove over to police headquarters, Stanton trailing us in the other car. In the detectives' room we found a badly frightened young man, surrounded by a group of plainclothes-men. The detectives were employing a deceitful method of flattery, but their victim was not rising to the bait. Gerrity curtly ordered the chap to be taken to his office. Then turning abruptly to the door, he strode off to his sanctum. Hand and I followed him in. We were quickly joined by Stanton and his prisoner.

Deliberately Gerrity sat down in his swivel chair behind the desk. Then he fixed the young man with a frowning glance. The poor fellow, endeavoring mightily to keep his gaze steady, fidgeted from one foot to the other. He did not, however, appear to be a shifty young person. He looked to me to be a badly-frightened boy under twenty who had talked himself into trouble and was seeing no way out of it. I felt sorry for him.

"What's your name?" snapped the inspector.

"Jimmie Delaney," he replied, his voice trembling.

"All right, Delaney. I want you to tell me the truth! Get that? Now what did you see Larry White doing last night? Speak up!"

"I—I don't wanna talk. Mr. White's a nice fella. He lives in our house, and he's always nice to all of us. I wouldn't o' said nothin' if I thought it'd hurt him."

"What you want to do, and what you are going to do are two different things! Come on now, I understand you saw Larry White in a jewelry store round eleven o'clock last night. You saw him give the proprietor a gold piece, didn't you?"

"Gosh, Mister," pleaded the boy, "don't make me talk."

"Talk or go to jail!" snapped Gerrity. "Come on, out with it!"

Jimmie Delaney hung his head.

"I seen him," he whispered. "He give old Max somethin', but I don't know what. Honest, Mister, I don't know what it was."

"It was a gold piece, wasn't it?" thundered Gerrity, leaning across the desk toward the boy. "Tell me it was, or you go to jail!"

"I—I think it was," stammered the boy, trembling from head to foot.

Gerrity leaned back with a satisfied smile.

"All right," he said, in a rather kindly tone. "Why didn't you say so in the first place? Where is this jewelry store?"

"It's on the corner, right below our buildin'," replied Delaney. "It's called the Diamond Shop. Gimme a break, Mister, don't say I told ya."

"You'll be protected, son," smiled Gerrity. "But you'll have to come along with us; we may need you. I'm going up to interview old Max, Hand. Want to come along?"

Hand nodded, and together we all left the office. Not long after we were climbing out of Gerrity's car before the little jewelry shop. Solemnly we filed into the store. A little old fellow with snow white locks came smiling forth to greet us. Something in our demeanor evidently warned him that business was not going to be so good as he had expected. The smile faded from his lips, and he glanced apprehensively at us.

"Ain't that watch working right, Jimmie?" he asked, anxiously.

"Yes, yes, it's fine, Mr. Silverman," replied young Delaney, hastily.

"Never mind the watch," growled Gerrity. "Silverman, where's that gold piece that young White gave you last night. Let's see it!"

"I—I don't know what you mean," whispered Silverman, fear creeping into his old eyes. He moved nervously over behind the counter.

"Take a look at this," invited Gerrity, displaying his badge. "I don't want any monkey-business now! If you want to keep out of trouble, produce that gold piece. It's blood money, and maybe you know it! Hand it over, and be quick about it!"

"Oh me! Oh my!" deplored the old man. "What have I done to deserve this? I ain't never had the police in here before, never! Fifteen years I am on this corner, and forty years on Third Avenue. The rent's just went up, and now the police! Oh dear me! Oh dear me!"

"Cut out the weeping!" snapped Gerrity. "Get me that gold piece, or I take you right down to police headquarters. Step on it!"

Silverman seemed unable to move. He stood with his trembling hands on the counter, opening and closing his mouth, but unable to say a word. Hand stepped up to him and patted him on one drooping old shoulder.

"Don't be so dismayed," he said. "The inspector has no intention of doing you out of your money. It may be that you have a right to it, and in that case you will get it back. But if it has been stolen from someone else, then you will have to lose it. What did Mr. White give it to you for?"

"He owed it to me," cried Silverman. "He owes me more than that, and now he's in jail and can't pay me! Poor feller, though. He's a nice young man, but he's poor. He's very poor. He's behind in his installments, way behind. But he's such a nice young feller. That's why I let him get behind in his installments. But I have to have money. The rent's went up, and business is poor."

"What was he paying installments on?"

"The ring! The ring he gave his girl. A fine diamond with hardly a crack in it. I couldn't ask him to get it back, now could I? Such a nice young feller, it would break his heart. I didn't keep after him for money, honest. I told him the other day that I didn't know for how I was going to pay the rent, and he just come in last night and paid me something. I didn't want to take it; he seemed to be so broken up. But I got to have money soon to pay the rent."

"Get the gold piece, Mr. Silverman," said Hand, in a kindly tone. "Give it to Inspector Gerrity. You don't want to be guilty of disobeying the law. If we find that the money rightfully belongs to you, you will get it back again."

Silverman glanced dismally from the friendly eyes of Christopher Hand to the angry orbs of Inspector Gerrity. Mumbling dolefully to himself and sadly shaking his old head, he moved over to a safe in the rear of the store. He crouched before it, manipulating the combination. Then he straightened and, with a great effort, pulled the door back. Once again he crouched before the safe and took from it a little drawer. For a moment he fumbled round in it with his fingers. Then, with a heavy sigh, he lifted something out and returned the drawer to the safe. Shuffling over to Gerrity, he held out a twenty-dollar gold piece.

"There it is," he said, a suspicion of tears in his eyes. "Twenty dollars I can't afford to lose. If it's mine, you'll bring it back, yes?"

"All right," agreed Gerrity, a note of kindness creeping into his gruff voice. "Sorry to have to do this, but I can't help it. I'll look out for this."

Hand once more addressed the old fellow.

"Mr. Silverman," he said, "did I understand you to say that Mr. White seemed perturbed when he was in here last night?"

"No!" replied the old jeweler, vigorously shaking his head. "I don't know what you said, but I said it not!"

"You mean you don't understand me. Well then, did Mr. White seem excited when he was here? Did he seem to be afraid of something, or was he just as usual?"

Old Silverman threw back his shoulders and looked Hand straight in the eye.

"I did not see," he replied. "He was all right by me. I would not have touched his money, because I know it is hard for him to pay his own rent. But he said he had more, and I have to have money. The rent's went up, and—"

"What time was he in here?" asked Gerrity.

Silverman looked quickly at Jimmie Delaney; then he shrugged his shoulders resignedly and glanced down at the floor.

"He came here just as I was closing up," he said. "I close up at eleven; so I guess it must have been about eleven o'clock. Poor feller!"

Gerrity walked quickly over to Hand, who was standing beside me.

"Do you think I ought to lock these two up as material witnesses?" he asked. "This is a strong link in my case, and I'd hate to have them run out on me."

"It might be well to keep the young fellow for a while," replied Hand. "Old Silverman, I should say, will not run out on you. If your case shapes up to the point where you want to make charges you can find him easily."

"All right. We won't bother you any more, Mr. Silverman. I'll look after this gold piece, and if it's all right you'll get it back. Come on, I want to go down and see Larry White."

Gerrity left Jimmie Delaney in the hands of Stanton, with orders to detain the boy at police headquarters. He also ordered the detective to get Silverman's full name and address. Then he, Hand and I got into the car and were driven to the Tombs. I was furiously trying to think up a new excuse for Larry White, but I had utterly no success. Somewhere in that great city, among its hurrying millions, lurked Filipo. My one hope for White was that we could find him. And yet I could blame no one but myself that Filipo's steps were not at the moment leading him into our waiting nets. I had frightened him away, and the prospects of our ever finding him again seemed hopelessly remote.

We found Larry White gazing dismally through a small window in his cell. As the door was being unlocked for us he turned languidly. Then he walked slowly over to his cot and sat down, eyeing the inspector uneasily. Gerrity planted himself firmly before him and looked down upon him in a most ominous fashion. White averted his eyes and gazed at the floor.

"Well!" barked the inspector. "We've got the goods on you at last. Come clean, now, what have you done with that money?"

White clasped his hands between his knees and slowly shook his head.

"The more trouble you give us," snapped Gerrity, "the worse it's going to be for you. We've found Amesbury's body, right where you threw it in the basement under your laboratory!"

He paused and observed the effect of this shot upon his prisoner. White caught his breath and glanced startled from one to the other of us.

"Amesbury!" he cried. "You—you found Jeremy Amesbury's body?"

"Come on," prompted Gerrity. "We may be able to help you if you'll give us half a chance. Damned foolish of you to try to hold out on us. Sooner or later you're going to crack. We've got all the information now. Ready to speak?"

But White, gazing unseeing straight at the wall of the cell, shrugged his shoulders and slowly shook his head.

"I told you we had the goods on you," said Gerrity. "I wasn't trying to kid you, Mister! It didn't take you long to start spending that money, did it? That was where you made your first mistake, son."

White gave a start. He glanced quickly up at Gerrity. It was plain to be seen that the inspector had penetrated him. He turned his eyes away to the wall, and his breathing became rapid and nervous.

"You'd have done better to spend some of the bills instead of the gold," sneered the inspector. "Come on, where did you put the rest of it?"

The prisoner set his jaw and maintained his silence. He became more and more agitated, until I could hear his breath hissing through his teeth.

"You might as well speak up," prodded Gerrity. "I'll give you another chance, son, come on. I'd like to help you out. See, look at this gold piece. Ever see it before? There's blood on it; you can't see it, but there's blood on it, all right enough! It's dirty money, my boy. You'd better do what you can to clean the blood off your own conscience. That's right, look at that gold. It's got blood on it!"

Larry White had undergone a remarkable change. Half rising from his cot, he stared at the gold piece resting in the inspector's huge hand as though he were looking straight at the electric chair. All at once he reached out fiercely to snatch the coin from the inspector. But Gerrity, too quick for him, whipped his hand holding the gold piece behind his back.

"Give me that!" shouted White, hoarsely. "Give it to me, I tell you!"

"Oh, no," said Gerrity, with a nasty laugh. "That's going to get the truth out of you. Sit down or I'll knock you down!"

But Larry White was on his feet, shaking his trembling fist at the inspector, his eyes flashing enraged defiance at him. Hand stepped quietly up to him. He placed a hand on the young man's shoulder, and looked steadily into his eyes. White slowly ceased his trembling, bowed his head, and with a groan dropped to the cot. He buried his face in his hands and sat motionless. My friend motioned Gerrity away. The inspector, with a lingering glare at his prisoner, walked over and leaned up against the wall. Hand looked down again at White.

"You know where we got that coin?" he asked.

White nodded, but he did not look up.

"We got it from Max Silverman," said Hand. "It puts you in a very bad light, Mr. White. I advise you, if you can, to explain how this coin come into your possession. You will damage your chances by remaining silent, I assure you."

The prisoner raised haggard eyes to Hand, but he shook his head. With a helpless gesture, he dropped his hands to the cot.

"I have nothing to say," he answered.

"Come, Mr. White," I cried. "Surely you have some explanation for once having possessed that gold piece. Think what you are doing!"

"Sure he has an explanation," sneered Gerrity. "He got it out of a money-belt. He got a lot of money out of two money-belts. If I knew where they are, I'd go easy on him. Come on, young fellow, where are they?"

White, with a return of spirit, flashed a contemptuous glance at Gerrity. Then he looked over at me and shook his head.

"I can't tell you," he said, steadily. "You can stay here all day and all night asking me, but I can't tell you. I know you are trying to help me, Mr. Clark, but you can't do it. I guess it's all up with me. You might as well go now, all of you, for I won't say another word!"

"Maybe you won't," growled Gerrity. "Let's see this!" Roughly he took hold of White's coat and unbuttoned it. He carefully inspected each of the buttons, grunting with satisfaction as he twisted the top one in his fingers.

"Who sewed that button on for you?" he barked.

"None of your business!" flared White.

"Isn't it? You'll soon find out whether it is or not. You lost that button in the basement when you threw Amesbury's body in there. I have an idea who sewed that button on for you, and I'll bet she did it last night, *after ten thirty!*"

It was Gerrity himself who suggested that we leave. With a sigh of regret I followed the others out of the cell. The nets were certainly closing tighter and tighter about Larry White. The last I saw of him he was sitting on his cot, dismally holding his head in his hands.

14

UNMASKED

Outside the Tombs Hand looked at his watch. Then he turned to Gerrity, who was chewing his lip as he descended the steps.

"I shouldn't be surprised, Inspector," he said, "if Amesbury is now waiting for me at the rooms. I left word at his hotel for him to call on me, and I told Mrs. Flemming to admit him to the living-room if I were not there. Would you care to have an interview with him?"

"I would," replied Gerrity, quickly. "I'd like to hear what he has to say about that affair in the restaurant today. Blast it all! Are these people all in league? I have a clear case against White; there's that old fake of a cripple with his box full of gold and bills; and then there's Amesbury with that precious friend of his Filipo. There's something in that; there must be! But who am I going to suspect?"

"If you handled a case the way I do," smiled Hand, "you wouldn't have so much trouble. I suspect everybody. Get much further that way. But, Inspector, I don't want you to mention that affair in the restaurant to Amesbury."

Gerrity growled something unintelligible and got into his car. We got in after him, and directing the driver where to take us, rode in silence up to the rooms. There we found Amesbury, roving round the living-room like a lion in captivity. As we entered he leaped excitedly toward Hand and grasped him by the arm.

"What's the latest?" he demanded. "Have you figured this thing out yet?"

"We are making progress," Hand assured him. "There is nothing definite yet, however. How have you been employing yourself?"

Amesbury glanced at Gerrity, who was regarding him narrowly.

"Well," he growled, "I've had a fellow trailing me round the past two or three hours. I can tell you that! If you care to step over to the window you can see him standing on the other side of the street. I called up police headquarters and asked for you, Inspector. They said you were out; so I reported it to somebody else."

"Oh, yes," said Gerrity, uncomfortably.

I stepped over to the window. Across the street I saw lurking in a doorway one of Gerrity's headquarters detectives. When I looked back at the inspector, he coughed and turned away. Hand covered up the silence.

"Have you been threatened in any way, Mr. Amesbury?" he asked.

"How's that?" said Amesbury, quickly. "Oh, no. Of course not."

"Sure about that?" asked Gerrity, cocking an eye at the client. "If there's a man following you round it looks funny. Better be careful."

"I am being careful," retorted Amesbury, quite ominously. "But I'll tell you something else more important than that. Mr. Hand, I think that my uncle is dead. In fact, I am quite sure that he is dead."

"My word!" I exclaimed. "What makes you think that?"

"Yes," added Gerrity, grimly. "What ever put that into your head?"

"It is the most mysterious thing," began Amesbury. "I was out for a while after lunch this afternoon. When I got back to the hotel they told me at the desk that you had called, Mr. Hand. They gave me your message to meet you here. Then they said that some other fellow had been trying to get me. Called me twice, they said. He refused to give his name both times, but they were sure it was the same man."

"Ah," said Hand, "but he called again, later, when you were in?"

"He did. He told me that my uncle was dead!"

This caused a good deal of astonishment. Gerrity, who had seated himself in my easy chair, leaped to his feet and leaned over the table tensely to Amesbury.

"Who was it?" he cried excitedly.

Amesbury shrugged his shoulders and looked puzzled.

"That's the mysterious part of it," he said. "I don't know who it was. I tried every way possible to get the fellow's name out of him, but he refused to give it. He said he was a friend, and that's all."

"Did you recognize the voice?" asked Hand, quickly.

Amesbury wrinkled his brow and cocked his head on one side.

"I've heard that voice before somewhere!" he said, vehemently. "I know I have! But I can't place it for the life of me. I've heard it before; I'm ready to swear that I have. But where it was I can't think."

"Can you remember exactly what he said?" pressed Hand.

"Pretty closely," replied Amesbury. "He asked me first whether I was very much concerned about my uncle, and whether I had been worrying a great deal over his fate. Of course I told him that I most certainly was greatly worried over my uncle's fate. Then he said that he always thought it was much worse to be uncertain like that, and that he thought it was his duty—his painful duty, he said, to inform me that my uncle was no more."

"Those were his exact words, as you remember them?" asked Hand.

"I think I can give you his exact words. He said: 'Perhaps I should not tell you this, but my conscience will not permit me to refrain from doing it another minute. It is my painful duty to inform you that your uncle is no more.'"

Gerrity had got to pacing up and down the room. Now he stopped before Amesbury and glanced intently at him, his head thrust forward.

"Did he tell you how he knew your uncle had been killed?" he asked.

"No," replied Amesbury. "I asked him all sorts of questions, but he would answer none of them. Finally he hung up on me."

"Do you remember Mr. Ackner?" asked Gerrity, quickly. "The husband of your uncle's landlady? That old cripple we saw last night."

"Why, of course," replied Amesbury, with a puzzled glance at the inspector.

"Could it have been his voice?" snapped Gerrity.

"How could it have been his voice?" countered Amesbury, with a derisive smile. "He can't even get out of his chair. But, hold on. His wife said she saw my uncle lying dead on the floor of his room. That's right! The old fellow may be sort of balmy. I'll bet that's who it was!"

"I'll bet that's who it was too," said Gerrity, grimly. "I think we ought to pay Mr. Ackner a visit right this minute! Perhaps it isn't so blasted balmy that he knows Amesbury's dead! What about it, Hand?"

Hand looked at his watch. He walked deliberately over to the table and picked up a cigarette. Idly tapping it on his thumb-nail, he stood gazing out the window. Twilight was falling. A sudden gnawing sensation reminded me that I had had nothing whatever to eat since breakfast. Events had moved so swiftly throughout the day that I had forgotten food. Hand turned slowly back to the inspector, who was waiting eagerly for his answer.

"I am expecting Dr. Richards at any minute," said my friend. "He should have been here by this time. I am very anxious to get his report."

"Do you mean that Dr. Richards is coming here?" demanded Gerrity, incredulously.

"Yes," replied Hand, lighting his cigarette. "I expect him to have some rather significant news. Do you suppose you can contain yourself until he gets here, Inspector? I think it will be well worth your while if you can."

Gerrity, growling some inferior opinion of Hand's being mysterious, threw himself into my easy chair. Amesbury commenced plying Hand with questions, which he soon found was a futile waste of time. I employed myself in jotting down notes concerning the case for future use. A half hour thus slipped by before there came a knock at our door. Gerrity, with an exclamation of hope, bounded from the chair and crossed rapidly over to admit the caller. He jerked open the door, and Dr. Richards strode quickly into the living-room.

All eyes were inquiringly on the doctor. Gerrity closed the door and walked quickly over to stand beside Hand. Dr. Richards carefully laid his little black bag on the table. Then he glanced sharply at Hand.

"Well," he said, with a shake of his head, "you were right. How you knew it I'm hanged if I know, but you were right. Makes me feel like a chump!"

"Right about what?" yelped Gerrity.

"Inspector," said Dr. Richards slowly, "my autopsy report on Nick Haggerty can be thrown away. He wasn't killed by a blow on the head; he was killed by drinking a pretty strong solution of cyanide of potassium."

"Damnation!" gasped Gerrity. "Then who struck him over the head?"

"I don't know," shrugged the doctor, "but I'll bet a dollar Hand does."

"You found whiskey in the stomach, too, Doctor?" asked Hand, ignoring Gerrity, who had turned balefully upon him.

"A small quantity," replied the doctor. "We examined every content of the stomach carefully. I didn't want to go making another mistake. I examined the contents of the stomach of that other body, too. That's what took me so long. But he hadn't been drinking any cyanide of potassium."

"What other body?" demanded Amesbury, quickly. "What does this mean? What other body is there?"

"It means," replied Hand, slowly, "that your uncle is indeed no longer living. We found his body in that basement under the laboratory where Nick Haggerty was found."

Mechanically Amesbury sat down in my easy chair. He stared dully across at the wall. Finally he drew a deep breath, pulled himself together, and glanced sharply up at Hand. He certainly appeared to have received a great shock.

"How did he die?" he asked, in little more than a whisper.

"One thing at a time," growled Gerrity. "I want to know, Hand, how in blazes you knew enough to put the doctor up to looking for poison in Haggerty's stomach."

Hand pursed his lips and sat down on the arm of his chair. Then he glanced quickly up at Gerrity, standing with jaw outthrust looking down at him.

"It's only fair to tell you, Inspector," said he. "I found a package of cyanide of potassium in Larry White's laboratory."

Again my heart sank. Lately everything that came to light seemed to accentuate the dark cloud of guilt that was gathering round the unfortunate young man. Inspector Gerrity was rubbing his hands in satisfaction.

"I knew it!" he cried. "He drank it in White's laboratory. He never went back to his room after he left that party last night. I knew I was on the right track from the start!"

Hand shrugged his shoulders and smiled over at Dr. Richards.

"You may be right," he said. "But the fact remains that there is a glass tumbler in Haggerty's bedroom this minute that contains a small quantity of whiskey and cyanide of potassium in solution. That stuff kills instantly. Haggerty fell dead the second he swallowed it, and the tumbler fell with him. The rug in his room was wet with it last night, and I detected the odor of whiskey in the room. If I were half as clever as Clark thinks I am, I should have paid more attention to it last night. There is a little of that deadly potion in the tumbler now, Inspector. I took a small quantity of it and analyzed it, but I was careful to leave as much as I took. The murderer picked that tumbler up from the floor where it had fallen with his victim. There are finger-prints on it, Inspector. Better have your men get to work on it."

The inspector was chagrined. He shook his head miserably.

"Why can't we get a clear-cut case?" he vociferated. "Everything we find is double-edged! But Larry White must be the poisoner!"

"Perhaps," said Hand.

"Of course he is," cried Gerrity. "You remember that shirt button we found in the closet of the laboratory. The body was robbed there!"

"Yes," said Hand, in a rather bored fashion. "But see here, Doctor, how about that knife-blade in that wound?"

"Oh, I found the knife-blade, all right. Here it is."

He took from his pocket a narrow, flat object about six inches long wrapped in brown paper. He carefully unfolded it on the table, and there was revealed to us as wicked a looking knife-blade as ever I have seen. It was freshly broken off at the handle end. The blade was almost as thin as a razor and looked fully as sharp as one. It glistened brightly under the light.

"That's it," said the doctor simply. "It struck a rib, just as I thought. Pierced the heart cleanly, though. The handle broke right off, you see."

Amesbury leaned over the blade. Then he raised a white face to us.

"Is—is that what killed him?" he asked, in a trembling voice.

Hand then told his client exactly how he had discovered his uncle's body, bringing in all the subsequent details. Amesbury shook his head and bit his lip.

Then Hand turned his attention to the knife-blade. He picked it up and turned it in his hand. After a moment he laid it down again.

"I looked that over already," said Gerrity. "It tells us nothing."

"On the contrary, Inspector," objected Hand, "it may very well be the clue that might lead us to the murderer. That blade is new. Hardly a scratch on it, and it has never been resharpened. It is the type of knife used in the pelting of animals. It is most certainly an unusual knife to find in these parts. Domestic manufacture. Perhaps the murderer brought it into the city with him. But if it was purchased here, it should not be difficult to find the seller. If you can do that you will have gone a long way toward clearing up this mystery."

"By thunder, you're right!" cried Gerrity. "I'll get to work on it at once."

"Don't you want to see old Ackner?" asked Hand. "I should like to take the doctor with us. Can you spare a few minutes, Doctor?"

"Yes indeed," replied Dr. Richards. "I'm getting all steamed up over this case myself. There seem to be a lot of intangible aspects to it."

"Yes!" exploded Gerrity, pointing an accusing finger at the knife. "How am I going to reconcile this thing with that blood-stained knife I found over at that blasted house? I suppose there's another dead body lying round somewhere! Besides that, the whole thundering neighborhood looks like a pack of murderers to me! I can make up a lot of cases, but the king pin is missing in every one of 'em. This thing is going too far!"

The disgruntled inspector took possession of the knife-blade, and we set out to call upon Mr. Ackner. On the way over Gerrity got to wondering again what the old fellow's part could be in the tragedy.

"I have his finger-prints, if you want them," said Hand.

"Where'd you get 'em?" muttered Gerrity.

"I have them on that nickel hand mirror that I was holding when he shook hand's with me last night. Of course I got nothing but the prints of the fingers on his right hand. But he is right-handed, and if he held that knife you found, Inspector, his finger-prints on that and those on my mirror should coincide. I don't think you will require them, however."

Before we confronted Ackner, Hand guided us to the basement of the building. Straight over to a pile of rubbish he went. Leaning over, he pulled aside a large piece of wrapping paper. Underneath it lay an old wooden box, all splintered open. Hand pointed to it with his long index finger and looked up at us.

"I want you to notice this," he said. "Just bear it in mind." Then we went up to Ackner's apartment. Mrs. Ackner admitted us. We found her husband seated in his invalid's chair, looking just as dismal and helpless as he had the night before. When he laid eyes on Christopher Hand he seemed to take a more cheerful interest in life. Gerrity, however, seemed to be no source of pleasure to him, judging by the hostile glance he bestowed upon the inspector. But Gerrity was eyeing him in a most unfriendly fashion.

"Ah, Mrs. Ackner," said Hand, turning with a smile to the little woman. "I see that the Skellys are not working at the picture house tonight."

"Oh, why, yes they are," she replied, wonderingly. "Unless you just saw them."

"No," said Hand, with a shake of his head. "But I was under the impression that you took care of their little girl while they were working. And here you are, you see."

"Oh," she smiled, "I just come down for a minute to see how Frank was getting on."

"You must be nervous about that little tot," said Hand, with more compassion than I ever thought was in him. "If she ever woke up all alone she'd be frightened to death. I'm going to have a chat with your husband. When I'm ready to leave I'll send Clark up to tell you that everything is all right."

It was plain to be seen that Mrs. Ackner was not sure that everything was all right then. She looked distinctly worried as, with her bird-like walk, she moved over to the door. After a last nervous glance over her shoulder, she went out and closed the door after her. I glanced quickly over at her husband. I could see that he was beginning to get excited again.

"Well, well, how are you tonight, Mr. Ackner?" asked Hand, heartily.

"I ain't so good, Mr. Hand," he whined. "This rheumatism does beat all."

"Pretty bad tonight, is it? Well, we're going to rid you of that right this minute! Do you see that man standing there with the little black bag. That is Dr. Richards, the foremost living authority on rheumatism."

"You don't say so," said Mr. Ackner, nervously.

Dr. Richards looked quite astonished. Mr. Ackner squinted suspiciously at him.

"Rheumatism is pretty bad tonight, eh?" said Hand.

"Oh, awful!" groaned Mr. Ackner.

"Cheer up. You are going to be rid of that rheumatism in about two minutes. Dr. Richards has almost uncanny—in fact they are uncanny curative powers. All he has to do is to walk into a room, look at a patient, and the next instant the patient is well. Now, I'll wager that after having been looked at by Dr. Richards you can walk as well as any man alive. Let's see you try it!"

"I—I just can't do it, Mr. Hand!"

"Certainly you can. Come on, try it!"

Hand pulled Mr. Ackner protesting from his chair and started him across the floor. Then he abandoned him, leaving the old fraud standing in the center of the room, blinking in consternation.

"There you are!" cried Hand. "Cured! Come on, walk about."

Unable to withstand Hand's commanding glance, Ackner walked dismally up and down the room. Dr. Richards became more and more astonished, and Amesbury's eyes were popping from his head. He glanced over-awed at the doctor. Gerrity, on the other hand, was filling with pugnacity.

"Splendid!" applauded Hand, to Ackner's discomfiture. "Wonderful! There is nobody like Dr. Richards to effect a cure. But, do you know, in my own way I'm quite as wonderful as he is. I am clairvoyant. Yes, Mr. Ackner, I am positively clairvoyant."

"You're what?" gulped Ackner.

"Clairvoyant. I see objects that are not perceptible. I can read your past, too."

"Not that!"

"I certainly can. I think you've lost a large sum of money. No, by Jove, you've just mislaid it! Am I right?"

"No, no, you ain't right!"

"Ah, you have forgotten all about it. I have it! I tell you I can see that money as well as though it lay on that table. I see it perfectly. Come on, all of you, and I'll show you where it is. I tell you, Mr. Ackner, this is a stroke of luck for you!"

He darted through the door into the bedroom. Ackner, with a cry of alarm, went speedily after him. There was no doubt that he was cured of his rheumatism.

Gerrity was quick to follow into the bedroom. Dr. Richards, Amesbury and I were right behind him. Hand was over at the side, tugging at a bureau set up against the wall. Ackner was hopping round him, protesting vigorously.

"There ain't nothing there!" he shouted shrilly. "Get out o' here!"

But Hand was not to be deterred. He dragged the bureau aside, revealing in the wall behind it a round opening about eight inches in diameter. A piece of cardboard had been fitted into it, closing it up. At sight of it Mr. Ackner became even more agitated. Far from being a helpless cripple, he was fast taking on the characteristics of a jumping jack.

"Ha!" cried Hand. "I knew it! Now to get that cardboard out. There we are, by Jove! A box, and there's something in it. This is just as I visualized it. Now what do you say, Mr. Ackner, am I clairvoyant or not?"

Mr. Ackner seemed to be thinking that Hand was something besides clairvoyant. My friend carried the box over to the table, the same table where Ackner had opened it the noon before. Ackner frenziedly elbowed his way up beside Hand. But it was plain to be seen that the situation was too much for him. He kept putting out his hands to grasp the box, only to drop them helplessly to his side.

Hand quickly removed the lid. Inside we saw the golden glint of the coins. Gerrity turned wrathfully to Ackner, who cowered before him.

"Where did you get that money?" he roared. "Quick, out with it!"

"Mr. Ackner has probably forgotten, Inspector," said Hand, quickly. "Now, Mr. Ackner, we shall just count this money, and see what good fortune has brought you."

The amount of money in the box was disappointing. Hand placed the gold, which was in coins of different denominations, into separate piles. Then he counted the bills, Gerrity aiding.

"A little over four thousand in all," said Hand. "One thousand and forty-five dollars in gold, and the remainder in bank-notes. Quite a tidy sum, Mr. Ackner."

"Where's the rest of it?" demanded Gerrity. "We've got to find it!"

"Aren't you satisfied with what we have here, Inspector?" asked Hand, in apparent astonishment. "I'll wager Mr. Ackner is, and he owns it. See here, Clark, just step upstairs and find Mrs. Ackner. I can just see that Mr. Ackner is dying to tell his wife the good news. Bring her down here, and let her see what we have found."

"Here!" cried Ackner. "Here! Wait a minute! Don't do that! Please!"

"I know what is the matter with you," smiled Hand. "You want to be the one to tell your wife. And you shall do it, too. But look at you, cured of the rheumatism and come into a fortune. It's not right to keep your wife in ignorance of it another second! Go get her, Clark."

"Oh, but—I know, but—" stammered Ackner. "Oh, my stars!"

A commanding glance from Hand sent me scuttling from the room. I had a bit of trouble finding the Skellys' apartment, but I soon located it. Mrs. Ackner, I found, had worked herself into a high state of excitement. She tried quite futilely to cover it up. From the bottom of my heart I pitied the poor little woman. But I was beginning to sense that Hand, without departing from his usual methods, was arranging to take a good deal of the load she had been bearing from her shoulders.

"Mrs. Ackner," I cried, "we have the greatest surprise for you!"

"W—what is it?" she asked, breathlessly. "Nothin's happened to Frank?"

"Your husband? Yes, indeed. Come and see; you'll be delighted."

Under a good deal of apprehension she followed me downstairs. As we entered the bedroom of her apartment, all the others were grouped about the table, just as I had left them. Ackner was vainly endeavoring to hide himself behind Hand. Mrs. Ackner stared incredulously at her husband. He dropped his eyes, abashed, and fidgeted painfully.

"Ah, there you are, Mrs. Ackner," cried Hand. "Look what we have here. Dr. Richards, here on my right, has cured your husband's rheumatism! He's as well a man as ever walked on two legs. Just think of that! Imagine how he will be able to help you round the house. Walk about there, old fellow, and show your wife how well you can do it. He's as well and sound as he ever was."

Ackner started shuffling disconsolately about. A low growl from the throat of Inspector Gerrity, however, brought an expression of alarm to his face and considerable vigor to his legs. He hopped up and down the room, keeping a troubled eye on the inspector. Mrs. Ackner clasped her hands, her face aglow with happiness. With the exception of Gerrity, who continued to glare at the erstwhile cripple, we all smiled upon Mrs. Ackner. She remained speechless, her eyes glistening with happiness, following the somewhat grotesque antics of her husband. Hand stepped over to the table.

"See here, Mrs. Ackner," he cried. "Your husband had all this money put away, and then he forgot all about it. We found it just now. It's all yours, every dollar of it."

Wonderingly, as one in a dream, Mrs. Ackner moved over to the table. Her eyes grew bigger by the minute. She reached out and timidly touched the gold.

"Mine? All mine?" she asked, looking unbelievingly up at Hand.

"All yours," he smilingly assured her. "Of course when money is found like this, it has to be investigated a little. Just a technicality. Inspector Gerrity will have to take it for a little while. Then you will get it back again. I don't think he will have to keep it long."

"Oh, ain't this just too lovely!" cried little Mrs. Ackner, tearfully. "With this money I can get a maid to help me, and with Frank able to work I can let the janitor go. We can begin to make a little money. I can get some new clothes and things! Oh, Frank, ain't this just too grand to believe!"

Evidently Frank did not agree. He glanced spitefully at Hand. I could see that my friend had lost one admirer in exchange for winning another.

"Well, Inspector," said Hand, briskly, "I think we had better be off. Put that money in the box, and let us go. You will get your money back very soon, Mrs. Ackner. I shall ask the inspector to see to it that you put it in your own bank account; your husband might lose it again. The inspector will also agree, I am sure, to have one of his men keep track of your husband's health. If the rheumatism returns, we'll just get Dr. Richards to come over and look at him again."

We left with Mrs. Ackner's half hysterical thanks ringing in our ears. Out in the hall Gerrity turned quite resentfully to Hand.

"What was the blasted idea of that?" he demanded.

"He's just a lazy old miser, Inspector. I didn't want you wasting your time on him. Clark and I heard him drop and break something. It was that broken box I showed you in the basement. It used to hold his money, I'm sure. He's been keeping his services and his money from his poor little wife for years."

Dr. Richards and I exchanged an amused glance. Even the deception of a husband was as tissue paper before the flame of Christopher Hand's perception.

15

MR. BOTHWELL

Inspector Gerrity suddenly remembered that he should, at this late hour, have the contents of the glass tumbler in Nick Haggerty's room analyzed. Accompanied by Hand, he went up to Haggerty's room to get the tumbler. Dr. Richards bade us good night and quickly left. Amesbury and I were left standing alone in the lower hallway. When Hand and the inspector had disappeared up the stairs, the client turned a puzzled face upon me.

"What should I do," he asked, "about this fellow who's been following me about?"

I realized, of course, that the chap must be a source of great annoyance to Amesbury. He must have been wondering whether his shadow was a representative of the police department or a henchman of Filipo. Either, I thought, would be about as unwelcome. I was unable to advise him.

"I'll fix him, if he's still there!" said Amesbury, grimly.

He opened the door and strode purposefully out into the open. Across the street, I saw the detective who had been following him. The fellow quickly presented his back to us. Hastily he applied a match to the cigarette between his lips. Amesbury, whom I had followed out to the steps, turned wrathfully to me.

"See that?" he demanded. "Lighting a cigarette that he was already smoking! By thunder, I'm going to give that fellow a piece of my mind!"

He walked quickly across the street, his fists doubled up. I decided I had better hear what was going on, and so I went after him. The detective immediately started strolling casually down the street. Amesbury, however, quickly caught up with him. Grasping the man roughly by the shoulder, he spun him round and glared into his face. The detective assumed an expression of righteous indignation.

"Hey!" he cried. "What's the big idea, brother?"

"You know what the idea is!" rasped Amesbury. "You've followed me round all you are going to, understand? It won't be healthy for you to do it any longer. Now get going up the street, and let me see the last of you!"

He gave the detective a shove that sent him spinning across the pavement. The fellow adjusted his coat, glared at Amesbury, and strolled on up the street. For a moment Amesbury stood frowning after him. Then he glanced quickly about. A dim light showed through the glass panel of the door to the Ackers' house, but there was nobody in sight in the hallway. Amesbury turned quickly to me.

"I have an appointment," he rapidly informed me. "Afraid I'll be a little late for it as it is. Tell Mr. Hand that I've gone. I'll try to get in touch with him later on. If he wants me, I'll be back at my hotel in an hour or so."

With that he turned and strode abruptly off. I was not just sure what I should do. A quick glance told me that the detective assigned to Amesbury had turned the corner in the opposite direction. Whether he would have the wit to follow his man I did not know. I could see little good of it, anyway. It is not difficult to throw a man off the track when you know he is following you.

There seemed to be less sense of my taking off after Amesbury. I quickly decided that the best thing I could do was to follow out his request, and at once I set off to inform Hand that his client had departed.

I found both Hand and the inspector in Nick Haggerty's room. Felty, who had not yet been relieved, was peering inquisitively in at them. I elbowed my way by him. Hand, evidently, had filled his little phial once again with the poisonous liquid from the tumbler. He was in the act of handing the phial to Gerrity. In his gloved left hand he held the tumbler.

"There you are, Inspector," he was saying. "I think—"

At that point I burst excitedly into the room. Before I could say a word, however, Hand turned and spoke to me.

"Clark," he said, "are you coming to report that Amesbury has gone off and left you?"

"Why, I—I—" I stammered.

"What's that?" roared Gerrity. "Amesbury gone? Gone where? Answer me, Clark!"

"I don't know where he's gone," I replied. "How should I? He just said he had an appointment and that he was afraid he'd be late. That's all I know."

"An appointment, yes," said Hand, his eyes shining with satisfaction. "Everything is working out nicely, Inspector. Perhaps Mrs. Ackner will get her money back tonight, who knows? Really, I am quite delighted."

"Did Amesbury tell you where he was going?" demanded Gerrity.

"Yes," replied Hand, with a chuckle. "But I'll wager that he didn't know it."

"What are you talking about?" snapped Gerrity. "What's this appointment of his, anyhow?"

"Come, Inspector," said Hand, briskly. "We are going out, and I'll tell you all about it on the way. We are wasting valuable time here. Take this tumbler; you'll want it examined for finger-prints, you know."

Gerrity quickly wrapped the tumbler up in his handkerchief.

"I'm carrying enough stuff!" he grumbled. "I've got over four thousand dollars in this box, and it isn't safe to carry that much money about. The department is forever discouraging it."

"Give it to the chauffeur, along with the tumbler and the knife-blade," advised Hand, as we passed swiftly down the hallway. "Tell him to take it all to headquarters. They can put the money in a safe, examine the tumbler for prints, and endeavor to find where that knife was purchased."

"But aren't we going to use my car?"

"By no means. Your car is entirely too conspicuous. We shall have to once again entrust our valuable lives to the mercies of a taxi driver. You know, Inspector, I believe the majority of these New York taxicabs were designed for the benefit of the amorous, but their dark recesses also do splendidly for sleuthing. Get rid of those things, and let's find a suitable cab."

Gerrity dispatched his car to police headquarters, and we set off in quest of a cab. As we passed before the parsonage of the Hendly Congregational Church, the same fellow I had seen lurking about it before slunk furtively into an alleyway across the street. I was about to mention something about him, but at that moment the inspector bellowed at a passing cab. We got in, and Hand gave the driver a number on Third Avenue. The inspector, something more than curiosity in his bearing, turned to Hand.

"Ah, Inspector, you want to know where I got that address. My eyes told me where Amesbury was going, and my imagination tells me what he is going to do there."

"Well, suppose you stop talking in riddles and tell me what your eyes and your imagination have told you. Nothing has told me a blasted thing!"

"Very well. While we were in Ackner's bedroom waiting for Clark to return with his wife, I saw Amesbury glance nervously at his watch. Then he took from his vest pocket a slip of paper and peered intently at it. He held it cautiously, but by good fortune there was hanging on the wall near his left shoulder a mirror. In it I read, in reverse, the address to which we are now going. All clear, Inspector?"

"How do you know that he's going there?"

"That is where the imagination comes in. When Clark told us of his experience in the restaurant this afternoon, it looked on the surface of it as if our friend Filipo had got clean away from us. But our contact with him is through Amesbury, and I reasoned that he would hardly let Amesbury out of his clutches so easily. I rather think, Inspector, that Filipo has communicated with Amesbury since and arranged a new rendezvous."

"And you think we're headed for that rendezvous now, eh? By thunder, I hope you're right! We might catch the pair of them at it red-handed! What do you think of my getting a few men down there, just in case we might need them?"

"I don't think we'll need them, Inspector. We three are armed, and we have handled similar situations before. If we resort to numbers more than likely we should merely frighten our bird right out of our hands. Besides, we have no idea of the physical features of the place where we must play our game. In such circumstances a small group can be maneuvered far more effectively than a cumbersome number of men. No, I am well satisfied with things as they are."

The physical features of the rendezvous, upon first sight, were not reassuring. It was a large tenement house. By the greatest good luck we had discovered out of the millions in the city an address, and now we found that the address was virtually a city in itself. Where in that huge pile of brick and mortar were the two men whom we sought?

"The thing to do," growled Gerrity, "is to get a couple of platoons of patrolmen down here and go through this blasted place from top to bottom!"

"Let's dismiss the cab," suggested Hand, "and make ourselves less conspicuous."

We entered the building and sought concealment in a darkened corner of the entrance hall.

"If we are at the right place," said Hand, "there are two possibilities. Either our men are here ahead of us, or they have not yet arrived. In either case they will have to use the entrances of this building. Clark, you stay here at the front entrance. If either Amesbury or Filipo enters, follow him to whatever floor he goes, mark the room he goes into, and post yourself in the hall. The inspector and I will find you. Now then, Inspector, you and I will reconnoiter and see how many entrances this building has. We'll meet here. Don't let yourself be recognized."

For several minutes I lurked alone in the gloomy hallway. Two men came into the building. Neither was Filipo, and neither could have been Amesbury. They passed right by without seeing me. Hand and the inspector rejoined me simultaneously. Hand took my arm.

"Fortunately," he said, "there are only two means of getting in or out of this building. They are at the extremities of this hallway. Come along, Clark, there is an alcove down here from which we can watch both doors without ourselves being seen. We won't have to separate, either."

We were soon ensconced in the dark alcove, like three thugs waiting for the arrival of a wealthy traveler on a lonely highway. Very soon after, a man silently descended the stairs and took up a station in the same corner that I had been standing in. He might have been a shadow, so silent was his progress. I was sure that it was Filipo.

With all his stealth, Filipo could still take a lesson from Hand. My friend, like an apparition passing through the gloom, moved off away from us and crouched beside the stairs. Gerrity and I remained breathless in the alcove.

The front door opened smartly, and a man stepped into the hall. He strode swiftly over to the stairs and mounted them. Still we could see the dim outline of Christopher Hand remaining motionless by the stairs. Another five minutes went by, and then came the protesting squeak that denoted another newcomer at the front. A vague form entered the hallway. Then a low, silky, ominous voice broke the stillness.

"You are late, my frien'," it said. "I thought you no show up."

"Oh, I showed up, all right," growled the voice of Woodford Amesbury. "Here, you dirty rat, take your money and don't ever let me see you again. I don't know why I'm doing this, but take it and get out!"

"Ah, not so fas', my frien'. I have a room upstair; we go up, eh?"

"I've been in enough of your filthy holes! Here, take your money and get away from me. In another minute I'll change my mind."

"Yes, you will change it and come with me, Mucker. I have what you call the goods on you, eh? You do not want me to send the leetle letter to the police. Come, we weell not be long."

"What the devil more do you want?"

"We will talk about that upstair, yes?"

We heard Amesbury growl something in an undertone; then they scuffled across the floor. A second later we heard them mounting the stairs. Hand moved silently off toward the staircase, and Gerrity and I followed him. But we waited out of sight until the pair we were following had left the stairs. Then Hand, motioning for us to remain where we were, set off in silent pursuit. Once again I marveled at his ability to get about anywhere seemingly without making the slightest sound. Those stairs had protested quite loudly when Filipo and Amesbury trod them. But Hand planted his feet close to the wall, and as he advanced his body seemed to slip upward, almost as though it were on wires.

He disappeared from our view at the top of the stairs. The inspector and I continued to peer up into the darkness. But Hand soon reappeared, motioning for us to come up. We made the ascent as silently as possible and joined Hand at the second floor. He glanced quickly round.

"I have them located," he whispered. "Follow me. No noise, now."

At length we stood in a gloomy corridor before a door. Hand and the inspector placed their ears to the panel. But even standing away from it, as I was, I could hear Amesbury's voice raised in bitter imprecation.

"I might have known you would betray me into a trap, you despicable cur!" he said. "So this is your gang of cut-throats, is it?"

"These are my frien's," replied Filipo's oily voice. "You do not like them, eh? But then, I did not theenk you would, Mr. Mucker Amesbury."

"Well," growled another voice, "what ya gonna do about it, big boy?"

"Since you ask," replied Amesbury, angrily, "I'm going to turn the whole pack of you over to the police the first chance I get!"

This was followed by a round of jeering laughter.

"Ya ain't gonna git the chance, fella," said one. "Quit the stallin'. What we're after is the fifty grand, get it? Ya got it stowed away somewhere, and we're on to it, see? Come across, or we'll take ya fer a nice little ride, Mucker."

"Ya don't even git no ride," corrected another. "Spill the info or ya go out o' this here room feet first, get me? Spill it, dam' ya!"

"Is it impossible for me to convince you?" shouted Amesbury, "that I haven't this dirty money you are after? I wouldn't give it to you if I did have it, you filthy rats! I'll give you one minute to open that door, and if you—"

"You'll give us one minute, will ya?" snarled a voice. "Ya got yer nerve with ya, guy. But ya can't bluff out o' this! Now I'll tell ya what we're gonna give you. We're gonna give you one minute to open up yer face, get me? Look down the little hole in this here rod. Yer gonna get somethin' out o' that in just one minute if ya don't talk! Either we get the dope in sixty seconds, or yer gonna take on a lot o' weight in a hurry. Now do yer thinkin', quick!"

Christopher Hand, like an expert cracksman manipulating the dial of a safe, was turning the knob of the door. He made not the slightest sound, and yet he was frustrated. The door was locked. A prickly sensation crept up my spine as I watched the little second hand of my wrist watch steadily advancing. Not a sound came from the room. Forty seconds had sped before Hand grasped me by the arm.

"All together," he hissed. "We've got to break down that door!"

Drawing our pistols from our pockets, we stepped back a pace. Then, at a signal from Hand, we hurled our combined weight against the door. It splintered from its hinges and flew into the room, all three of us hurtling in after it.

I lost my balance and fell on top of the wrecked door. Something was squirming beneath it. Hand and Gerrity charged by me. A quick glance showed me that three men besides Amesbury were standing in the room. With a cry of alarm, one made a rush for the single window. Another raised an automatic and aimed it at Hand. The third, Filipo, cowered in a corner, unable to flee or defend himself. Hand's pistol spat flame and smoke, and the fellow with the automatic dropped the weapon and howled with pain. Gerrity leaped across the room, seized the neck of the fellow attempting to escape through the window, and tossed him in a quaking heap on the floor.

The wriggling beneath the door on which I knelt increased in vigor. Glancing down, I beheld a hand protruding from under the door. Clutched tightly in the hand was a wicked-looking pistol. I leaped to my feet and brought my heel sharply down on the fellow's wrist. His fingers released the pistol, and from under the door came a muffled shout of pain. I quickly picked up the pistol. Leaning over, I grasped the door by its edge and threw it over. A rough-looking chap peered apprehensively up at me with eyes gleaming with fear. I fancied that he was the chap who had been talking so fiercely a moment before. There was nothing terrible about him now.

"Get up on your feet," I ordered him. "And it will pay you to be careful."

Rubbing his injured wrist, he got slowly to his feet. Hand and Gerrity quickly frisked all four of them. They stood dejectedly against the wall, flinching before Gerrity's baneful inspection.

"I—I say," gasped Amesbury. "Where in thunder did you fellows come from?"

"Never mind," snapped Gerrity. "It was a bit lucky we did come, I'll tell you!"

"Good heaven, yes!" agreed Amesbury, fervently. "I thought I was living my last minute. What a fearful set of ruffians they were a moment ago. But look at them now, will you! My word, I almost pity them."

"You do?" sneered Gerrity. "I don't! These birds are going to the cleaners."

Our prisoners shifted uncomfortably and dropped their eyes. Of all their dejection, Filipo's was the worst. He trembled from head to foot, his face twitching and his fingers jerking spasmodically. He glanced up fearfully, saw Hand's eyes gleaming at him, and all but cried out in terror as he hastily averted his face. Gerrity turned fiercely upon Amesbury.

"What'd you mean by sneaking off to this place?" he snapped.

"Never mind that now, Inspector," said Hand, crisply. "We must get these fellows into safe-keeping. Clark and I will stand guard over them while you go order a patrol wagon. Have your own car driven over here, too. You'll find a telephone booth on the corner below, I think."

Gerrity nodded curtly and left the room. I recognized, besides Filipo, two of the men who had stood guard over Miss Blake and me in the restaurant that afternoon. One of them, the fellow who had been pinned under the door, plainly recognized me. Regaining some of his lost bravado, he essayed to glare vengefully at me, a snarl on his lips.

"I wish t' Gawd I'd o' bumped ya off when I seen ya before!" he muttered.

"If you had," I retorted, cheerfully, "you would be having by now a life-sized picture of the electric chair. I'm not so sure that you won't get it, anyhow. Inspector Gerrity is very thorough about the pasts of men who fall into his hands. What a pity you fellows ruin your lives as you do!"

My words seemed to make them more uncomfortable.

Nothing more was said until Gerrity rejoined us. He eyed Amesbury even more coldly than he did our prisoners. I knew that he would have given much to get Hand's client off by himself.

"Questioned these fellows yet?" he demanded.

"Not yet," replied Hand. "There is only one that I care about, and I don't want to question him here. Your patrol wagon will arrive soon?"

"Any minute," replied Gerrity. "Which one of this bunch is that fellow Filipo?"

"There he is," I replied, pointing Filipo out to him. "The one with the little black mustache. I swear, Gerrity, if you make a move you'll scare him to death."

Amesbury appeared astonished that I could identify Filipo so readily. He began to appear rather embarrassed, although he bit his lip and tried to cover it up. I could see that Hand, out of the tail of his eye, was watching his client narrowly.

Filipo's rendezvous being not far from police headquarters, it did not take the patrol wagon long to arrive. When the bluecoats entered the room, Hand strode over and took Filipo by the arm. His prisoner shrank away from him.

"We'll take this fellow along with us, Inspector," said Hand. "He has some valuable information that he is going to give us. Better put the others away in the Tombs for the present. I don't think they are of any value to us."

Thoroughly disheartened, Filipo's three companions allowed themselves to be led quietly from the room. Hand, maintaining his grasp on Filipo's arm, turned to his client. I thought that Amesbury glanced back at him a trifle guiltily.

"I shall have to ask you to accompany us, Mr. Amesbury," said Hand. "I hope that we can soon clean up this mystery, and you should be present."

"Gladly!" complied Amesbury. "By thunder, I hope you are right!"

Gerrity looked thoroughly incredulous at this. Amesbury noticed it and turned away from him. Hand leading Filipo, we descended the stairs and went out to the sidewalk. The inspector's car was standing at the curb. We all crowded into it, and Hand, to my astonishment, ordered the driver to take us to the parsonage of the Hendly Congregational Church.

"Don't stop right before the door," he instructed; "pull up and let us out about fifty feet away from it. And don't waste any time."

On the way over Gerrity was as fidgety as an old hen with a cat lurking about. I guessed, and rightly too, that he had no more idea of what was going on than I had myself. But his dignity, together with his knowledge that it would most likely do no good, prevented him from asking Hand questions. Instead he took turns glaring first at Filipo and then at Amesbury. The client appeared astonished at this. Affected or not, he was distinctly resentful. Hand said nothing, and neither did I. Filipo gnawed his finger-nails and was careful not to glance in the inspector's direction. I was relieved when the car stopped down the street from the parsonage. Hand immediately leaped out.

"You fellows stay here for a minute," he said.

"Are we going to call on Mr. Bothwell?" demanded Gerrity, irritably.

"Yes, but I want to speak to someone first. Be right back."

He strode quickly up the sidewalk on the opposite side of the street from Mr. Bothwell's residence. Arrived at a point directly across from the parsonage, he paused and applied a match to a cigarette. He stood facing the parsonage, the light of the match beating upon his thin features.

Almost immediately a figure detached itself from a bush on the narrow strip of lawn in front of the parsonage. The window of Mr. Bothwell's study, which was just above the bush where the man had been hiding, was aglow with a soft light. The fellow vaulted the low fence and, quickly crossing the street, stepped up to Hand. They conversed for a moment; then they both turned and walked back to us.

I recognized Hand's companion. It was the same fellow I had seen skulking about the vicinity of the parsonage all day.

"Inspector," said Hand, "I could close this case right here, I feel sure. But Schurman here, who has been keeping watch over the parsonage for me, has just given me

some fresh information. In order that you may not mis-
construe what has taken place, I think we should allow
events to advance one step further. You have done a good
job, Schurman; come up to the rooms tomorrow, and I'll
give you a check. Better get home, now. This car is in the
wrong location. It wants to be headed the other way, and
we want to be on the other side of the parsonage from
this."

Hand leaped into the car, and the driver started up. He
drove to the end of the block, turned round, and drove
back until Hand told him to stop. The parsonage lay fifty
yards on ahead of us, and we were headed in the direction
one would take to go from the parsonage to the Blakes'
apartment house. All this was getting Inspector Gerrity
more and more mystified.

"What in blazes are we doing?" he growled. "What's
going on, anyhow?"

"Schurman," replied Hand, "was fortunate enough to
hear Mr. Bothwell talking over the telephone to Mr. Blake
a short while ago. He called a number of others, as well,
and it appears that he has arranged to meet them at Mr.
Blake's very soon now. The meeting is to be at a quarter
of nine, and it lacks ten minutes of that. He should be
coming soon."

Try as assiduously as he would, Gerrity could get nothing further out of Hand. Finally he fell into a sulk, and
from then on we waited in silence, broken occasionally by
a heavy sigh from Filipo.

At twenty minutes of nine Mr. Bothwell emerged from
the parsonage. Under his arm he carried a rather bulky
package. Passing through the iron gate, he turned sharply
and struck off down the street away from us. The motor of
Gerrity's car was idling silently. As Mr. Bothwell turned
the corner in the direction of the Blakes', Hand reached
out and touched the driver on the shoulder.

"Proceed slowly down the street," he said. "Just nose round the corner until we look over the situation."

We rounded the corner just in time to catch a glimpse of Mr. Bothwell ascending the steps to the Blakes' apartment house. He quickly opened the door and stepped inside. Hand ordered the driver to proceed on to the entrance of the house. As the machine stopped before the door, he turned briskly to the inspector.

"We will go in here," said he. "Bring Filipo with you, Inspector."

Gerrity and his prisoner bringing up the rear, we entered the building and immediately mounted the stairs. We passed along the corridor, pausing in a group outside the Blakes' door. As we stood there we heard men's voices raised in excitement, coming to us from inside the apartment. Hand knocked peremptorily, and quiet settled over the apartment.

The door was promptly opened by Mr. Blake. He flushed painfully when he saw who was standing at his door. Hand advanced unceremoniously by him, thus starting a stampede of the rest of us past the astonished Mr. Blake. He tried ineffectually to stem the tide; then he crowded into the living-room after us, complaining bitterly.

Beside a table in the center of the room stood Mr. Bothwell, his left hand resting on a covered shoe-box. I thought I recognized it as the bundle we had seen him carrying on the way over. Surrounding him were the stockholders in the Ajax Mining and Engineering Company. Hand strode up to Mr. Bothwell.

"Should you mind," he asked the minister, "if I open that box?"

Mr. Bothwell bowed his head. He remained thus for fully a minute. Finally he heaved a sigh and raised his eyes to Hand's.

"I suppose there is no alternative," he said, lifting his hand from the box. "Go ahead, Mr. Hand."

Mr. Bothwell, still with bowed head, stepped back from the table. Hand quickly reached forth and lifted the lid from the box. We edged up to the table, craning our necks to see into the box. Gerrity's breath hissed through his teeth. Inside the shoe-box, closely packed together, were two bulging money-belts!

16

THE LAST TRAIL

Christopher Hand reached into the shoe-box. He grasped
the money-belts and dropped them on the table, where
they struck with a heavy thud. One of the belts was heavily stained with blood. Inspector Gerrity turned belligerently to Mr. Bothwell.

"It was you!" he roared. "By thunder, just imagine!"

Mr. Bothwell lifted his hands, as if in protest, and then
he let them fall back dejectedly by his side.

"Hand," cried the inspector, "how in blazes did you
ever find him out?"

All at once there was a mild commotion. Judith Blake,
who had been standing with her mother in the background,
frenziedly pushed her way through the group of men. She
planted herself firmly before Mr. Bothwell, as though she
would protect him from the entire police force of New
York City.

"You shan't arrest him!" she cried, stamping her foot.
"I won't let you!"

Mr. Bothwell smiled sadly. A low growl of approval
rose from the men. Christopher Hand stood gazing down
at the money-belts, but I felt that he did not see them. He
briskly raised his head.

"Inspector," he said, sharply, "I find that I am forced to
play my hand. One or two threads yet dangle, but, as they

are unimportant, they can be gathered later. The theory, however, that forms the strongest link in my chain remains to be tested. I will not present my case until it is. But, quite fortunately, I think that I can test it in a very few minutes."

"What is it?" asked Gerrity.

"If you will accompany me to the laboratory," said Hand, "we shall see whether I am right. If my hypothesis does not fill the gap my case falls to the ground. I stake everything upon its being correct!"

Here was a departure, indeed. Never before had I seen him willing to expound his case before every aspect of it had been thoroughly proved. Perhaps Miss Blake's kiss had stirred him more deeply than I had supposed.

I could see that Hand's suggestion had left Inspector Gerrity in something of a quandary. From the way he was regarding them in turn, I could see that he was mightily anxious to keep Filipo, Amesbury and Mr. Bothwell all very close to him. Something was certainly bothering him, and I could easily imagine that it was how this was to be accomplished if he went off to the laboratory with Hand.

Hand seemed not to mind Gerrity's predicament. He turned and started for the door. Judith Blake said nothing, but a determined light, that I recognized only too well, had come into those brown eyes of hers. She immediately set off in Hand's wake. As if that were a signal, the whole roomful of people started for the door. Gerrity, who with his prisoner was being carried along in the press, set up a clamor of objection.

"Hand!" he shouted. "Hey, Hand! Everybody's following you."

My friend turned in the door and glanced back over the mass behind him. He glanced down at Miss Blake, who was crowding right behind him in a most determined manner. His eyes twinkled as he glanced back at the harassed inspector.

"I fancy everyone is rather interested," he said. "I have no objection, Inspector, although if I am wrong this time there will be no keeping my failure a secret. I should suggest that you bring the money-belts with you, as well as Filipo."

With a mutter of vexation, Gerrity whipped about to peer sharply at the table. So did everyone else. The money-belts, to the vast relief of the stockholders, still lay on the table. Gerrity, pulling Filipo with him, struggled through the crush round him and gained the table. He placed the money-belts back in the shoe-box. Then he picked it up and followed after the rest of us, who were trooping through the door.

As we passed through it, Mr. Zinger's corridor resembled the entrance to a subway station. The little superintendent opened his door and thrust his head out, just as Gerrity was leading Filipo by. Mr. Zinger's face blanched, and he made a hoarse sound in his throat. Then he hastily withdrew his head and slammed his door.

The policeman guarding the laboratory door unlocked it for us. We all entered as quickly as possible, and Hand switched on the light. Gerrity glanced apprehensively about, located Amesbury and Mr. Bothwell, tightened his grip on Filipo's arm, and relaxed a little. Hand leaned against the work-bench and frowned into space. A silence quite appalling ensued as we stood expectantly regarding him. Finally he stirred and peered sharply over at the inspector.

"I have steadfastly held," said he, "that the key to this mystery lay here in this laboratory. Although efforts to locate it have come to naught, I have always been positive that there exists a secret means of leaving this place."

"Impossible!" cried Gerrity. "Don't think that I have ignored that theory. The walls, floor and ceiling of this room have been thoroughly examined. There is no possibility of a secret exit being concealed in the walls! There is no trap-door in the floor, and every board on the floor is securely nailed down!"

"I quite agree with you, Inspector. Everything you have said is entirely correct."

"Then you have abandoned the theory that there is a secret means of leaving this laboratory?"

"On the contrary, I am more certain than ever that there is one."

Inspector Gerrity smiled pityingly.

"You haven't been working too hard, have you, Hand?" he asked.

"No," grunted Hand, with surprising abruptness springing away from the work-bench. "As I said, Inspector, I have had no opportunity to put my theory to the test. That is not altogether regrettable; it provides me with the opportunity of demonstrating to you the power of the imagination in the solution of crime. But I am forced to admit that the foundation of my hypothesis rests upon one or two significant details that I was fortunate enough to detect. Here, Clark, help me move this work-bench a few inches."

Together we shifted the bench about four inches in the direction that it faced. Hand stepped behind it, and everyone moved round in order to keep him in full view. He reached out his foot and tapped his toe on one of the wide floor-boards. It was one of the boards upon which the workbench rested, and it extended out behind the bench a distance of approximately five feet.

"That board," said Hand, slowly, "is the secret means of leaving this laboratory."

"But that board is nailed down!" objected Gerrity. "There are four nails in it on this side of the bench, two on the sides and two on the end of it. You can see them plainly enough!"

"So it would appear. But here is one of the indications upon which I base my hypothesis. Notice this indentation in the board."

He pointed to a mark across the board directly on the line where the work-bench had rested upon it. I had noticed the mark before.

"That mark," said he, "was made by the bottom edge of the work-bench cutting into the board. There is no other such mark in these other boards that the bench rested upon. It must have been made by the board being forced against the edge of the bench."

"Maybe it was," conceded Gerrity. "But the fact is that the board is securely nailed down, and, if a man pried it up and dropped through it, it isn't possible that he could have nailed it down again from the top. It wasn't nailed from below; my men would have detected that!"

"The board is certainly nailed down, as you say, but it was nailed neither from above nor from below. The energy that nailed it down is contained in the board itself. Here again my hypothesis was aided by detection together with known facts. Mr. White complains that someone stole a hammer and file from this laboratory. They were both used on this board, and now they both lie among the rubbish in the door-well beneath the porch outside the laboratory door. The murderer stole them from here. Then he carried them, at night, I imagine, into the basement beneath us. He stood upon a box, wrapped a cloth round the hammer, and hammered this board up. The box with the marks of his shoes on it is still in the basement, and by going out to that door-well you can see for yourself the cloth-wrapped hammer."

"And then what?"

"Then he proceeded to file the nails in this board flush with its under-side, thus leaving the heads convincingly hammered into the top of the board. To all appearances the board is just as securely nailed down as it ever was."

"But the board *is* nailed down, I tell you!"

"Undoubtedly. I tested it. But it nailed itself down, Inspector. Our man hammered two nails, I should say, into the end of the board, from the under-side, between the two nailed through from the upper-side that he had filed off. Then he filed the heads off the nails he had driven into the under-side. More than that, he filed sharp points on them. Thus he had two double-pointed spikes, the upper parts half way through the board, and the rest of them protruding from the under-side of the board at its end. Do you follow me?"

"Yes, yes. I begin to see what you are driving at."

"Bear in mind that the heavy work-bench rested upon the other end of the plank. By forcing the loose end up a powerful spring action was obtained. Suddenly released, the board would fly back to its flat position, driving the spikes in its under-side into the floor-beam below it. Thus it would actually nail itself down."

"Could it be possible! For heaven's sake, Hand, pry it up!"

Hand quickly complied. He seized a large screw-driver from the work-bench and advanced to the end of the board. The screw-driver, a huge, strong instrument nearly two feet long, he inserted into the crack between the end of the board in question and the one that abutted it. Slowly he drew back on it, and the floor-board moved up an inch. Obtaining a new bite with the screw-driver, he pried against the board again. Working the screw-driver under the board, he at length was able to get his fingers under the board.

"This is not the first time this board has been pried back, Inspector," he said, looking up at Gerrity.

"No; I saw that the edge of that abutting board was crushed down, just as you're crushing it down now with that screw-driver. Hurry up! Pull it up so that we can see whether you're right."

The plank was thick and solid. It took all Hand's strength to force it back. But he did bend it slowly back, until, with a quick movement, he propped it back by thrusting the screw-driver under it, bracing it lengthwise between the floor-beam and the board.

Hand stooped quickly and glanced sharply under the curved board. As he stepped back I knew instantly that he had vindicated his theory. His eyes kindled with triumph, and he rubbed his long hands together with satisfaction.

Everyone crowded forward and inspected the under-side of the board. Excited exclamations of astonishment and admiration rose from the group. There was only one instance where Hand's hypothesis had erred. There were three spikes in the end of the board instead of two.

"I think, Inspector," he said, quietly, "that I am now ready to present my case."

"And by thunder," growled Gerrity, "I'm more than ready to hear it!"

"Do you mean to say that you are still in doubt as to the identity of the murderer?"

Gerrity scowled darkly, first at Amesbury, then at Mr. Bothwell, and finally, with a great deal of malignancy, at Filipo.

"Well," he growled, "he's right here in this room!"

"I'm afraid you are mistaken, Inspector," sighed Hand, sadly shaking his head. "The murderer of Nick Haggerty was Jeremy Amesbury."

A mixture of reactions greeted this amazing announce-ment, among them astonishment, incredulity and, in one

or two cases, open resentment. Inspector Gerrity resignedly shrugged his shoulders.

"I'm afraid you'll have to prove that to me," he said.

"As I said before," pointed out Hand, "I am now in a
position to do it. It would be just as well, I think, to treat
this matter in its proper chronological order. We shall
deal first with the character of the man whom I have just
accused. It was distinctly criminal. He served two terms
for swindling in San Quentin Prison, the first in 1914 and
the second in 1921."

"My word!" I gasped. "How could you determine that
on such short notice? Why, the murder occurred less than
twenty-four hours ago!"

"I was led to the discovery of that," smiled Hand, "by
Mr. Bothwell."

"I—I told you that?" stammered Mr. Bothwell, in confusion.

"Not exactly," replied Hand. "You keep a file, however,
containing data on everyone in your congregation. Last
night when we called on you I pilfered Jeremy Amesbury's
pigeon-hole. I thought that there might be something of
interest in it, and there was. He wrote Mr. Bothwell in
1914 from San Quentin Prison. The burden of his cry was
that he had been jailed on false testimony, but I imagine the testimony was quite authentic. He was asking for
funds in order to engage legal talent. By the address on
the envelope, Mr. Bothwell at the time was the pastor of
a church in Salem, Massachusetts. At the first opportunity I dispatched a wire to San Quentin Prison, asking for
particulars. Amesbury was known to them as Arthur Jack-
son, but Mucker Amesbury was one of his aliases. They
are sending me his finger-prints, Inspector, according to
the wire I received from them. We can check them with
Amesbury's."

"You—you stole that letter right under my nose?" asked Mr. Bothwell, as if he could not comprehend it.

"Not quite," smiled Hand. "When I took it both Inspector Gerrity and Clark were unconsciously screening me. When I put it back this afternoon Clark was standing between you and me. He politely stepped out of the way and all but left me exposed to discovery. I am bound to say, in justice to Mr. Bothwell, that he probably thought he had completely Christianized Jeremy Amesbury, and therefore he had no compunction about letting these people invest their money with him."

I glanced at Woodford Amesbury. He had hung his head, but these glaring accusations Hand had levelled at his uncle seemed to rouse no anger within his breast. Gerrity was so amazed that he all but forgot to cling to Filipo.

"So you see," went on Hand, "I had taken a long step toward the solution of the case. But the way lay in darkness, with here and there a beacon of evidence illuminating it. From the information I had received from San Quentin, I was certain that Jeremy Amesbury was as resourceful and cunning a criminal as we are likely ever to encounter. I began to reconstruct his plot.

"There is on Mr. Blake's living-room table a piece of what appears to be a specimen taken from a vein of gold ore. When we dropped in at the Blakes' last night I examined it intently. I thought I detected something peculiar about it. When I wired to Alaska for particulars on Amesbury and Haggerty, I suggested that the assayer give Amesbury's ore a second test, with a view to determining positively whether it had been salted. Salted, I might explain, is a term used to designate bogus ore. It is accomplished quite simply by discharging a shot gun loaded with particles of pure gold into a vein of rock. I received two telegrams from Alaska, one verifying the presence of

Amesbury and Haggerty in Alaska last spring. A subsequent wire, which I received this afternoon, verified my suspicions concerning that ore. It is salted."

"Then the mine is no good!" cried Mr. Blake.

"I'm afraid not. But I did not wait for verification; I assumed that Amesbury's gold mine was a myth. It was merely part of his nefarious scheme. But why should he have come to New York when he might have played his game on the west coast? His record was bad there. Here he could play the part of an honest prospector without fear of detection. I paid little attention to the story he told of accidentally coming across Mr. Bothwell's name in a newspaper. In fact, I paid little attention to any of his stories, including that of the desperate battle with the Portuguese. His nephew and Mr. Bothwell considered him a romancer, but I considered him a liar. His stories lent color to his plot; they were enticing to his victims. There is published each year a book containing the names and churches ministered to by them of every clergyman in the country. It was simple for Amesbury to locate his boyhood friend who, if I may be pardoned for saying so, he probably knew as being quite innocently gullible. I have set a number of inquiries afoot to determine whether Amesbury actually did honestly seek to obtain money before he laid his proposal at the door of the Hendly Congregational Church. I have yet to hear from a single financial house that he did. It was quite apparent that he and Haggerty came to New York intent upon swindling Mr. Bothwell's congregation."

"Then what in blazes did he want to kill Haggerty for?" demanded Inspector Gerrity.

"There came a hitch in his plans. He raised the money quite easily, and he was also fortunate in persuading these people to let him take fifty thousand dollars away in cash on a very flimsy excuse."

"Oh, I have been blind!" cried Gerrity.

"But then came the hitch," went on Hand. "Mr. Anderson, by the grace of good fortune, lost his job and elected to go to Alaska. I am quite certain that Jeremy Amesbury did not persuade Mr. Anderson to go to Alaska with him. He had no intention of going to Alaska. It was decidedly inimical to his plans that any one of the stockholders should leave New York with him. He had to switch his plans hurriedly, and I must say that he did it adroitly. Haggerty was the victim of his new plot. Such is the honor among thieves."

"Of course, of course!" said Gerrity. "Go on, Hand."

"Things fell out nicely for Amesbury. Larry White was desperately trying to raise money. Upon his shoulders the guilt should be directed. Amesbury dropped in here recently, no doubt, and, when White was not looking, purloined the hammer and the file. That was where he made his first mistake; he should have bought them. Then he proceeded to arrange this floor-board in the manner I have demonstrated. What held his hand until the final evening before their departure, we can merely guess. When Haggerty returned from the Blakes' party last night, Amesbury, who on a pretext had left early, had fixed him a drink in his room. It was the deadly potion that we found in the tumbler. Haggerty drank it and fell dead. Thereupon Amesbury tied a rope round his body and lowered it out the bedroom window to the courtyard below. He threw the rope out after it, and quickly left the room."

"Is that guess-work?" asked Gerrity.

"By no means. Several strands of hemp are caught in the bricks outside Haggerty's bedroom window. They were torn from the weighted rope as it passed over them. The window-sill is slightly scored where the rope was paid out over it, too."

"Why didn't I see that!" exclaimed Gerrity, with an expression of annoyance.

"After lowering the body out the window," went on Hand, "Amesbury just had time to skip back to his own room to play a rather grim trick upon Mrs. Ackner. It was a drama in which he depicted his own murder. This he did by the expedient of breaking the blade from a knife, lying prone on the floor, and affixing the knife-handle to his chest to simulate his having been stabbed through the heart. When the desired effect had been produced upon the landlady, he rushed out of his room and down the stairs. While she was gone after the policeman, Amesbury put a slight cut in his wrist and smeared the blood from it over the blade of his bowie-knife. This he threw into the closet under the stairs in order that you, Inspector, might be aided in your deduction concerning the murder."

Gerrity was all but gnashing his teeth in mortification.

"Then," went on Hand, "Amesbury went out to the courtyard through the back door of the Ackners' building. He shouldered Haggerty's corpse and carried it over to the laboratory. There he laid it down while he climbed up to the window and broke in here. The rope served again to haul the body into the laboratory through the window. There are more pieces of hemp clinging to the bricks outside this window. They are among those beacons that I mentioned which throw their light along the trail. There being no further use for the rope, it was untied from the body and thrown over into that corner of the laboratory where it now lies. Amesbury carried the body into that closet, provided himself with a hammer from the workbench, and with it crushed in Haggerty's skull. Then he took the money-belt from it.

"I think that Filipo can verify part of what I said. Filipo, tell us what you saw out of that window next door."

Filipo's face gleamed whitely. As he became the center of attraction he shrank back and glanced fearfully about. Gerrity shook him roughly.

"Speak up, you!" he growled. "Be quick about it, if you know what's good for you!"

"I tell you," whined Filipo. "I tell you everything. I see Mucker Amesbury on the street, but he did not see me. I know he ees up to something, and I rent the apartment to watch heem. Las' night I see Mucker, but he ees mad that I fin' heem, and he tell me nothing. But later I see heem carry a man across the open out back. By gar, eet ees Nick Haggerty—dead! Mucker break into the laboratory, just like you say. I open the window in my apartment and climb out. Mucker has take Nick into the laboratory, and he has close the window. I climb up, but I can see nothing. I theenk Mucker come out; so I climb down and wait. But he deed not come out. At las' I rush all over. I try to find heem, but he ees gone. Then, today, I see Mucker walking weeth you. He ees disguise, he look younger, but Mucker could do that. I try to get heem to geeve me money. Then you capture me. That ees all I know."

"No," disagreed Hand, peering sharply at Filipo. "I think you can tell me something else. As you watched Mucker Amesbury carry Nick Haggerty across the court out back, what did you see in Mucker Amesbury's mouth?"

Filipo's own mouth dropped open, and his eyes gleamed with awe.

"In hees mouth?"

"Between his teeth."

"It—it look like a knife! I theenk he was carry a knife in hees teeth. It was shiny, but it was a ver' funny looking knife."

Hand veiled his cold eyes, and a suggestion of a smile passed momentarily over his stern lips. Then his eyes flew open again.

"Now let us get back to where we left Jeremy Amesbury in the laboratory," he said. "He had been wearing gloves in order to keep from leaving his finger-prints about.

After securing Haggerty's money-belt, he took them off. You will find them, Inspector, in the drawer of that work-bench. Then Amesbury slipped through the floor in the manner we have seen. Here two other costly mistakes took effect. He had neglected to provide himself with an electric torch. Groping about in the dark below here, he lost his way among those confusing old walls. Mr. Zinger did identically the same thing this morning, and Mr. Zinger had a light. At the end of the space between the walls where Amesbury lost his way lies the old furnace pit. Moving blindly forward, Amesbury tumbled into it.

"And that is where the second mistake cost him his life. Had he safely disposed of the blade he broke from the knife-handle, he might have made good his escape, and we should never have found him. A blade without a handle is a treacherous thing for one to have about him, especially a thin, keen blade such as that. Placed in a pocket or thrust under a belt, it could very easily wound the bearer. It was equally dangerous in the money-belt, as Amesbury contemplated climbing through the laboratory window and then through the laboratory floor. I reasoned that the safest place for him to carry it was between his teeth. This he did, I believe, until he had dropped through the laboratory floor into the basement. Having climbed through the window and dropped through the floor, there was no further justification for his carrying the blade between his teeth. It cannot be supposed, in fact, that he would walk through the streets of New York carrying a knife in such an outrageously conspicuous manner. He took the knife-blade from between his teeth and carried it in his left hand. His supreme mistake was in not placing it immediately in a pocket. He still held it in his left hand when he pitched head-foremost into the furnace pit. As he fell, he followed a natural instinct, putting his hands out before him to break his fall. He must have been carrying the blade point upward. He struck full on his chest, and his left arm, you will recollect, was doubled under him. The knife-blade was forced through his left hand, inflicting a deep cut on the palm. This wound bled profusely. For that reason, of course, I was convinced that Amesbury had not met his death in his bedroom, where there was no blood-stain to be found. No, Inspector, he died in that pit. He fell heavily on the knife, and the blade was driven deep into his heart. A just Providence killed him instantly."

Hand finished speaking, and a heavy silence fell upon the laboratory. Gerrity, at length, cleared his throat noisily.

"I agree with everything you have said, Hand," he said. "But there is something that you have left unexplained. If Amesbury died in that manner, why do we find the money-belts in Mr. Bothwell's possession. That is something that has got to be explained to me!"

Never have I seen a man look more helpless than did Mr. Bothwell at that moment. He glanced beseechingly, pleadingly at Hand.

"My story would never be believed," he said, with a dismal shake of his head. "My motives, however misguided they may have been, were in the interests of my flock. Mr. Hand, you are a veritable Prophet. If you could explain my actions, coming from your lips there is no one who could doubt them. I implore you to explain what I did, for if I tell it, Mr. Gerrity will never believe me!"

"I shall be delighted to try," smiled Hand. "If I stray from the facts, you will correct me. Mr. Bothwell, Inspector, is by no means a bad criminologist. As a logician I am afraid you would find it hard to show me his peer in the police department. I fancy that we gave him a nasty shock last night, when we told him that Jeremy Amesbury and the funds of the Ajax company were both missing. He readily conceived, I imagine, that perhaps he had not made such a Godly man out of Mucker Amesbury after all. His trend of thought was similar to mine. He reasoned that if Amesbury were at the bottom of the tragedy, Larry White was the logical person for him to cast suspicion upon. I have found out from the men who were working here on the case for you last night that Mr. Bothwell came over and made inquiries. The result of his investigation convinced him that, if indeed Amesbury had made an escape from the laboratory, the basement was the logical place for him to look for evidence to that effect. He went there. He could tell us whether he got lost among the walls, or whether he determined to explore all parts of the basement. The fact is, however, that he came upon the furnace pit. He had a small, but nevertheless effective electric torch. He did not fall into the pit, but he saw Jeremy Amesbury's body lying in it. The thought that attracted him most was to secure the money and carry it to a safe place.

"He removed the money-belt from Amesbury's body. It is the one that is stained with blood. He picked up the one belonging to Haggerty. Amesbury had not strapped that round him; it would have been blood-stained if he had. Mr. Bothwell's natural instinct was to conceal the belts on his person until he got home. He unbuttoned his coat in order to don the money-belts. In his agitation he snipped a button off his coat. Having put on the money-belts under his coat, he swiftly repaired to the parsonage. With a good deal of relief, I imagine, he put the money away in a safe spot. Then he began to repent his rash act.

"It is not hard to conceive of an impractical man following an unwise course in such a circumstance. How was he to explain having the money in his possession? How was he to explain not having reported at once his having discovered the body? He felt that by, tacitly at least, recommending Amesbury to his church-folk he was morally responsible for the money they had invested. He determined to hold on to the money at all costs, believing that the body would soon be discovered, anyway.

"But as time wore on, Mr. Bothwell's conscience began to tell on him. There was Woodford Amesbury, terribly concerned over the fate of his uncle. Mr. Bothwell had every reason to believe, and so have I, that Woodford Amesbury considered his uncle an upright, honest man. And here was Mr. Bothwell in full knowledge of Jeremy Amesbury's fate. He successfully resisted the urge to put an end to Woodford Amesbury's terrible uncertainty until this afternoon; then it got the better of him. He called Mr. Amesbury and anonymously informed him that his uncle was no more. He used the term no more, and that gave me a clue to his identity, for he had used the same term with much the same connection last night.

"Woodford Amesbury, however, was not the only one on Mr. Bothwell's mind. He was also thinking of all these people, who were desolate at what they considered the irretrievable loss of their money. Finally he could keep them in ignorance no longer. He called them up this evening, and arranged to meet them at Mr. Blake's. Of course it is obvious that he intended to return the money to its owners. I fancy, too, that he intended to ask their advice concerning what course he should follow regarding Jeremy Amesbury's body, which, so far as he knew, remained undiscovered."

"But," asked Gerrity, "what was he doing when we discovered him in the basement this morning?"

"I should imagine, Inspector," replied Hand, "that he was looking for the button that he had discovered had been lost from his coat. He probably realized he had dropped it in the basement, and he was afraid that it would incriminate him."

"Bless my soul!" exclaimed Mr. Bothwell. "You have astounded me, Mr. Hand! Surely the Lord put you on this earth for some good purpose. But how, from a few meager traces of them, you can deduce a man's past actions so far surpasses my understanding that I am unable even to begin to comprehend it. I regard it as a miracle! Why, there is not one thing that I can add to or detract from your recital of my connection with this deplorable affair!"

"Just the same," growled Gerrity, "you should have informed the police that you had possession of the money."

"I don't know, Inspector," smiled Hand. "There is nothing so unusual in the treasurer of a company's having its funds in his possession. But now let me wind this case up. I think the only aspect that yet need be expatiated is that of our capture of Filipo. I feel that this is essential in order to show that my client was merely a victim of sinister circumstances. I was quite positive that Filipo had witnessed Jeremy Amesbury enter the laboratory last night, and I felt equally certain that from that point on Filipo lost track of him. He knew Amesbury of old, and, even though he perhaps had not received certain knowledge of it, he felt sure that Amesbury's crime had been committed for money. He was quite anxious to locate Amesbury in order to blackmail him. Reasoning thus, I hoped that Filipo would make the mistake of taking Woodford Amesbury for his uncle in disguise. In this, of course, I placed my trust in the remarkable resemblance between uncle and nephew.

"It was in this connection that I asked you to keep secret the discovery of Jeremy Amesbury's body. Had Filipo learned of it, you may be sure that he would straightway have disappeared, and we should have lost our eye-witness. As it was I felt confident that sooner or later he would get in touch with Woodford Amesbury, and if he did, I meant to have him."

"That is all very well," said Gerrity, "but what was Woodford Amesbury doing handing five hundred dollars over to this crook?"

"I suppose I was foolish," said Amesbury, hanging his head. "But the fact was that this fellow intended to blacken my uncle's name if I didn't pay him. He refused to believe that I was not my uncle. He had newspaper clippings concerning my uncle, and although they were old and faded, they certainly gave my uncle a vile reputation. He threatened to send them to the newspapers and the police, together with the information that my uncle had murdered Nick Haggerty. Of course I refused to believe that, but then, Filipo refused to believe me!"

"Hum—m, well," growled Gerrity, "it's a mighty good thing for you that Christopher Hand investigated this case! Well, Hand, you have made a complete job of it. There is left only one bit of evidence to be uncovered."

"You refer to the knife-handle, of course."

"Yes. It was not in Amesbury's pockets, and it was not in his room. I'll swear that it was not in that closet under the stairs. But we must find that."

"I think it will present no problem. Obviously he intended to carry it away with him. I should look for it in his money-belt."

Gerrity quickly handed the box containing the money-belts to me. I laid it on the work-bench and extracted the blood-stained belt. Hastily running my fingers over its bulging pockets, I felt an object in among the bank-notes. I opened the pocket and pulled it out. It was a knife-handle with the blade broken cleanly off.

"I think the knife-blade you have at headquarters will fit that," said Hand. "And now, as a final bit of advice, I suggest that the Ajax Mining and Engineering Company be dissolved and its funds returned to the stockholders."

"It is rather dubious, flying in the face of your advice, Mr. Hand," said Mr. Bothwell. "But for some time past we have discussed putting money behind Larry White. Mr. Patcher is with the National Electric Company and, therefore, knows a good deal about electrical appliances. He says that Larry White has a marvelous idea for an electric furnace. I should not be surprised if we put our resources behind him so that he can perfect it. I feel positive that such an act would enrich us all."

"I think it will too!" cried Hand. "It is a splendid idea."

"Say," said Gerrity, suddenly, "I was just thinking about—but then, I suppose there really is no reason why Larry White shouldn't own a twenty-dollar gold piece."

"I should say not!" cried Judith Blake. Then she colored slightly and dropped her voice. "I gave it to him for good luck," she said, shyly. "Maybe it will bring him good luck now."

"It certainly will!" I said, grasping the inspector exultingly by the arm. "See here, Gerrity, I presume that you are about to take Filipo to the Tombs. I told Larry White not long ago that I'd bring Miss Blake down there to unlock the door to his liberty. Any objections if we go down with you?"

Judith Blake clasped her hands and peered anxiously at the inspector. As he looked back at her a grin spread over his face.

"Come along," he heartily invited us. "And, by thunder, we'll let Miss Blake unlock the door of that cell herself!"

"In that case," said Christopher Hand, to my utter astonishment, "I think I shall go to the theatre."

"What?" I said, weakly. "Do you mean to say you are going to the theatre at this hour, and all by yourself?"

"Precisely," he stiffly replied. "I shall go to the theatre where you had me last night. We missed the last act, did we not? I shall be just in time to make it. This case has convinced me that there is a fallacy in my theory concerning the deterioration of the criminal mind. By the time the performance is over, my dear Clark, I should have it all straightened out."

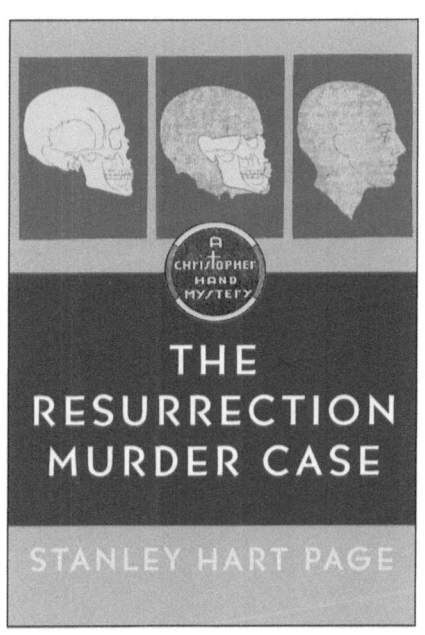

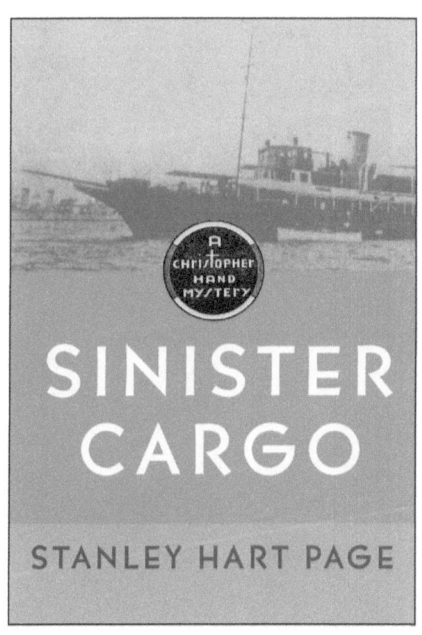

COACHWHIP PUBLICATIONS

COACHWHIPBOOKS.COM

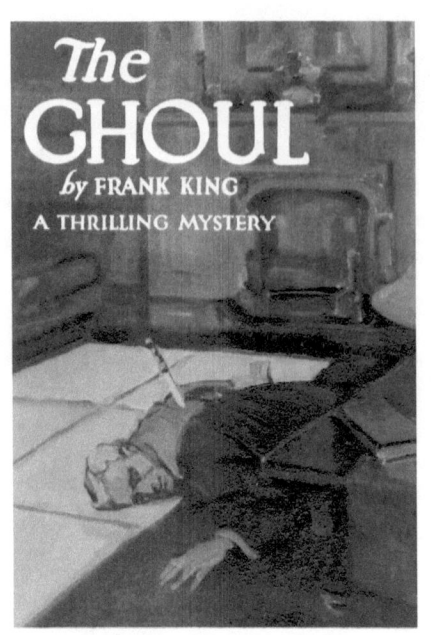

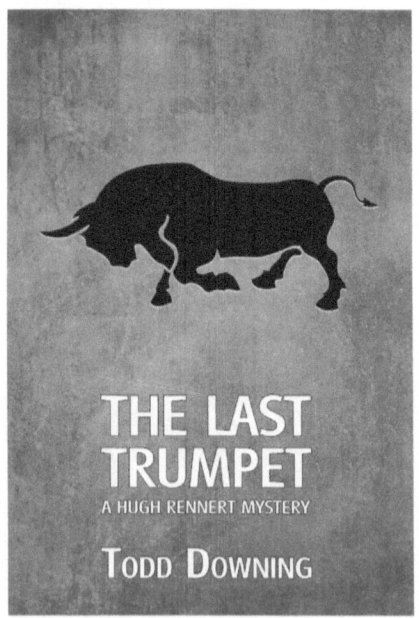

COACHWHIP PUBLICATIONS

COACHWHIPBOOKS.COM

FEAR OF FEAR

FLORENCE RYERSON
COLIN CLEMENTS

MURDER IN THE FAMILY

NICE PEOPLE MURDER

Mary Hastings Bradley

3 DETECTIVES
FEMMES AUDACIEUSES
MERWIN · SOMERVILLE · FOOTNER

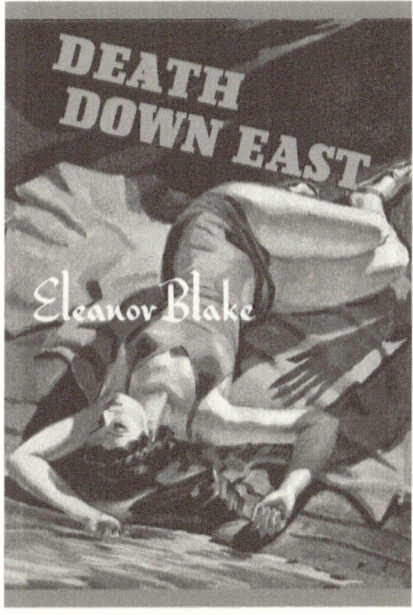

DEATH DOWN EAST

Eleanor Blake

COACHWHIP PUBLICATIONS
COACHWHIPBOOKS.COM

THE
MYSTERY
OF THE
FOLDED
PAPER

HULBERT
FOOTNER

The
Hollow Tree
Mystery

MADELON ST. DENIS

VIRGINIA RATH

FERRYMAN,
TAKE HIM ACROSS!

NO FACE TO
MURDER
EDITH HOWIE

COACHWHIP PUBLICATIONS

COACHWHIPBOOKS.COM

THE QUINNY HITE
MYSTERIES

CHINESE RED · HERE LIES THE BODY

RICHARD BURKE

I'll Hate Myself in the Morning

Murder on the Left Bank

Elliot Paul

MURDER'S COMING

GRAVE WITHOUT GRASS

BY
DONALD CLOUGH CAMERON

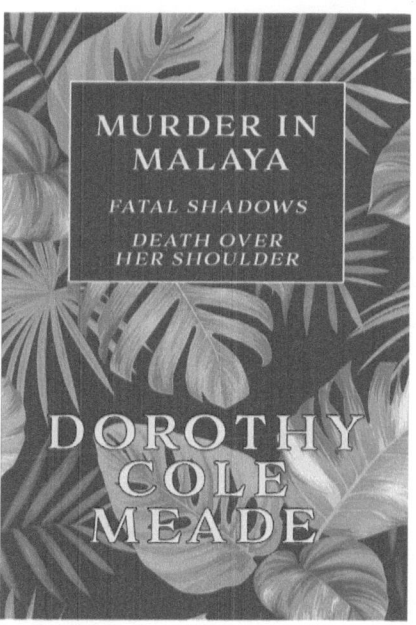

MURDER IN
MALAYA

FATAL SHADOWS
DEATH OVER
HER SHOULDER

DOROTHY
COLE
MEADE

COACHWHIP PUBLICATIONS

COACHWHIPBOOKS.COM

COACHWHIP PUBLICATIONS

COACHWHIPBOOKS.COM

THE FIRES AT
FITCH'S FOLLY

KENNETH WHIPPLE

DRESSED
TO KILL

Emma Lou Fetta

GRIMM
DEATH

THE
GROUSE
MOOR
MURDER

JOHN FERGUSON

COACHWHIP PUBLICATIONS

COACHWHIPBOOKS.COM

MURDER AT DRAKE'S ANCHORAGE

E. LEE WADDELL

MURDER AT THE KENTUCKY DERBY

CHARLES PARMER

MURDER ENDS THE SONG

ALFRED MEYERS

3 DETECTIVES
MURDER ON THE RAILS
WHITECHURCH • THORNE • TORGERSON

COACHWHIP PUBLICATIONS

COACHWHIPBOOKS.COM

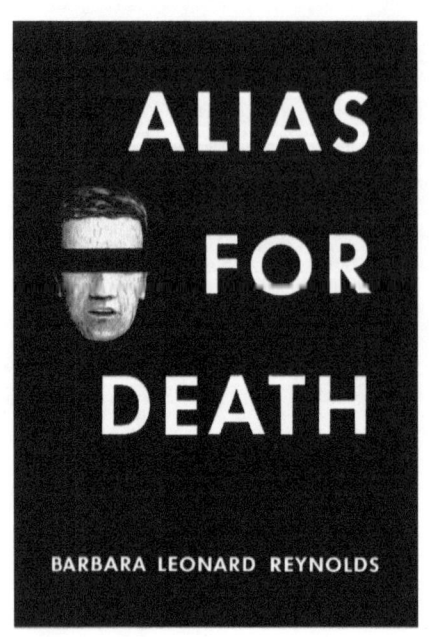

ALIAS FOR DEATH

BARBARA LEONARD REYNOLDS

THERE IS NO RETURN

THE ADELAIDE ADAMS MYSTERIES

ANITA BLACKMON

Jack Dolph

MURDER MAKES THE MARE GO

FEAR CAME FIRST

VERA KELSEY

COACHWHIP PUBLICATIONS

COACHWHIPBOOKS.COM